# FATED CURSE

SHIFTERS OF RAGNAROK BOOK TWO

## SKYE MALONE

WILDFLOWER ISLE

FATED CURSE
*Book Two of the Shifters of Ragnarok Series*
by Skye Malone

© Copyright 2021 - Skye Malone

Published by Wildflower Isle
P.O. Box 129, Savoy, IL 61874
www.wildflowerisle.com

Paperback ISBN: 978-1-940617-82-4
Hardcover ISBN: 978-1-955991-00-1

Library of Congress Control Number: 2021903169

Find out about all new releases:
**Join Skye's mailing list at skyemalone.com/mailinglist!**

# TITLES BY SKYE MALONE

ADULT PARANORMAL ROMANCE
The Shifters of Ragnarok Series
The Demon Guardians Series

YOUNG ADULT PARANORMAL ROMANCE
The Awakened Fate Series

YOUNG ADULT URBAN FANTASY
The Kindling Trilogy

# AUTHOR'S NOTE

A number of the words in this series are taken from actual Norse mythology, albeit with some slightly altered spellings. The ulfhednar, seidr, and the draugar are just a few.

While this series is a work of fiction, and as such, I have taken artistic liberties with all of these concepts, I highly recommend reading more about them from nonfiction sources. Their history is fascinating.

1

---

# LINDY

Ｉf she didn't leave now, everyone could die.

Keeping an eye on the exit from the barracks, Lindy folded a small scrap of paper and set it on the rough gray blanket. Somebody would find the goodbye note, but it wouldn't be soon. This cot was far from the front of the underground bunker, and there were plenty of barrack rooms to fill before any survivors were assigned space back here. By the time anyone spotted the note, let alone brought it to her best friend, Hayden, Lindy would be long gone.

Hopefully.

Guilt colored the thought. Hayden wouldn't understand, not at first. But maybe, with enough time, her best friend would at least forgive her. Lindy had done all she could to protect Hayden's parents when the world fell and fire came from the sky. She'd done everything she could to protect everyone else in Mariposa too, mostly from herself. But the spells Hayden put around this place made seidr fill the air now, permeating everything with magic, and the

1

curse was gnawing at the edges of Lindy's mind in response. It was only a matter of time until the darkness inside her won.

So she had to go.

She hefted her backpack higher on her shoulders, checked her switchblade in its customary position in her pocket, and then headed for the door. Two hundred people filled the bunker, give or take. Survivors of the world's collapse and all that was left of the population of Mariposa, Colorado.

Easy enough to get lost in the shuffle.

*Watch for moments of distraction or confusion. These are to your advantage, as your prey will not be ready when you strike to kill.*

Her steps hitched and she stopped, hot rage bringing pointless tears to her eyes as she tried to banish her mother's voice from memory. The woman had done enough damage to her childhood. She had no right to lurk in Lindy's mind now.

Especially given the circumstances.

Drawing a steadying breath, she made herself continue into the hallway. Based on conversations she'd overheard from the ulfhednar—otherwise known as the werewolves who owned this underground safe haven and the luxurious manor above it—the bunker was extensive. A metal-walled complex filled with barrack rooms and private rooms alike, along with multiple kitchens, a gym and dojo, and storage areas galore. A prepper's fantasy, really. But in addition to countless generators and water filters and enough food to last for years, the place had three exits, just in case one or another became inaccessible.

And the one nearest to Lindy led to the garage.

The people organizing everything had thought it

strange when Lindy asked for a cot this deep in the complex. They didn't know she had no intention of remaining here.

Keeping her head tucked down, she hurried through the metal halls, hoping her thick winter coat and knit cap made her look like just another survivor on her way to a place to stay. With any luck, no one would pay her any attention, and the ulfhednar would be so busy helping people at the main entrance or coordinating with the soldiers who'd come to help guard this place, they'd never notice Lindy slipping away.

*Without* any luck, she'd have to use seidr.

Nausea stirred in her stomach, and she tried to ignore it. If it came down to it, she wouldn't use much. Just enough to disguise her to whoever was guarding the door. She'd be okay.

So would everyone else.

Breathing slowly to stay calm, she rounded the corner. At the end of the next hall, she spotted a stairway leading upward.

Bingo.

Glancing around swiftly, she didn't see anyone standing guard, and so she hurried toward the stairs. Old habit made her keep her footsteps silent as she scaled the steps, but resignation hit her when she reached the heavily fortified door.

Palm-print lock. Dammit.

She cast a quick look back down the stairs. Going out the front wasn't an option; there were too many people to get past easily, even with magical help. And the other exit from the bunker opened into the forest, which would only leave her needing to traverse the woods back to the garage anyway.

And God knew what was waiting out there.

Gritting her teeth against the fear and frustration that still made her want to cry, she pressed her left palm to the panel and felt the seidr spread through her body like an insidious, invisible smoke, carrying out into her hand. Under her breath, she snarled the spell.

Darkness whispered within her, seething and churning at the edges of her mind like a toxic black cloud on the horizon, waiting to swallow her whole. On her right wrist, her Allegiant tattoo tingled faintly beneath the leather band she wore to hide the mark.

A barely audible click came from the door. She yanked her hand back, releasing her hold on the seidr as fast as she could.

The darkness receded inside her mind.

She trembled. Even if she couldn't feel it anymore, she knew the poison wasn't gone. It never would be. The curse was only waiting.

But it hadn't taken her yet.

With a steadying breath, she pushed the door out from its frame and peered through the gap. The garage was nearly the size of a small warehouse, filled with everything from sports cars to SUVs to what looked like a vintage Army truck.

"—ready in a few minutes."

She ducked back at the sound of a young man's voice. Through the narrow opening, she caught a glimpse of one of the ROTC soldiers standing near an SUV.

"Sounds good," another voice replied.

Ice shot through her. She knew that deep, entirely too-tempting voice.

Wes.

Lindy hesitated behind the door, debating, while the

sounds of something heavy being moved came from the garage. The forest exit meant more seidr, more risks. Those zombie-like bastards, the draugar, could be anywhere. Hell, the Order could be too. But the egress was still tempting, considering this one led her right near that damnably hot wolf with his rugged good looks, tattooed body made of muscle, and eerily intense eyes.

Eyes she'd caught lingering on her more than once whenever she'd run into him, and God help her for how *that* made her feel.

Cursing silently to herself, she reached into her backpack and drew out her mask. The air outside was still terrible, weeks after fire had burned the forest, the town, and probably half the damn world. Pulling it on, she kept an eye to the gap between the door and the frame, careful not to make any sounds. Ulfhednar hearing was incredible, as was their strength and sense of smell. But she'd distracted Wes once with seidr, back before the world went mad. He and his friend Connor had come by to help her and Hayden after one of the Order broke into their apartment.

Shudders rolled through her. That guy was dead, but others were out there, as well she knew. The Order had always been everywhere, ready, waiting. Before the advent of Ragnarok, they'd secretly occupied everything from jobs as janitors at gas stations to CEOs in corporate high-rises, though most people didn't even know they existed. And now they were out in the open, marching through the wreckage and celebrating how they'd torn down the world while they unleashed hell on all who survived its fall.

*When the day comes, the righteous shall rise to wreak justice upon the corrupt and the fallen.*

Her skin crawled. Death-cult bastards.

Pushing the memories aside, she eased the door open

wider, grateful at least that the ulfhednar kept the hinges oiled so it didn't make a sound. As she slipped through the gap, she eyed the vehicles again. None of them were options, not with a wolf nearby. But there were cars and trucks out in the courtyard, brought by the survivors and left with their keys inside in case anyone needed to make a fast getaway. No one wanted to be trapped without a way of escape, even in this place.

Not after everything they'd all seen in the past few weeks.

But the cars and trucks would presumably be empty now that most everyone was inside, which meant all she needed to do was take one and everything would be fine.

Hopefully, anyway.

She slipped past the door and then eased it closed behind her. Placing each foot carefully in front of the other, she crept along the side of an SUV. The massive garage door gaped wide ahead of her, a view of the expansive courtyard and burned forest beyond it.

Two people stood near the entrance, their backs to her.

She swallowed hard, hesitating in spite of herself. Wes waited at the garage opening, his eyes on the burned forest. The guy to his right was even bigger than him, though they both were built like towering trees from before everything went to ash. She recognized the man too, though she hadn't caught his name. One of the ulfhednar. The one so huge and tall, he had to bend just to get through doorways. He was currently hefting a box down from the back of an Army truck, casting short glances around the garage as he moved.

Damn, damn, damn.

Gritting her teeth, she drew the seidr up inside again, her eyes on Wes even more than his friend. His dark hair was trapped beneath a black knit cap, and tattoos peeked past the collar of his coat. Even beneath his winter gear, he was clearly solidly built, and he eyed the destroyed forest like he was challenging it to attack.

She inched toward the door. While the defenses around her would suppress her scent and quell any trace of sound, more than one person in history had lost their lives by trusting their defenses so much that they stopped being cautious. For that matter, Wes didn't even have a mask on, which was reckless of him given all the grit and toxins possibly lingering in the air.

The better to smell her with...

Anxiety tangled in her stomach like snakes. Creeping forward, she inched toward the door, attempting to stay as far from the two men as possible. Her eyes never left Wes, for all that she knew there was the other, larger wolf less than three feet beyond him.

But somehow it felt like, if anyone was going to pick up on her presence, Wes would be the one who—

His head turned her direction, and she froze. For a heartbeat, Wes paused, a flicker of consternation passing over his face. His nose twitched in a way she recognized from all the times Hayden tried to pretend not to be sniffing something with those heightened senses of hers.

"Odin's *fucking* eye," the bigger man swore incredulously.

Wes's attention snapped to his friend, and warily, Lindy followed his gaze. Beyond the two men, a trio of little boys were running through the courtyard.

"Dammit," the larger man said, moving to put down the box he was holding. The cardboard bottom started to give way and the guy shifted his grip quickly to keep the contents from falling. The sound of bottles clattering against each other came from inside.

"You okay?" Wes paused in the act of reaching to help him.

"Yeah, uh—" The big guy glanced between the kids and Wes, a question in his eyes.

Wes hesitated. "It's okay." His voice was tinged with reluctance. "I've got it." He walked out toward the boys, calling to them as he went.

Lindy watched the bigger guy for a moment to see if he reacted to her presence. When he didn't look away from Wes and the boys, she cautiously crept onward, not drawing a full breath until she was over a dozen yards beyond the garage.

The ulfhednar never looked toward her.

Quickly and silently, she hurried around the corner and then let the seidr die, trying to ignore the way it felt like a faint electrical current was fading from the green-black ink of her tattoo. Biting her lip, she scanned the forest and then hurried toward the car at the far end of the courtyard and closest to the road away from the manor. The dark-brown jalopy wouldn't win any awards for design, but that wasn't the point. No one would miss it, because unlike the trucks and SUVs and newer cars, she wasn't taking anything the survivors would desperately need. It was bad enough she was stealing a car in the first place, but at least she wasn't stealing anything else. No food at all, and only her own bottle of water and a blanket in her bag.

But if there was anything to be said for being raised by an apocalypse-obsessed cult, it was that they'd taught her to survive just about anything. She could find what she needed out on the road, even in the hellscape the world had become, and nobody here would suffer because she left.

Or because she stayed.

She grasped the handle, pulling it slowly to minimize any sound from the door. Old fast-food wrappers littered the floor of the vehicle, and an empty pack of cigarettes was crumpled in the middle console, while a cup of soda lay on the passenger seat, the fate of its long-dried contents still visible in the discolored patches on the fabric.

Lovely.

She looked back toward the manor. They'd be okay. All of them. The Order didn't stand a chance trying to breach this place on their own, and between Hayden's powers, the wolves' ability to kill the zombie-like draugar, and all the security on the underground bunker itself, the place might as well be a fortress.

Her eyes crept skyward. Amid the lingering smoke and cloud cover, five black gashes shredded across the heavens, their interior as dark as the depths of outer space.

Against that, even a fortress wouldn't be enough.

But it was better than nothing.

Lindy swallowed hard, tearing her eyes away from the impossible lines, an ache taking up residence in her chest. There'd been a time—just a few *weeks* ago, there'd been a time—when she really thought she'd made it. She'd built a life in Mariposa. Undergrad was behind her and grad school was waiting, and all her future could really be her own. She'd been setting off to Harvard—*Harvard*, of all places!—with grand plans for making a positive impact in the world.

But she'd been kidding herself. Her life ended when she was twelve years old; she just hadn't understood it then. And now there was nothing except this.

She turned away from the manor. The people here would survive, and her family would too. She'd get to Minneapolis, and she'd find her dad and brother. They wouldn't be out there alone, unprotected from the draugar and the Order and the whole damn world. This ulfhednar bunker near Mariposa was the safest place on earth now, so this was where they needed to be. She'd get them here where Hayden's defenses would protect them, and after that, it didn't matter. She'd leave. Throw herself off a cliff, if she had to. She'd do whatever was necessary to make sure the curse couldn't hurt anyone else when it took her, and then...

She'd die knowing the people she loved would be okay. That was the important thing.

A shuddering breath entered her lungs, and she forced herself to focus. Silence had served her so far; now came the time for speed. The wolves would hear her start the car no matter how quiet she tried to be, so now the only thing that mattered was getting out of here before they realized what she was doing and tried to stop her from leaving.

Swinging into the vehicle and ignoring the crunch of old wrappers beneath her, she cranked the engine and then shoved the gearshift into drive. With a foot to the pedal and her hands clenched tight on the wheel, she floored it away from the manor as quickly as the old jalopy could carry her.

2

# WES

"Yes, I know it's crowded underground, but you still can't be out here." Wes struggled to hold his voice level as the little human boy glared up at him. "And I know *you* know why."

"But my uncle says those bad things can't get us here."

Wes glanced at the forest in spite of himself. The seidr defending the manor and its surroundings wasn't visible like it had been in town. No glistening shield of defense shone in the forest now. But their resident crazy woman— or seer, as she called herself—Ingrid assured them that the power their alpha's mate, Hayden, controlled was still keeping this place safe.

As much as it could be, anyway, given that there were now nearly two hundred humans filling what *had* been the wolves' sanctuary. There weren't a lot of places left in the world where the ulfhednar could know they were safe from humans—or that humans were safe from *them*. Now even the manor was gone.

Everything was gone.

"Your uncle needs to be more careful too, then," Wes said to the boy. "Letting down your guard gets people hurt."

The kid blinked, blood seeming to drain from his face. Wes struggled to hold in a grimace. He sucked at this. Reassuring kids. Talking to kids. Hell, even just talking to humans. And now it was only worse, considering that the outright fear that all those humans *should* have felt around his kind was gone.

Didn't they understand how dangerous this was for them? Being near the ulfhednar, *staying* with his kind? Sure, the fact that the world was now full of undead monsters—monsters only the ulfhednar could destroy— probably contributed to the trust they were all suddenly displaying in wolves they most likely would have slaughtered less than a month ago, but...

Still. It was reckless. Foolish. Yes, the other wolves were safe enough to be around. He trusted his pack implicitly and knew they'd never harm a single human soul.

Unlike him, they hadn't been made into an ulfhednar by a monster.

"Go back inside," he continued to the kid. "All of you."

He included the boy's friends in his pointed look and was rewarded a moment later by the children glancing at each other and then retreating toward the manor at top speed.

Thank the gods.

Watching the kids until they were safely through the door, he drew a breath of air and then cleared his throat uncomfortably, regretting leaving his mask back in the bunker. But if there was a threat out here, he wanted to be able to smell it coming, for everyone's sake.

"That go okay?" Marrok asked when Wes walked back into the garage. Arranging the last box of food stores safely on a cart, the large wolf eyed Wes.

"Yeah, fine."

He could feel Marrok's suspicion, but the male didn't say anything more. His pack shared his discomfort at their sudden proximity to humans, if not all of his reasons for it. They knew he hated this, even if he understood how their options had been limited.

Leave the humans to die or bring them back to the manor.

Forget *limited*. Those options were shit.

Beyond the garage, he heard an engine start, followed a moment later by the sound of a vehicle driving away. He tossed Marrok a questioning look, only to find confusion on his pack brother's face.

"You remember anyone saying they were heading out?" he asked Marrok.

The male shook his head.

Wes walked back outside and peered around the corner of the building. The courtyard was an expanse of cobblestones that led down to a long drive away from the manor. Whoever had been there, they were long gone.

Trepidation prickled through him, and the wolf inside him stirred. Major Rolston and the ROTC kids who'd survived the fires wouldn't have left without warning, and the rest of the humans certainly hadn't seemed in any rush to leave, considering the manor and the bunker below it were the most secure places they'd seen in weeks. And the pack bond that let him feel where his friends were wasn't giving him any indication some of the wolves were gone.

That left one option, and it wasn't good.

He strode back toward the manor. "You okay to keep watch out here for a moment?" he called to Marrok.

His friend nodded.

Wes continued toward the bunker entrance on the far side of the garage. They'd done their best to guarantee Allegiants weren't among the survivors—checking the wrists of anyone Hayden couldn't vouch for in search of those damned tattoos—but short of commanding every human to pull a full-blown strip search, there was only so much the wolves could do.

They all suspected the Order of Nidhogg would make another move eventually. Yes, the wolves stopped one guy, but those bastards were everywhere.

Wes had just hoped they'd have more time to prepare.

He reached the bunker entrance and pressed his palm to the panel on the wall. The door opened and quickly, he hurried inside, pausing only long enough to tug the thick metal closed behind him before jogging down the steps. Connor and Hayden were on the opposite end of the bunker, most likely still helping the humans get sorted into their various barracks and rooms.

Weaving through the crowds and the halls, he cursed the minutes it took him to make his way through the complex. The place was huge, but now that every surviving human for miles around filled the bunker, it was enough to make him claustrophobic, and he found his pulse flying from more than nerves about the Order.

Gods, he could barely breathe down here.

By the time he reached the area they'd taken to calling the front room, if only because it led straight up into the manor above, it was all he could do not to start shoving past the humans. Over the heads of the survivors, he caught sight of Connor with Hayden beside him. Recently elevated to alpha of the Thorsen pack, Connor had taken to the leadership position with aplomb.

But even he had a harried edge to his expression now.

"—in the *western* barracks." Connor pointed, and the human couple near him looked toward the hall. "*That* way. Last door on the left."

"Yes, security has already checked the rooms," Hayden assured a young girl clinging to her arm. "I promise no draugar are there."

"Connor!" Wes shouted over the crowd.

His friend looked toward him, concern flashing across his face. "What is it?"

"Can I borrow you for a sec?"

Connor glanced at Hayden, who nodded quickly and then returned to reassuring the human girl who had yet to let her arm go. Maneuvering through the throng, Connor walked up to him. "What?"

Wes eyed the humans warily, and he kept his voice low as he said, "We might have a problem. Anyone mention to you that they were heading out of here?"

Connor gave him a skeptical look. "No…"

"Someone took a car. Drove away pretty damn fast too. It wasn't any of us, and Levi didn't mention the soldiers planned on leaving, so…"

"Shit."

Wes nodded.

Connor scrubbed a hand through his hair. "Okay, head upstairs. Find Tyson. He was working on a few of the cameras. Ask him if any of them caught a glimpse—"

"Hayden!"

Wes turned. A gray-haired human woman rushed through the crowd, a frantic look on her face.

Hayden hurried toward her. "Johanna, what's wrong?"

Pushing a folded bit of paper into Hayden's hands, Johanna seemed on the verge of tears. "I went to check on her because she seemed... I knew something was off earlier, but I didn't want to pry and— Oh, sweetie! She left!"

Blinking, Hayden took the note. "What?" Horror spread through her expression as she read the contents. "Oh my God." She looked at Connor. "Lindy."

Chills shot through Wes while, inside him, his wolf went utterly still. Lindy was... what was she? Human. Intriguing, beautiful, unbelievably attractive, and... human.

Also known as *off-limits* to him. In the two decades since a sick bastard attacked Wes and turned him into an ulfhednar, he and the rabid wolf inside him had come to an uneasy truce. Wes would accept what he was, could shift and live in the pack and *cautiously* be all the things that the wolf could be, but only if the wolf accepted there were rules—the cardinal one of which was he never got involved with a human. He couldn't risk it. If even a trace of that bastard's corruption had become a part of Wes when he'd been bitten, it meant Wes might be driven to do that to someone else. The ulfhednar doctors swore they didn't think such a thing was possible, but that didn't equal rock-solid certainty, not in his book. And while Wes had worked hard to control the wolf inside him, if that control slipped... if the wolf bit a human and did to them what had been done to him as a child...

His stomach twisted. It would be hell, and not just for him. With that one bite, he would have stolen everything. Their life as they'd known it. Their dreams and anything they might have been in the human world. Now, they would only be a wolf, forever outside society, forever at risk of being killed by humans who would never understand what he'd forced his victim to become.

He couldn't do that to someone. Take everything they were out of pure selfishness, just for the sake of companionship or sex or even some half-assed attempt at a relationship. It wasn't an option.

So *stay away from humans* was the number one rule.

And yet, right at this moment, his wolf didn't give a shit about the rules. Adrenaline flooded through his body in an instant, screaming for him to race out the door after her. The damn creature pushed at his skin, wanting him to shift if only to move faster. His wolf had been drawn to Lindy since the moment Wes first laid eyes on her—one little apocalypse and a couple of weeks ago in the flower shop where she'd worked with Hayden. And sure, he'd tried to play it cool ever since. Kept all their subsequent interactions to a minimum and never so much as hinted at how his cock hardened just at the sight of the gorgeous, feisty woman with honey-brown hair and dark, sharp eyes that he suspected saw a lot more than she let on.

"What about Lindy?" he managed with a flash of pride for how neutral his voice sounded.

Connor glanced at him sharply, curiosity in his eyes.

Fuck.

Speechless, Hayden extended the paper scrap to her mate and then glanced at Johanna. "Go find my parents. See if she said anything to them, okay?"

Johanna nodded and hurried away.

Ignoring them, Connor read the message quickly and then offered the note to Wes, a guarded expression on his face.

Wes unfolded it and skimmed the neat, curving letters in blue ink.

*I'll be back if I can. I'm sorry. - Lindy*

He looked up at Hayden, shivers racing through him. "What the hell is this?"

"I don't know."

"Why would she leave?" Connor asked.

Hayden floundered. "I..." She turned away, running a hand over her hair. "I mean, I don't... I told her no one would hurt her here. She..." Her eyes went back to her mate. "I have to go after her. She—"

"You can't," Connor told her, a strained note of apology in his voice. "Without you at the manor, the defenses on this place won't hold. We can try to send some of the soldiers—"

"And if the draugar are out there?" Hayden countered. "No, it has to be a wolf and—"

"I'll go."

Connor and Hayden both turned to Wes, appearing alarmed and relieved in turns.

"Alone?" Connor replied.

Wes shrugged. "What other option is there?"

His friend grimaced. Wes knew what he said was true, though, even *without* his wolf pacing back and forth like a neurotic windup toy in his brain. Their pack brother Tyson was repairing the cameras and technology-based security of this place. Kirsi was working with the human soldiers on guard rotations, and Marrok would be furious if asked to leave her. Luna was helping the doctors with the wounded while all the other wolves of the larger Thorsen pack were busy getting the humans settled into this place.

And that left him, the one guy who could go.

The one guy who really shouldn't.

"She's not been gone very long," he made himself continue. "I'll find her, figure out what's going on, and then we'll head back here. Okay?"

Hayden smiled at him. "Thank you."

Connor sighed. "Do you have any idea where she would have gone?" He addressed the question to his mate.

Hayden's brow shrugged. "No. I mean…" She paused. "Her family. They're all the way in Minneapolis, though. Surely, she wouldn't…" The disbelief on her face faded into nausea. "Oh, God."

Wes's wolf strained inside him like a rabid dog on a leash. Northeast was good. Better than good. He needed to be heading that way sooner than yesterday, ripping with teeth and claw through every damn thing that blocked his path to her, so why the hell was he still standing here?

He shoved the feeling aside, trying to focus. The damn creature was delusional and would latch on to anything that might lead to the human woman. "I'll start in that direction, then."

"Hayden?" her mother cried, hurrying through the crowd with Hayden's father on her heels. "What's this about Lindy being gone?"

"Did she say anything to you?" Hayden asked.

Her mother shook her head, and Hayden's father did the same.

Good enough for him. "I'll be back soon," Wes said, starting for the door.

Connor caught his arm. "We won't have any way to reach you out there. Tyson and the others are trying to get the radios working, but even shortwave is barely functional. You'll be on your own."

"Then the sooner I get going, the better."

Connor stared at him for a heartbeat and then exhaled,

releasing him. "Take extra gas, food, and some blankets, just in case. We don't know what the roads are like beyond town."

Wes gave his friend a nod. "I'll be back before you know it."

# 3

# LINDY

The apocalypse didn't make for the best driving conditions.

Gripping the steering wheel of the brown jalopy, Lindy wove through the abandoned cars on the highway, silently begging the old tires to hold on to the icy road despite her speed. The fire that had poured from the gashes in the sky weeks ago seemed to have reached here as well, turning the snow that used to cover the terrain into a muddy sludge that had frozen in the bitter cold. It had burned the cars too, charring the vehicles around her into blackened sculptures of twisted metal with corpses inside.

They'd tried to flee, the passengers. Scrambled toward the windows or shoved open doors. Whether anyone had survived was impossible to tell, but she doubted it. If the fire here had been anything like Mariposa, there wouldn't have been time to escape, let alone anywhere safe to go.

Memories of screaming flickered through her mind. That day had been the first time she'd used that much seidr in years, and even then, her defensive spell had barely held. In a shimmering bubble of light around her and Hayden's parents, she'd channeled all the magic she could while fire fell from the gashes in the sky and killed everyone in the neighborhood around her, burning them alive in their homes.

And afterward, the decade-old tattoo on her wrist scorched her like a brand, warning of the cost.

Of the curse whose time had come.

She shifted on the uncomfortably hard seat. If nothing else, the blackened bodies around her were motionless, and as horrible as it was, for that she was grateful. The zombie-like draugar weren't created by a virus or bacteria, though a bite could still be a problem if the person died. But they were creatures of myth—similar, in a way, to the ulfhednar. Except while werewolves had lived in secret for centuries, no one had seen anything like the draugar in over a millennium.

That was the thing about Ragnarok. There was no telling what all it might have brought out to play.

She eyed a charred minivan as she sped past, its side door standing open with at least three bodies inside. Apocalypse or not, myth typically held that greed, discontent in life, envy, or other such things were responsible for making a body rise and return as a draug after death. There was no firm estimation on how long that took—days, weeks, months? Anything was fair game—but the ancients had employed all kinds of rituals to make sure the dead stayed dead. And while dying bloody in a burning car probably *discontented* someone a fair bit, apparently these corpses were so sufficiently turned to charcoal that they couldn't rise even if they wanted to.

A blackened hand stretched past the shattered window of a pickup truck ahead of her, clawing feebly at the air.

Lindy floored the gas pedal and veered wide of the vehicle.

Hours passed before the half-burnt ruins of a sign finally told her she was nearing Denver. The sight was only partially reassuring. Denver meant supplies, sure. Gas too, which would be welcome considering the little warning light had just flickered to life on the dashboard.

But the city was practically guaranteed to be crawling with draugar.

She chewed her lip. She'd be quick. Get blankets and supplies enough to siphon some gas from whatever vehicles survived and then head onward. Maybe grab food while she was at it, if it wasn't too much of a risk.

Her stomach rumbled as if in commentary.

The road twisted through the outskirts of town, lined by the wreckage of apartments and assorted stores. The farther she drove toward the city, however, the better the condition of the buildings became. On the apartments, siding was still intact. Color remained on vehicles and signs alike. She couldn't see any people, but then, there weren't many corpses either.

She eyed a strip mall on her right, the expanse of its parking lot easily visible from the elevated highway. A discount department store anchored one end, with a stretch of smaller stores beside it, and several cars appeared generally untouched in the lot.

Good enough.

Keeping an eye out for any sign the draugar were nearby, she steered her car toward the off-ramp and then down past a dead stoplight. Driving slowly, she scanned the lot as she pulled up in front of the store.

Nothing moved.

Releasing a slow breath, she studied the store entrance.

A random assortment of items from inside lay scattered on the sidewalk—evidence looters had already made quick work of this place, she suspected. Trampled boxes and shattered bottles hinted at an interruption to their efforts, however. And beyond the shattered glass of the sliding doors, the interior was a black abyss.

This could go bad *so* quickly.

Still keeping an eye to her surroundings, she bent across the middle console and tugged open the glove compartment. A minor avalanche of crumpled papers tumbled out, and she cursed beneath her breath as she shoved through it. Whoever owned this car clearly had the organizational skills of a hoarder, but maybe that could work in her favor.

Her fingers bumped into a small, hard cylinder. Prying it out, she thumbed on the pocket-sized flashlight and allowed herself a small grin at the beam of light that resulted. It wasn't much; the batteries were clearly weak. But it was damn well better than nothing.

Tugging on her mask and then pulling her knit cap into place, she debated putting her gloves back on too, but between handling her own knife and anything she grabbed in the store, she'd need dexterity. Better to be cold than fumble something at the worst possible moment.

Trepidation swirled inside her. Glancing around the lot one more time, she pushed open the door.

Silence greeted her.

For a moment, she didn't move, waiting for anything that might charge from the shadows. When nothing did, she snagged her backpack from the vehicle and then shut the door carefully. Warily, she crept forward, one foot placed gently in front of the other to minimize any sound while she aimed the flashlight beam into the depths of the store. Ransacked shelves glinted back at her, their contents scattered across the tile floor. The air was eerily still, without the hum of a heater or refrigerator, and it felt stale on her skin, stripped of the previously ever-present energy of life. Beyond the meager gray light from the overcast day outside, the dark aisles lurked like a black labyrinth hiding hungry, decaying death.

Straining to hear even a whisper of movement in the darkness, she didn't take her eyes from the rows. If the layout followed the logic of every other discount store she'd ever encountered, hardware would be toward the far back corner, home goods toward the middle. Food would be somewhere along the sides, presumably, and hopefully she'd encounter it along the way.

But barring that, gear for siphoning gas was definitely the first priority, with blankets and any other warm items she could snag coming in immediately second. Even driving as much as she could, she was still looking at a few days before she reached Minneapolis.

No way she'd survive the cold without some additional coverings to keep her warm.

Drawing a steadying breath, she headed deeper into the store. The main aisle split ahead of her, part of it continuing on straight while the rest branched left with a display of children's clothing arrayed to one side. Sequined shapes of owls and raccoons sparkled from shirts and sweaters, catching the beam of her flashlight, while little mannequins posed among the racks of clothing, faceless.

Eyeing the mannequins, she shuddered and kept walking, sweeping the flashlight behind her as much as to the front. Not far beyond the clothing and cash registers, rows of food waited, and carefully she took cans and a box of utensils from the shelves, ignoring the rotting baskets of produce nearby.

Her skin prickled with anxiety, and she swept the flashlight beam behind her again. She'd swear she was being watched, but the light found nothing and she couldn't hear a thing beyond the short, sharp sounds of her own breathing behind the mask.

Paranoia was a bitch, but it was definitely time to get moving.

Shifting the backpack onto her shoulders again, she walked back out to the main aisle with the faint whisper of her footsteps on the tile as the only sound. The grocery section fell behind her, and then the pharmacy did too, and the deeper into the store she walked, the less ransacked the shelves became. Looters hadn't made it this far.

Lindy tried not to think of why.

Tools glinted ahead of her and cautiously, she sped up. In the back corner of the building, red plastic gas containers stood on a shelf, untouched. She eased one down without making a sound. A short distance farther on, she removed a bundle of tubing from a display and shoved it into her bag before veering toward the center of the store where blankets might be, sweeping her flashlight around her as she went.

A hand lay outstretched at the end of an aisle.

She froze, snapping the flashlight beam back. Pale and splattered with blood, the hand was motionless.

Lindy glanced around, straining to hear any hint of movement in the dark. An aisle of blankets waited just beyond the hand on the ground, and circling through the rest of the store to avoid the corpse wouldn't help anything. She'd just end up back here.

Swallowing hard, she checked around once more and then inched forward.

Three bodies lay in the aisle. A trio of guys who'd probably been in their mid-twenties before they had their throats ripped out and their insides chewed on. They were dressed in camouflage gear, though without any rank or particular military insignia. Boxes of electronics were scattered around them: game systems, laptops, cell phones.

Idiots cosplaying apocalypse, right up until it got them killed.

They hadn't come entirely unprepared, though—not that it'd done them much good. Rifles and a handgun lay on the ground beside them, along with a machete, of all things. The blade had no blood on it, and whether they'd gotten off any shots was anyone's guess.

She bit her lip behind her mask. Guns wouldn't stop a draug but a machete might, and bullets would still be useful for other things.

Cautiously, she set down the gas container and eased her bag from her shoulder. Sweeping the beam of the light across her surroundings one more time, she inched forward and then reached down. The handgun lay only inches from the nearest body, and she snatched the weapon up, checking it swiftly.

Still loaded.

Tucking the gun into the back of her heavy winter pants, she stayed as far from the bodies as she could while she crept forward again. The corpses hadn't risen yet, but that didn't mean they wouldn't. Meanwhile, the machete lay beside the base of the shelves, as if it had tumbled there when the guys died. Watching the bodies warily, she wrapped one hand around the hilt and drew the machete up. The blade was awkward, weighted wrong. Probably homemade or bought from some cheap cosplay dealer more interested in looks than actual efficacy. From the haphazard scratches on the blade, she imagined one of the guys had tried to sharpen it, though. She adjusted her grip as she straightened, taking a step back from the bodies before turning toward the aisle.

A draug stood right in front of her.

The creature's ear-piercing shriek cut the air, its rotted mouth gaping wide. One eye dangled loose from its socket and flesh hung from its decaying limbs. Rotted clothes sapped of all color were nothing but rags on the draug's emaciated body.

It lunged for her.

Years of training took over in an instant, her muscles reacting before her mind could do more than register alarm. Shifting her weight quickly, she dropped the flashlight and threw her body into a two-handed slash at the draug.

Her blade ripped through the creature's neck, the draug's forward momentum helping the cheap machete. The creature tumbled to the ground while the flashlight clattered around the tile, its glow bouncing madly off the corpses and the fallen draug alike.

Casting a frantic look around, Lindy strained to hear a sign any other creatures were coming for her.

Something grabbed her ankle. Twisting fast, she yanked her foot away as the flashlight beam caught on the headless draug still fumbling around on the floor.

She stared, her heart pounding, while the creature's body attempted to drag itself past the other corpses toward her. Bending fast, she snatched the flashlight from the ground and swept the beam around while she retreated into the aisle.

Nothing else moved.

Shudders ran through her. Fucking *zombies.*

Crouching quickly, she set down the light long enough to snag a blanket from an endcap display, stuff it into her backpack, and then return the bag to her shoulders. Maneuvering the flashlight around, she managed to clasp it and the handle of the gas container in one awkward grip before rising to her feet again.

Time to get out of here.

The store was silent as she strode swiftly through the aisles, keeping the machete in front of her. Beyond the clothing displays and freakish mannequins standing motionless in the dark, the glow of the overcast day beyond the entrance beckoned her.

A crash came from deeper in the store. Shrieks followed.

*Shit.*

She rounded the corner and bolted for the entrance, the heavy backpack thudding painfully against her spine. Debris crunched under her feet, and after the dense darkness, the light glared in her eyes when she raced past the shattered glass doors.

A pair of ravens sat on the roof of the car, and as she ran toward the vehicle, they took off, cawing loudly.

As if in answer, shrieks rose from deeper in the parking lot.

Her heart climbed her throat, and she raced for the driver's side. Siphoning gas would *so* have to wait. She set the gas container down and shoved the flashlight into her pocket, freeing a hand to yank open the door. The keys were still in the ignition. She just needed to—

The brand on her arm surged to life, burning like acid and making her cringe away from the car.

A green-black rope of smoke slammed into the vehicle right where she'd been standing, sending the jalopy lurching sideways. Lindy stumbled back, looking around wildly.

From between a row of cars in the lot, a woman stepped into view.

Nothing about her looked human anymore.

Ice shot through Lindy's core, and for one horrible heartbeat, she thought it was over. Her mother had found her already. They were a thousand miles from the commune, but the distance hadn't mattered.

Ragnarok was here and somehow Carolyn was too. Dal Hegnar's righthand woman, come to unleash the curse and reclaim Lindy once and for all.

Surrounded by draugar, the dark-haired woman paced closer, the decaying monsters snarling at her side, and Lindy's paralysis drained. The woman was too young. Her face wasn't Carolyn's. Green glowing smoke twisted around her limbs like toxic auroras, chased by shadows that slipped in and out of her body like eels cresting and then disappearing beneath the surface of a lake. Darkness pooled in the hollows of her cheeks and eyes, giving her face the appearance of a skull, while her body lurched and jerked like a marionette jolting on its strings.

Reaching out, the woman stroked one hand down the rotting cheek of a nearby draug and smiled at Lindy. "Well, well... poor little poppet, all alone. Would you like me to spare your life, little poppet? I can make you a beautiful deal. You won't even feel it when—" She cut off, pleasant surprise flickering over her face. "Oh, wait now. I know you."

Chills shot through Lindy. *Shit.*

"They showed us your picture. Showed it to everyone

before the world went dark. You're Melinda." Her lips pulled back in a skull-like smile. "The one who's lost."

The woman paced closer. One hand still gripping the machete, Lindy reached for the handgun, despite the fact the weapon probably wouldn't do her a damn bit of good. The woman was Order. Succumbed entirely to the changes they'd wrought upon themselves, but Order all the same. She'd attack before Lindy ever made it within a dozen yards with the blade, and the power she controlled would stop any bullets as well.

Darkness whispered at the edge of Lindy's mind, promising a death bloodier than this mere ordinary Allegiant could ever dream.

A shudder raced through Lindy, and she retreated warily, gripping her weapons. She couldn't fight the woman like that. Couldn't use seidr to stop her. Sure, Lindy would win.

But they'd both die.

"She's looking for you, did you know?" The woman's voice was saccharin sweet. "Them too. That traitorous bastard who stole you away from us, and your sweet little brother. So misguided. So *alone*. We'll fix that, though." She shook her head chidingly. "But it's not going to be pretty what the Second will do when she finds your daddy."

Lindy's blood went cold as her last hope died. She'd thought, maybe, if she was lucky, her mother would leave her family be. That sure, she'd be out here somewhere, searching for Lindy—because of course she would be. But that Carolyn would focus on her and not on Andrew or Frankie, leaving only the draugar and the whole goddamn mess of Ragnarok as the worst things her dad and brother had to handle.

But no. Her mother was after them too.

There was no telling what she'd do when she got her hands on them.

Heart racing, Lindy scanned the lot in short glances. More draugar were lurching toward her on the right, waiting on the woman's command to charge. To the left, the strip mall came to an end in an open lot with a restaurant at the center.

"Come back with me, Melinda. Maybe your mother will spare them if she sees you've returned to the fold."

Lindy ignored her. If she ran, the draugar and the woman would chase her; of that, she was fairly certain.

But if she could lead them away from here... If she could get far enough ahead to circle back to the car and get the hell out of this place...

The woman and the draugar came closer. "Here, little poppet."

Lindy ran for her life.

# 4

## WES

I f nothing else, Wes's wolf was convinced it knew where he was going, which only went to prove the damn creature was insane. There were only so many paths to Minneapolis, after all. Of course, Lindy took one of them.

But gods, he hoped he'd picked the right one.

His wolf was convinced of it. The damnable creature paced and whined in his head, making it nearly impossible to concentrate. But all it wanted to do was go northeast onto this particular interstate, rather than any other road past Denver, and so—for fear of developing a splitting migraine if he *didn't*—onward Wes drove.

But he was starting to fear he'd missed her. For hours, he'd been steering the SUV along icy highways. Surely he should have caught up to her by now. Yes, she knew exactly where she was going, and he didn't. And, fine, so there were different routes she could have taken out of Mariposa and up toward Minneapolis. For all he knew, she'd gone straight east instead of north, trying to avoid the worst of the snow that had covered the area for months despite the fact it was technically almost June. And never mind the fact—if she was in a smaller vehicle—she would have had an easier time getting past some of the burned vehicles blocking the road than he had in the bulky SUV. But still, by this point, surely she wasn't *this* far ahead of—

His wolf thrashed inside him, nearly making his arms rip the wheel into a turn. Gods above, it wanted to get off the highway *now*. Head that way, down into the city, because Odin's eye, it was *important*.

Snarling at the damn thing, he slowed, looking toward the city. There was nothing, though. Empty streets. Abandoned cars. Some strip mall with a bunch of damned draugar milling about in the—

A surge of glowing green smoke ripped across the strip mall parking lot like a battering ram, slamming into a brown car near one of the stores.

*Holy hell.* His foot hit the brake. That was the Order. The virulent green smoke was the same as what another one of their bastards used to try to kill everyone in Mariposa. But what the hell were they—

A petite figure raced away from the brown car, running like hell for the end of the strip mall.

Lindy.

Wes floored the gas pedal, too shocked to bother questioning the wave of recognition. The woman was easily over half a mile away, and bundled up to near anonymity in winter gear same as everyone these days. But it didn't matter.

Somehow, he just knew it was her.

The SUV charged down the off-ramp and whipped around the corner. The damn road was too long, the entrance for the parking lot too far off, and now he couldn't see her anymore. Pointless fast-food restaurants and other bullshit were in the way.

Gods, if the draugar caught her... if the Order of Nidhogg did...

His wheels jumped the curb as the SUV sped into the parking lot. She'd been racing toward the side of the building, so that's where he headed, driving as fast as he could while bracing to hit the brakes and hopefully not hit her if she ran out in front of him.

Where was she? Where the hell—

She darted across the road up ahead, draugar on her heels. More of the creatures emerged from behind a restaurant across the road, their bodies seeming fresh enough that they probably had been diners from inside the building before something killed them.

Lindy skidded, trying to change direction fast. The monsters grabbed for her.

Oh gods, Wes wasn't going to reach her in time.

Whirling quickly, she slashed out with what he'd swear was a machete. The head of a draug tumbled away, but she didn't stop. Her other hand held a gun, and the crack of weapons fire was audible even from inside the SUV. Bullets tore through the legs of the draugar, precise and rapid, and each creature that came close to her lost its head with deadly speed. Bodies collapsed to the concrete all around the woman moving like a trained fighter amid the horde.

Holy *shit.*

One hand fumbling for the window control, he sped up, charging toward her, and then whipped the wheel around as he hit the brakes. The SUV skidded to a stop only a few yards away.

"Get in!" he shouted through the open window.

She gave the SUV an alarmed look. The draugar charged.

Her blade struck instantly, cutting the monsters down. But for an eternal moment, she didn't move toward the SUV. Incredulity flooded him. What the hell was she thinking?

Lindy's face twitched behind her mask like she was swearing to herself. She ran for the vehicle and scrambled inside.

Wes floored it, leaving the draugar shrieking in their wake.

# 5

# LINDY

H undreds of miles, one itty-bitty apocalypse, and somehow, this damn smoldering-hot wolf still found her.

Lindy ripped off her mask, glaring at him. "What the *hell* are you doing here?"

Wes glanced at her, an eyebrow rising over his dark eyes as he steered the SUV away from the strip mall. "You're welcome."

She turned away, fuming. Screw him. Yes, she'd been in trouble back there. Yes, there'd been even more of those monsters than she anticipated. But this wasn't an improvement.

The draugar would just kill her. Wes was a wolf. He'd not only kill her but tell his pack about her too, and then maybe they'd turn on Hayden. Her friend's parents. Anybody.

*Remember, Melinda. With their every breath, shifters lie.*

Lindy fought the urge to shift on the seat. Thanks, Mom. Like the Order was so much better?

God, what the hell was he *doing* out here? Tracking her? Hunting her down? For all she knew, he'd already learned everything about her past. Maybe Hayden told him. Yeah, she'd promised Lindy she wouldn't, weeks ago when Lindy had been forced to reveal what she was or else watch her friend die, but... dammit...

Maybe the truth was out, so Hayden's safety wasn't at stake. Lindy's family might be in danger instead. Wes might just be biding his time. He hadn't killed her already or left her to die, after all.

Maybe he wanted information first.

"Where'd you learn to fight like that?" Wes asked.

Ice shot through her, his question a confirmation of all her fears. Any second now, he would tell her he knew what she'd once been, or demand to see her wrist beneath the coat, seeking the only evidence he'd need that she was everything the ulfhednar sought to kill.

Not that she could blame them, exactly. The Order of Nidhogg had damn near annihilated his kind. They'd driven the wolves to the brink of extinction, determined to relegate the ulfhednar to the history books, right alongside bear shifters and anything else that had once inhabited the world.

But for the Order, that was the point.

*We kill them so the world will die.*

Lindy swallowed hard. "Martial arts classes. Self-defense or whatever."

He was silent. She watched him from the corner of her eye.

"Impressive."

She couldn't find the words to respond to that. "How'd you find me?"

Wes hesitated. "Got lucky."

Her gut twisted, and she couldn't put her finger on why. There was just something odd in his voice.

He shifted his grip on the steering wheel. "Hayden thought you might be headed for Minneapolis. This was the fastest way there."

She was silent. So Hayden said that. What else had she told this guy?

Wetting her lips, Lindy measured her words carefully. "Well, if you want to just drop me off somewhere, I can—"

"What?" Wes scoffed, glancing at her askance and then returning his eyes to the road. "We need to head back to Mariposa. You—"

"Excuse me?"

"We can get help. Reinforcements. More supplies."

Her brow furrowed. "For what?"

"Rescuing your family."

She blinked.

"You're going after them, right?"

She stared at him, speechless.

Wes threw her a short glance, his dark eyes becoming guarded as he turned the SUV onto an on-ramp toward the southbound interstate. "*Right?*"

Why the hell would he help her rescue...

Lindy pushed her incredulity aside. "Listen." She kept her voice level. "I'm not going back to Mariposa yet. But thanks to that Order bitch and the draugar, I need another car. So if you'll just drop me off here, I can—"

"Not happening."

She tensed, keeping her breathing steady as she inched her hand toward her gun. "So... what? You take me hostage and drag me back to—"

"*What?* No!" He looked at her incredulously.

She froze.

He steered the SUV onto the highway, weaving around an abandoned car. "I—" His head twitched toward the city behind them. "I'm trying to help you. And your family. I swear."

She eyed him warily.

"I just think this would go better with backup, so we should get to Mariposa as soon as we can."

Shivers raced through her, laced with darkness and all the myriad reasons that was a terrible, *terrible* plan. Simply having Wes here was dangerous, and not just because of how—even now—he looked like a goddamn tattooed model, all sharp angles to his face with piercing, dark eyes that did absurd things to her insides.

But she could kill him. Kill anyone near her, for that matter. If she lost this fight and couldn't hang on...

"No," she managed. "It'll take too much time. Just drop me off—"

"How many times do I have to say that's not an option?"

"You have no idea what you're messing with here! You —" She clamped her mouth shut, turning away.

The thud of the wheels rolling over the pavement was the only sound.

He drew a deep breath. "Then I'll come with you."

"*Not* happening."

His dark eyes brooked no dissent. "It's that or I head back for Mariposa right now. I'm not leaving you alone out here."

"I don't need a babysitter. Just let me out somewhere. I'll grab another car and be on my way."

"While I do what? Go back to my best friend and say you were fine when I left you, but the gods know what's happened since then? That you could be dead in a ditch for all I know?" He shook his head. "What about *your* friend? You think Hayden wasn't terrified, knowing you were out here alone?"

Lindy looked away, her stomach twisting. *Bastard.*

But the words worked all the same. Guilt gnawed at her, despite how she knew she couldn't have explained more to Hayden. Not without risking the other wolves learning about her past. If she wanted a safe place for her family to return once she found them, no one could know what she was. What she and her father and brother had *all* been, for one reason or another, even if they weren't exactly that anymore.

Anxiety stirred her stomach. Her dad would be okay. Frankie too. Her baby brother had scarcely been out of diapers in those days, and whatever initiation rites Mom had done on him wouldn't be enough to hurt him now.

Hopefully.

Pushing her worries down as best she could, she inched her eyes toward Wes. He wasn't acting like he wanted to interrogate her, or even like he was suspicious of her, really. Confused, yeah. But not like he was waiting to attack.

*Shifters lie.*

So was she.

"What are you saying?" she asked.

Wes let out a breath, his hands working on the steering wheel. "We'll travel fast. That's what you're after, right? Reaching them as soon as possible? And what's your plan after you get to Minneapolis?"

She hesitated, dropping her gaze away. "Bring my family back to Mariposa."

"Great. Let's do that, then."

She couldn't quite bring herself to look at him for fear

he'd somehow see in her expression a hint of the *rest* of her plan. Specifically, the part where she had to die.

"I'm not leaving you alone out here, Lindy," he said as if reading something in her silence anyway.

Stupid, pointless quivers of heat radiated from her insides at the sound of him saying her name, and furiously, she smashed them down too. Being attracted to this wolf was madness. Hell, all of this was madness, and she had to find a way to end it.

"Whatever," she said.

She looked back to the window, fixing a cold expression on her face, for all that she could feel his attention on her like a fingertip brushing her skin. But after a moment, the SUV slowed and carefully, he steered it across a mud-covered median and onto the northbound lane.

Lindy didn't look back. She'd wait for her chance because sooner or later, it would come, and somehow, she'd get Wes to leave. For his sake. For hers.

She had to.

# 6

## WES

Wes could guarantee Lindy was trying to figure out how to make him leave.

In silence, he maneuvered the SUV through the obstacle course of the interstate, following his gut instinct and innate sense of direction more than the road signs to know they were heading the right way. Somewhere out on the other end of this was Minneapolis, but even if he drove top speed for hours, the city would still take days to reach.

Days which she'd spend trying to get away from him.

His wolf growled, stewing in frustration. Taking her hostage, she'd said. Merciful gods, he wasn't trying to do that. She had every right to do whatever she wanted, including crossing this entire hellscape of a country with nothing but a machete and a handgun, if that's what she chose. And sure, it would be sheer *lunacy*, but her family was out there.

If it was his pack, he'd be doing the same.

He just couldn't turn away, was all. On some level, he

knew he should. She resented the hell out of his presence, for one. He barely knew her, for two. More than that, it wasn't safe for her to be this close to him, for a million reasons that began and ended with the words *human* and *wolf*. And while his insides curdled at the thought of hurting her, that wasn't enough. He couldn't afford a mistake, not one, especially not with a human woman whose scent kept making his skin want to shift and his cock threaten to grow hard.

Trusting his damn wolf around *this*? Not an option.

His eyes twitched toward her. Even in the middle of the fucking apocalypse, she looked beautiful, her cheeks flushed by the cold and the wavy locks of her amber hair curling past the shoulders of her thick winter coat. Meanwhile, the fire in her words and actions intrigued him and his wolf both, like some ulfhednar version of catnip. He wanted to know more about her. Wanted to know everything because damn if she wasn't an enigma and a half. As a result, simply turning around and leaving her out here was totally off the table. Never mind that he would have struggled at the thought of abandoning a total stranger in all this. But her?

Impossible.

Who the hell *was* she, anyway? From what little he'd gathered from his pack—not wanting to seem suspicious by asking about her too much and all—Lindy had been a close friend of Hayden's for years, worked in the flower shop with her, and was the female's roommate for quite some time too. They seemed nearly as close as sisters, which automatically ruled out any fear she'd be Order. Any member of that group would have killed Hayden on sight. From what he understood, up until a few weeks back, she hadn't even known Hayden was a wolf or that the ulfhednar existed. An attack by a bastard from the Order necessitated telling Lindy the truth, and honestly, she'd reacted to the news of shifters and murderous secret societies about as well as anyone could be expected to.

Which was to say, she'd been tense. Suspicious. Nervous and snappish and ready to retreat.

Rather like now, minus the machete and handgun.

Had Hayden known her friend could handle herself like that? She'd seemed terrified for Lindy back at the bunker. And, sure, even if Lindy was a clearly consummate badass, the world was a *bit* much right now for anyone short of an army—which would be a good reason for Hayden's fear.

But still.

Wes returned his attention to the road. Wherever Lindy had learned to fight, she'd obviously learned well because, gods, she'd been incredible today. On edge but ferocious, equal to any wolf he'd ever seen. Now that his fear for her life was fading, his blood heated at the memory. The thought of her in danger was horrifying. But the sight of her fighting, of her speed and prowess...

Damn him, it was hot as hell.

He shifted on the seat, bashing down the useless, idiotic arousal. Lindy wanted as much to do with him as she did with a draug, so letting himself get distracted like this was only going to make things more difficult. He wouldn't abandon her even if she despised him, because he couldn't stomach the thought of her dying out here when maybe he could have done something to stop it. So no matter what, he needed to keep his guard up because the moment he slipped, she'd take off.

And then he'd be stuck chasing her once more, hoping

to all the gods that she didn't get killed before he found her again.

The highway rumbled on, the only sound as the hours crept by. After a time, he stopped to refill the tank from the containers in the back of the SUV, watching her all the while in case she bolted. Later, when he brought out a few of the cans of food he'd brought with him, she eyed him like maybe they were poisoned before retrieving her own supplies from within her backpack. They ate in silence and she barely looked at him, but whenever she did, the steely distrust in her eyes was enough to cut stone.

Minneapolis felt as far away as the moon.

As the miles passed, the gray sky shifted toward darkness, the light fading swiftly until everything became an endless abyss. Even in Mariposa, there'd been some small measure of illumination from the security lamps around them. But here... there was nothing. No billboards in the darkness. No glow of a city on the horizon. The moon and stars were gone, swallowed by the overcast sky that never seemed to change, and only the gods knew if those distant lights were even still up there.

He hoped so, though the myths of Ragnarok said even the moon and the sun would disappear in the end.

His skin crawled and he swallowed hard. He and his pack had trained relentlessly in the wilderness, prior to moving down to Colorado. Eighteen months in the wilds of Alaska meant plenty of nights where they'd stayed up, needing to keep watch while being hunted by any number of predators—and humans most of all. He'd long since learned to go without sleep if necessary, so driving all night didn't worry him.

But he still had a sneaking suspicion he'd made a colossal mistake.

The world was an abyss, and the SUV's headlights were like two lonely candles trying in vain to pierce the black. Beyond the windows on either side, nothing was visible—though what lay ahead was bad enough. Abandoned cars loomed out of the shadows, appearing in the beam of the headlights like obstacles in a nightmarish video game. Draugar skulked between them, reaching for the SUV while he raced by. And even setting aside the reality that he would eventually need sleep, they'd have to stop to refuel at some point. The containers in the back would get them another hundred miles or so, but not through the whole night. Which meant they'd need to somehow siphon gas from whatever vehicle they found and then fill the tank in utter darkness, hoping all the while that the draugar didn't attack.

Stupid.

He maneuvered the SUV around an abandoned vehicle, and around another, and then veered farther over still as a draug staggered onto the road, its rotted mouth gaping.

Damn this. Damn him.

Adjusting his grip on the steering wheel, he eyed the highway. There had to be an exit at some point. A while back, they'd crossed into Nebraska—otherwise known as an abyssal stretch of damn near nothing on a good day—but there still had to be *something* out here. He didn't need a metropolis. Just somewhere to park the vehicle that hopefully would be out of sight of anyone or anything that might do them harm.

Minutes ticked past. The headlights caught the edge of an off-ramp ahead. He slowed.

"What are you doing?"

He glanced over, Lindy's voice the first thing he'd

heard besides the rumble of the tires for hours. "We need sleep."

She gave him a look full of suspicion. "We *need* to keep moving. Either keep going or pull over and let me drive."

"And when we need to refuel in the dark? Or if we get stuck? We've been lucky the interstate hasn't been completely blocked by cars already."

Lindy looked away, her jaw muscles jumping.

Well, okay then.

He steered the vehicle along the ramp and then slowed at the end. A country road stretched away on either side, nothing visible beyond the beam of the headlights.

Left or right...

Scowling, he chose a direction at random and hoped it was a good call. If nothing else, there weren't any draugar on the road.

Yet.

Drawing a steadying breath, he kept going. The road was straight as an arrow and flat like a sanded board, and beyond the headlights, only a few trees stood like surreal shapes in the darkness. The terrain hadn't burned here, and pockets of snow covered the ground, remnants of the ridiculously unseasonable cold that had gripped the world before everything went to hell. But as the minutes crawled past, he started to feel like maybe they weren't moving at all, if only because of how same, same, *same* everything appeared.

He shifted his grip on the wheel. Much longer, and he'd turn around for fear of getting so far from the interstate that draugar could block the way. The last thing the two of them needed was one of those undead monsters getting stuck in the grill of the—

The headlights caught on a farmhouse up ahead.

Relief drove the air from his chest. The house was dark, but at least it was still standing. A driveway wrapped around the building, possibly extending toward a garage, but the layout would give them cover from being spotted until dawn.

With any luck, anyway.

Shoving the thought aside, he turned into the driveway and circled around behind the house. The building was two stories, white-sided with blue shutters that had hearts cut out in the middle. In the daylight, it probably was a cute house beloved by its occupants.

Who hopefully were still alive and not planning to shoot at the two of them.

He pulled to a stop with the headlights aimed at the house, watching the building cautiously.

Lindy moved to open the door.

"Hold it." He reached over, placing a hand to her upper arm.

She froze.

His wolf strained at his skin, urging him to draw her closer. He released her immediately.

"If there's something in there"—he kept his voice meticulously level while the wolf whined inside his head —"we don't want to get trapped with it."

"That place is a lot more defensible than this thing." She nodded to the SUV. "We clear the house, and then we'll have solid walls between us and whatever might be out here."

His brow twitched up. She sounded like a tactician.

Who the hell was this woman?

He pushed the thought aside. "The house isn't mobile. If we're attacked, the SUV gives us a faster escape."

"There could be supplies in there. Maybe weapons too."

"So we check in the morning."

Lindy's jaw worked around. "Fine." She released the door handle. "You get some sleep, then. I'll keep watch."

Wes restrained a scoff. Right, like *that* was trustworthy.

"That's okay." He gave her a smile. "You had a run-in with the draugar this morning. All I did was drive. You sleep first."

She met the friendly expression with a dark look, but after a heartbeat, she held up her hands in surrender. "Suit yourself."

Shoving away from the seat, she climbed into the back, brushing close to him as she passed.

His whole body froze. Vanilla and gunpowder, sugar and the salt of sweat, her scent twisted within the smell of ash and soot on her coat, teasing his senses, making his cock hard. For the barest of moments, he thought she hesitated midmotion, but then the pause was over and she was past him, moving quickly to situate herself in the back.

He cleared his throat. "Blankets behind you," he managed. "Sleeping bag as well."

Saying nothing, she reached over the seat and tugged out the thick blankets and sleeping bag he'd brought from the bunker, just in case it took more than a day to find her.

"Mind if I get one of those too?" he added.

Lindy thrust a bundle of wool between the seats.

"Thanks."

She just eyed him, silent.

Burying a frown, he made himself turn. Staring at her like a damn stalker wasn't helping anything, and the icy look on her face wasn't either. His wolf grumbled, wanting to reach out for her like that would solve the damn problem, when really it would just make everything a thousand times worse. And never mind the fact that the minute he fell asleep, she might well try to leave him here and slip away to hijack another vehicle.

He frowned at the darkness. Sleep wasn't an option. Not tonight. And tomorrow, he'd set himself to figuring out some way to get her to trust him.

Even if right now that seemed impossible.

A sigh left him. Tugging the blanket around himself, he settled deeper into the leather seat.

This was going to be a long night.

7

## LINDY

L indy would bet every can of food in her backpack he didn't intend to swap places with her tonight.
The asshole.

Lying on the back seat, a pile of blankets on top of her, she kept her eyes on the ceiling, refusing to give him the satisfaction of acknowledging his presence. Stopping was idiotic. Stopping made them a target and gave the Order and whatever the hell else was out here a better chance to find them. And, sure, fine, so the guy may have had a point about the roads, but that didn't mean stopping was the better plan.

*Stopping.* God, what was that man thinking?

Furiously, her eyes snapped over to him before she could help herself. She couldn't even *see* him in this darkness. How the hell did he intend to spot any threats? With the headlights off and the world swallowed in night, they might as well have been in a sensory deprivation tank.

But then, he was a wolf. Maybe the bastard was planning on hearing them. Seeing hints of their movement.

Smelling them.

She yanked her eyes away from him, for all that it didn't change a thing. She knew he was there. Heaven help her, she could practically smell him too.

And he smelled good. Better than anyone in the apocalypse damn well had the right to smell, and when she'd climbed past him, brushing up against him for that one little heartbeat…

She bundled the blanket around herself tighter, quivers radiating through her. It made no sense, this way her body reacted to him. The irrational flutters in her stomach. The involuntary way her breasts tingled or the flesh between her legs heated at the thought of him. She'd never been *this* turned on by anyone in her life, and like everything else, it was utterly idiotic too.

He was ulfhednar. He was the single, solitary *worst* person she could ever have found herself this goddamn attracted to, and the moment he learned what she was, he'd probably try to rip her throat out. It didn't matter if he was being friendly now or that he'd volunteered to cross this hellscape with her—and for seemingly altruistic reasons, no less. It didn't matter that he'd been nothing but kind to her, even while she snapped at him or ignored him. The moment he learned the truth, all that would go away.

And these weird, erotic reactions from her body? They'd probably get her killed.

Which meant Frankie and her dad would die too.

Fear tangled in her belly, joining the anxiety that seemed to have become a permanent resident. She couldn't let down her guard, now or ever, no matter how damn attractive this rugged, tattooed model of a gigantic wolf might be. She had one last job to do, and it mattered more than anything. Frankie and her dad had to be saved from the draugar and Ragnarok and whatever the hell *else* might be out here too.

And her mother—because, God, what that woman would do to them.

So Lindy had to stay alive, at least for now.

Carefully, her hand slipped down her side to her pocket and then withdrew her switchblade knife. Gripping it tightly, she watched Wes in the darkness as the minutes ticked by and exhaustion sank little fishhooks into her muscles and bones, dragging her down.

She wouldn't attack him if he didn't attack her. That much, she could promise herself. But there was no way in hell she'd trust him.

Or think herself safe, even for a second, as long as he was around.

She opened her eyes to the feeling of someone's hand on her shoulder, and instinct took over before her mind caught up. Her knife flicked open, stabbing directly at whoever had touched her.

"Whoa!"

Her vision cleared. His hands up and his eyes wide, Wes stood several feet away from the open door of the SUV, as if he'd leapt backward.

A rough breath entered her lungs. Easing the knife down, she glanced around while he lowered his hands.

It was morning.

Of *course* it fucking was.

Keeping the knife ready, she shifted around on the seat

until she was facing him. "You thought I'd leave, didn't you?"

He eyed her warily. "Crossed my mind."

Her teeth clenched. "I'm not your prisoner."

Wes gestured like he agreed. "Didn't think you were."

"Then why did you—"

Seething, she cut off. This was pointless. What's done was done, and she'd been right about him anyway.

Flicking the knife closed, she shoved the blankets aside and climbed out of the vehicle. "You check the house already too, then?"

"No."

She reached back into the SUV and snagged the handgun from where it had rested near her on the seat. Without a word, she shoved it into the back of her winter pants, grabbed the machete, and then stalked toward the building, leaving him to follow.

Only a heartbeat passed before she heard the crunch of footsteps behind her.

She ignored them.

The morning was silent around her, and to her right lay only empty fields and a few trees sheltering the property. To her left, the garage was closed, no light showing past the windows in the door. Two ravens sat atop the small building, one bird glancing around, the other motionless. When she spotted them, they seemed to turn at once, their beady eyes locking right on her and their heads cocking in eerie synchronicity.

Though surely that was just her imagination. As was the fact they looked like the pair she'd seen near Denver.

Because that was probably impossible.

In a burst of motion, both ravens leapt into the air, cawing loudly as they flew away.

She shuddered, watching them until they disappeared beyond the trees, and then made herself continue on.

A cement stairway led up to the back door of the farmhouse, the steps still covered in snow. With a wary glance at the windows nearby, she tried the handle on the white-painted door, twisting it slowly for fear of making a sound. The knob turned, the mechanism inside clicking softly as the latch gave way, totally unlocked.

Her lip twitched. God bless country living.

Slowly, she pushed open the door and peered in. A spacious kitchen waited inside, complete with an island with pots and pans hanging above it. A collection of dishes filled the drying rack next to the sink, and a coffee cup sat on the island, a stack of mail neatly arranged beside it. The hardwood floor creaked faintly as Lindy stepped one foot past the door, and she hesitated, waiting for a shriek from the draugar or a shout from anything else.

Silence.

Her eyes darted around, taking in the hallway leading deeper into the house and the doorways on either side, one standing open to a laundry room, the other to what looked like a stairway to the basement. The cabinets nearby would probably have food, and more winter gear and blankets might be farther within. The house felt cold, almost the same temperature as the air outside, which couldn't be a good sign. But then, the electricity might be out.

She bit her lip. If the people who lived here were still alive, then sneaking in was a brilliant way to get shot. If they weren't, then making any noise at all would probably prompt an attack by them or whatever killed them. Yet, if the draugar *were* here, drawing them out into the open would be safer than stumbling upon them when she was trapped by halls and stairwells.

Hopefully.

"Hello?" she called. "Is anyone home?"

Nothing.

"I'm not here to hurt anyone." She eased farther past the doorway and tucking the machete out of sight behind her. "I'm just..." Looking to steal their food? She grimaced at herself. "I'm wondering if you could help me."

The silence didn't change.

Letting out a slow breath, she walked into the kitchen, casting a short glance back as Wes followed her inside. Gone was his friendly expression. Now, he looked all predator, an air of almost preternatural menace radiating from him, promising to make a chew toy out of anything idiotic enough to fuck with him. In swift glances, his dark eyes scanned the open doorways and hall as if daring them to attack.

Lindy swallowed hard, wishing she hadn't gone ahead so swiftly and left him at her back.

"I'll check for food," he murmured.

She managed a nod, moving to put distance between them. Peering around the corner, she looked down the length of the hall while Wes quietly opened the cabinets.

The front door was open.

Shit.

Not taking her eyes from it, she drew the machete out in front of her, gripping it with both hands. Wes paused behind her.

"What—" he started.

She hissed at him to be quiet and then nodded to the hall. There was a screen door beyond the opening, and at night, it would have been difficult to tell the door wasn't shut, at least from the outside.

But it explained the cold air... and possibly the silence too.

She shifted her grip on the hilt, grateful that they had stayed in the SUV the night before. The open door didn't mean anything was in here.

It didn't mean something wasn't.

Carefully, she inched forward. There was a dining room to her right, the table cleared and the porcelain dishes in a glass cabinet untouched behind it. A closet waited below the stairway to her left, the shut door blending with the hallway walls paneled in oak. Pictures framed in cheerfully blue-painted wood hung along the corridor, showing a smiling young couple, some older people who may have been their parents, and countless adventures skiing or fishing or visiting Disney World.

Lindy trembled, hoping for their sakes they'd made it out somehow. Casting a short glance over her shoulder, she studied the shadowy recesses of the second floor above the stairway before creeping farther down the hall and peering into the living room at the front of the house.

She froze. They hadn't.

Two corpses sat on the couch, both of them positioned as if they were watching the lifeless television. Their bodies were desiccated, their skin gray and toughened like leather, pulled tight across their skulls. A few tufts of hair clung to their heads while more lay in piles on their laps, and they held hands as if sharing a private moment, even as their mouths gaped open in horror.

"Lindy?" Wes's whisper carried from the hallway, making her flinch.

She didn't look back, her eyes darting across the spacious room. This wasn't the work of the draugar, and she'd never heard of the Order doing anything like this. Which left... something.

And she didn't want to run into it herself.

Soft footsteps came from behind her. "Oh, shit," Wes breathed.

"Yeah." Lindy backed toward the hall, gripping her machete. "We need to get out of—"

"Help me?"

She whirled at the small, desperate voice.

A woman walked down the steps, her legs seeming unsteady beneath her. She was pale with long brown hair that hung past her waist, and her eyes were like black pools. Tottering down the stairs, she braced herself with one hand on the banister.

And she was naked. Stark naked, with her long hair covering her breasts and not much else. Breathing in short, ragged gasps, she staggered from the steps, her eyes locked on Wes like he was water in a wasteland.

She never even glanced at Lindy.

"What the hell?" Wes looked around fast and then pointed to an armchair. "Grab her that blanket." He started toward the woman. "What happened to you? What's wrong?"

Warily, Lindy slipped past the woman and hurried over to the chair.

"Please?" the lady begged. "I don't know where I am. Please tell me where I am."

Snatching up the blanket, Lindy turned back quickly.

And froze.

The woman's back wasn't human. Wasn't even like any animal Lindy had ever seen. Her skin was like tree bark, and a tail like a cow curled up along her spine as if tucked out of sight.

"Please?" The woman stretched out her hands as if to grab on to Wes for balance. He reached for her. "Where—"

"Don't touch her!" Lindy cried, dropping the blanket.

Wes pulled back immediately, alarm flashing over his face.

"*Please?*" The creature staggered toward him faster even as he retreated, her voice becoming strident. Hungry. "Where am I? Where *am* I?"

Wes backed away, his eyes darting across the room. The woman was between him and the hallway, and she was coming closer with every second.

Lindy yanked the knife from her pocket, flicking it open. "Wes!"

She tossed the blade, only to have panic grip her. He might not know how to catch—

Wes snagged the knife from the air effortlessly, whipping it between himself and the creature with lightning speed.

The blade sliced her palm, and the woman howled, recoiling. Hugging her hand to her naked chest, she glared for a heartbeat and hissed at Wes like a snake.

And then she lunged.

He swiped the blade at her again, retreating fast, but there wasn't anywhere to go. The corpses on the couch toppled to the side as he bumped into the sofa, trying to stay on his feet.

Lindy swung her machete hard. The blade slammed into the woman's back, lodging in her tree-bark skin and going no farther.

The creature screamed.

Lindy's hands released the machete and clamped over her ears against the high-pitched, deafening sound. Whirling fast with the blade still stuck in her back, the woman snarled and then jumped at Lindy like a wild animal.

Scrambling backward, Lindy retreated behind an armchair, moving fast to keep it between herself and the creature. She didn't know what would happen if that thing touched her.

The corpses seemed a good indication.

Wes spotted the woman's back, and his eyes went wide. "Holy—"

"Run, goddammit!" Lindy pulled out the handgun and opened fire.

Bullets ripped into the creature's chest, making her stagger, but she didn't fall. Her lips curled back, her face distorting as the motion continued, stretching her mouth like a demented clown and widening her eyes until the whites showed on all sides.

The gun clicked empty. Lindy's heart raced as her gaze darted around the room. There had to be a way past this thing. A way that didn't involve seidr. If she could make it to the front door—

Wes grabbed a wooden TV tray from next to the sofa. "Hey!"

The woman whipped around.

"Get the hell away from her," he snarled.

Swinging hard, he slammed the wooden stand into the creature's head. The woman stumbled to the side as the tray shattered.

"Go!" he shouted at Lindy.

She didn't need the encouragement. Darting out from behind the armchair, she bolted toward the hallway.

Like a cobra striking, the woman lashed out, catching her forearm.

Beneath her leather band, the tattoo on Lindy's wrist

flared white-hot, the pain piercing down through her skin until it felt like it scorched into her bones. She screamed even as the creature did too, and the woman fell to her knees, releasing Lindy immediately.

Wes didn't waste a second. Grabbing Lindy's shoulders, he hauled her away and pushed her ahead of him as she stumbled toward the door.

An ear-splitting shriek came from the living room behind them. Cringing, Lindy clamped her palms over her ears again as she raced out the back door and down the steps toward the SUV. Wes climbed swiftly into the driver's seat while she rounded the vehicle and scrambled in on the passenger side.

The woman ran from the door, her distorted mouth gaping wide in a scream.

"Go!" Lindy cried.

Wes floored the pedal, sending gravel and snow spitting in their wake as they flew away from the farmhouse.

# 8

## WES

"Are you all right?" Wes asked, throwing a fast look to Lindy as he sent the SUV careening back onto the road. Her scream when that creature grabbed her had sent his heart into his throat, and he still didn't feel like it'd come down.

Holding her right arm to her chest, she didn't answer.

"Lindy?"

He could see her grip shaking where she held her arm. Worried, he reached for her. "Lindy?"

She jerked away from him like his hand burned. He froze.

Rapid breaths entered and left her for a moment, and then she shifted on the seat, a steely cast coming over her face. Releasing her arm, she gripped the side of the door, her body rigid with tension and her eyes locked on the world beyond the passenger side window. "I'm fine."

He cast short glances at her as he raced the SUV down the road. Sure she was.

Though, really, who could blame her for being shaken?

What the *hell* had that thing been? Bullets couldn't hurt it, neither could a damned *machete*?

And those corpses...

Old memories of long-forgotten mythology classes played back as his heart slowed down. He hadn't been raised among the ulfhednar, at least not until after he was bitten and had nowhere else to go, but once he joined the pack, he'd been tutored with the rest of the kids. Connor's father had always insisted they learn mythology, which annoyed the hell out of most of them because how would *that* ever be relevant, and now...

"A fucking *huldra*," he muttered, incredulous.

From the corner of his eye, he caught sight of Lindy glancing at him.

"That was a huldra," he explained. "They're forest creatures. In myth, I mean. They've got a cow's tail and a back like tree bark and they..." Shudders ran through him. That creature had looked at him as if he was Sunday dinner and she hadn't eaten all week. "They seduce people, and if they're not, you know—" His eyes flicked toward Lindy and then back to the road, and he cleared his throat with discomfort. "Satisfied, they... they kill them."

Lindy looked away again, not saying anything.

His brow furrowed. She didn't seem shocked or confused. More like distracted, and her fingers had begun itching absently at the sleeve on her right wrist.

"You sure you're all right?" he asked.

She stilled her hand, placing it back in her lap. "Yeah."

He steered the SUV onto an on-ramp for the interstate, not sure he believed her. "Thanks for the knife," he said. "And the warning."

Lindy flinched again, as if he kept pulling her from her thoughts, and her gaze inched toward him. After a heartbeat, her head dipped in a small nod. "Thanks for the TV tray."

His lip twitched. "You're welcome. You were pretty impressive with that gun."

She looked away sharply, locking her eyes on the window at her side. "Anybody could hit a target three feet in front of them."

His mouth moved, but against her cold tone, he had no idea what to say. Blinking with consternation, he turned back to the road.

He didn't know what to make of her, except to think she disliked him for some reason. But then, she'd also saved his life, more or less, considering what might have happened if that creature touched him.

And what might have happened to her.

"You sure your arm is okay?" he tried again.

Her eyes snapped to him. "I said it was."

He held up a hand peaceably.

Blinking, she looked away slowly like she wasn't sure she should take her eyes off him.

A breath left Wes. Maybe it wasn't him specifically she disliked. Maybe it was anything or anyone inhuman. For all that she'd been friends with Hayden for years, she hadn't known the female was ulfhednar. She probably hadn't known anything outside of the so-called "normal" world existed.

Then she found out about "werewolves" only an hour or so before the world ended and everything from draugar to huldra to the-gods-knew-what-else came out to play. And that didn't even bring the Order into it.

All things considered, she was keeping it together amazingly well. But it was no wonder she was edgy.

Maybe he just needed to give her time to realize he wasn't actually…

His thoughts trailed off. What, a monster? Who was he kidding? He wasn't, but that didn't mean he was safe for her. That he could ever let down his guard for even a heartbeat, for her sake and his.

Gods, he was thinking like they could be… what? Friends? More?

Shifting position on the seat, he shoved the thoughts aside. He needed to focus on driving, not woolgathering over the beautiful enigma of a woman who could never be anything more than an *extremely* distant acquaintance to him.

No matter how much the delusional wolf inside him paced and grumbled about it.

Time crept by as he steered the SUV along the highway, stopping a few times to siphon gas with a tube Lindy produced from her backpack and endlessly veering wide of the draugar roaming the terrain. Slowly, exhaustion began to seep through him despite his efforts to fight it. He hadn't slept in two days, and barely slept the day before that. Meanwhile, the world around them was a monotone expanse of white and gray, with barely a curve in the road to provide variation. Whatever adrenaline he'd gotten from surviving the huldra's attack was long since gone, and his limbs felt almost as heavy as his eyelids.

This was absurd. Surely she wouldn't leave behind the SUV—and him—if he simply let her drive for a while.

At least long enough for him to get a bit of rest.

"Listen," he said. "Any chance you'd mind taking over a bit so I could get some sleep?"

She looked over at him, and for a moment, she said nothing. "Yeah, okay," she allowed. "I could…"

Her eyes went beyond him, alarm breaking past her closed-off expression. He followed her gaze.

For a moment, he couldn't tell what she'd seen. The landscape ahead looked burned—as if, like in Mariposa, this part of Nebraska was another place where fire had inexplicably poured from the gashes in the sky. But in the distance, it was encased in white fog, rendering the horizon a uniform blur.

Almost uniform.

Leaning closer to the steering wheel, he strained to see the strange object in the distance. It was tall. *Too* tall. Last time he checked, Nebraska didn't have skyscrapers, especially in the middle of nowhere.

He glanced over as they flew past the burned remnants of a highway sign. Most of the markings were charred, but he thought it said thirty miles to Lincoln, Nebraska.

Way too far for that to be a structure inside the city.

Apprehension bubbled through him. Maybe the road would curve away from it. Maybe it was just a trick of the weird, overcast light... or lack thereof.

With every mile marker, he thought they would come upon it, but still, the structure remained shrouded by fog, far in the distance and yet growing larger with every moment.

Gods, it had to be *huge*. How had they not passed it yet?

Gradually, the highway curved, carrying them on an angle away from the thing. But as the minutes passed, the fog began to thin. The expanse was hazy, but he began to be able to make out a shape.

His mouth moved. "What the *fuck*..."

A person stood in the open fields, towering taller than the Empire State Building. Its back was hunched, its gray skin mottled like the surface of the moon, and its long arms dangled down beside its ragged loin cloth and knobby knees. On its face, it bore a beard that looked made of snarled seaweed and dead trees, the tangled mess covering everything below its bulbous nose and pinprick eyes.

It was a frost giant. It had to be. In enormous, lumbering strides, the thing walked along the countryside, billows of fog rising like a smoke machine all around it.

And suddenly, he realized why.

In an instant, the ash-covered highway turned to a sheet of ice and snow, and the windows frosted as if from a sudden temperature drop. He pumped the brakes, trying to find traction where there wasn't any, while the SUV slid on the wintry road, careening wildly.

The tires made a crunching sound. The SUV tipped as they left the road behind.

And then came the ditch.

# 9

## LINDY

L indy groaned, grimacing as she opened her eyes.
One minute they'd been driving, closing in on that
towering nightmare on the horizon, and the next...

Slowly, she leaned her head away from the hard surface
beside her. She hurt. All over, she hurt, and gingerly, she
lifted a hand to her head.

A painful lump throbbed beneath her questing fingertips, dried blood crusted on it.

Dammit.

She looked to her left and then paused, confusion
hitting her. Wes was stirring at her side, groaning too, but
he seemed higher than her. The whole cabin of the SUV
was tilted, and beyond him, she could only see snowy gray
sky and no sign of the monster walking across the countryside.

"You okay?" Wes asked, worry in his voice.

"Yeah. You?"

He started to nod and then winced with pain. "Yep."

The guy barely sounded it, but she didn't argue. They were alive. It was enough. It meant they could keep going.

Away from the thing that could only be a goddamn frost giant, somehow wandering the scorched Nebraska fields, turning them into the arctic.

She swallowed hard. Icy roads were probably only the beginning of what that thing could do.

Moving slowly, Wes reached up and tried to start the SUV. The engine grumbled but didn't turn over. "Shit," he muttered.

A shiver went through Lindy. No. No, she needed this vehicle. *Any* vehicle, but out here, where she'd seen nothing but the SUV for miles...

Looking around, Wes seemed to orient himself, and then he grabbed the handle and shoved at the driver's side door, leveraging it open despite the way it kept wanting to fall closed.

Taking a deep breath, Lindy turned, trying to do the same.

The passenger door wouldn't budge.

Her heart began pounding harder, her blood pressure rising. Scrubbing her arm across the fogged window, she tried to see past the glass, but all she could find was snow. Grunting hard, she shoved at the door again.

"Hey."

She shoved again.

"Lindy!"

Whirling, she looked back to find Wes reaching toward her.

"Here." He stretched his arm as far as he could. "Come on."

She reached out and grabbed his hand. Bracing himself, he pulled her with him as she clambered across the seats and out the door. Swinging down from the opening, she landed on frozen dirt and snow.

And slipped.

Wes caught her.

Lindy froze. She was right up against his chest, so close she could feel his warm breath on her cheek. Her hands clutched his coat where she'd grabbed him for balance, and his face was only inches from her own. A sudden, irrational compulsion gripped her to reach up and run her fingers across the dark stubble on his jawline. The smell of sandalwood and musk surrounded her, lessening the panic and fear of a moment before, leaving only the desire to bring him closer, breathe him in, and God, yes, let him do all manner of amazing things to her. Heat rushed through her body, making her throb and bombarding her with insane impulses that were impossible. Suicidal.

Overwhelming.

"Are you okay?" he murmured, his deep voice only inches from her ear.

A full-body shudder coursed through her. God, she... she wanted...

Exhaling sharply, she retreated, not looking at him as she braced herself on the side of the SUV. A heartbeat passed before she could find her voice, the sound strained to her own ears. "Fine."

When he didn't respond, her eyes crept up in spite of herself.

Wes's head twitched in a nod, a tight expression on his face. He probably thought she was nuts.

Better that than a threat.

She tried to refocus, looking at the SUV, because for goodness' sake, now was not the time for any of this. Not even the *person* for any of this, by far. What the hell was wrong with her?

*Focus*, dammit. She had to focus. The world around her was a charred wasteland buried in snow, and their vehicle was stuck in a ditch. The sooner they got it out of here, the sooner she could rescue her family from her mother.

And get away from this disastrously tempting, *distracting* wolf.

Taking another breath, she forged along the side of the SUV, using the vehicle for balance as her boots sank into the snow. The driver's side seemed fine, but when she reached the front of the vehicle—with Wes way too close behind her for comfort—she spotted the other wheel on the passenger side.

Her body went cold.

"Dammit," Wes muttered.

The axel had snapped, and the right front wheel was lodged sideways under the vehicle. It was only a miracle the SUV hadn't flipped.

Trembling ran through her. There was no fixing this. Ragnarok didn't feature a maintenance shop. And they were miles from Lincoln, let alone Minneapolis, with nothing but miles of the burned and frozen wasteland around them.

Beneath her leather wristband, the tattoo itched like tiny teeth biting into her skin. Ever since the huldra grabbed her, it hadn't stopped, and even now, she could feel the shadows at the edge of her mind roiling like amorphous monsters who thought their time had come.

Did she have days left? Or was it only hours—*minutes*, even—until whatever was holding back the darkness finally collapsed and the curse took her? Before she was gone? Too late to save her dad, her brother. Too late to save anyone from what she would become.

Tears stung her eyes. She'd run all the way to Minneapolis if she could.

"Guess we're walking," Wes said. His feet sloughed through the snow as he headed for the back of the vehicle.

She didn't move, her trembling growing worse as rage and sobs and a scream all boiled up inside her. So, what? He thought they had all the time in the world then? And fine. Sure. Walking was the only choice, but would it be enough? Could she be fast enough to stay ahead of the monsters, when the monsters were in her own body, slowly devouring her soul?

*On that day, you shall know neither pain nor sorrow nor joy. You shall only be our weapon as we lay waste to the corrupt world.*

"Lindy?"

A shudder ran through her. She couldn't take her eyes from the SUV.

"We'll just—"

A scream left her. Wildly, she kicked the fender.

"Holy—" Wes forged through the snow back to her. "It's okay. We can—"

Her boot slammed into the SUV again.

"Lindy—" He reached out to grab her.

She yanked away from him. "It's not fucking okay!"

"What—"

"Nothing is fucking *okay!*" She stared around at the empty wasteland. There wasn't anything she could do to stop herself if the curse took her. No gun. No machete. Just endless fucking snow and the hope Wes would give the knife back before she killed him too.

"Lindy, we can still—"

"No." She shook hard, her muscles longing for something to punch. Something to *do*, if only to change this. With every ounce that remained of her soul, she wanted to fly straight to Minneapolis this moment, where her dad and Frankie would be alive, and safe, and Carolyn wouldn't have found them.

Yet.

Shudders racked Lindy's body. "She's going to kill them. She's going to... And I can't..." Her voice choked. "There's no time to..."

She hugged her arm to her chest, her body caving in on itself as the tears burned in her eyes.

"Who's going to kill someone?" Wes's voice was quiet behind her.

Trembling racked her. She dashed the moisture from her eyes and tried to ignore the way her skin itched and the shadows roiled in her mind. There wasn't time for this either.

For anything.

Turning fast, she shoved through the snow toward the back of the SUV. Yanking the rear hatch open, she set to shoving supplies into bags. Warm things, she would wear. Food, she could carry. And maybe—*probably*—she wouldn't make it, but...

Dammit, she knew she was going to die.

But she wasn't dead yet.

A FEW MINUTES PASSED BEFORE SHE HEARD CRUNCHING ON the snow behind her, and a short glance back confirmed it was Wes following, a backpack slung over his shoulders with a rolled-up sleeping bag on top.

She returned her attention to the road, her eyes darting over the icy expanse as time ticked by. That frost giant was gone, somehow vanishing over the horizon during however long she'd been unconscious, but God knew what else could be out here. Beneath the snow, every vehicle she passed looked burned to charcoal, which might mean draugar, might mean something worse. She wanted to think the flat fields and endless snow would at least give them a chance to see a threat coming, but myth held too many monsters for her to be sure.

"Someone's threatening your family," Wes said, his soft voice breaking the quiet. "Aren't they?"

She didn't respond. Another minute crept by.

"Who?"

She walked faster.

Wes sighed. "Lindy, if there's anything I can do to help you, I—"

"You can't."

"Why?"

She gritted her teeth. She shouldn't have spoken. Shouldn't have lost control, either, back at the SUV because, damn this wolf, he probably wasn't going to stop asking. Or wondering. Or staring at her with those deep, gorgeous eyes, waiting for a chance to pry into—

"Listen," he started.

"My mother, okay? My mother."

He was silent. She scowled.

"Why is your mom going to kill your family?"

Seething, she looked away. Screw him. Nosy, prying, *goddamn* wolf with his gentle questions like this was *so* easy to explain. Like he even had a right to know.

Like he wouldn't kill her over the truth.

"Has she tried before?"

"Dammit, this isn't any of your—" She spun at him, furious, only to have her words falter at the look in his eyes.

The concern was palpable. A gentle care for her, for her *family*, and it hurt, somehow. Hurt like a knife slipped between her ribs, stabbing whatever was left of her heart, because it couldn't remain, not if he knew the truth. Wes was ulfhednar—and not one like Hayden who hadn't been raised by the wolves, who didn't think the way they all did. Even if Dad and Frankie had never been part of the Order like Lindy had, they'd still joined. Not because they believed, really. But because they didn't have a choice.

But that wouldn't matter. Not to a wolf. He'd leave them to die.

Two less Order members in the world.

"I just want to help, if I can," Wes said.

A painful scoff rose in her chest, and she swallowed it back down. That wouldn't happen if the truth came out. But she'd also seen enough of him in this past day to know the persistent bastard wouldn't quit asking, no matter what.

He'd followed her halfway across the country on less than this, after all.

Cursing to herself, she started walking again. "My mother is dangerous," she allowed, choosing her words carefully. "She... She thinks Dad stole us from her after their divorce. And before all this happened—" Her hand twitched toward the world around her. "Dad had ways of keeping us safe. Courts and video recordings and threats of restraining orders. But now..." A shiver ran through her. "I'm sure Dad's considered she might be coming, but...

Mom is *ruthless*. She wants my brother back. Me too. And if Dad gets in her way…"

For a long moment, Wes didn't say anything. "Is she why you learned to fight like that?"

Lindy's eyes flicked to him, wary, but there was only sympathy in his gaze. "You could say that."

She returned her attention to scanning their surroundings for enemies, hoping he wouldn't pry any further. A highway sign remained standing up ahead. Snow caked most of its surface, but a sheet had fallen away, revealing enough bubbled paint and surviving markings to show Lincoln was still miles off.

Tugging the bag higher on her shoulders, she tried to walk faster.

"I get it," Wes said quietly.

She looked over at him.

"My, uh…" He cleared his throat. "My folks weren't the best, and, um… after I was changed"—his head bobbed while he searched for words—"they didn't take it well."

She hesitated. "Changed?"

"Bitten. When I was eleven. And when I shifted for the first time…" He scrubbed a gloved hand over his face. "See, my parents had this church. Real hardcore kind of place. Nothing like those nice churches who feed the homeless or whatever. Dad was the preacher; Mom was the dutiful wife, and when they saw their son turn into a wolf…" He laughed. There was no humor in the sound. "They decided Satan had gotten me. Turned me into a demon. So they tried to exorcise it. And when that failed…" His brow shrugged. "Kill me. Because, you know, they thought I was a monster."

She stared.

"I got away. Obviously. But I guess my point is… I get

it. Kind of, I mean." Wes met her eyes. "We'll find your dad and your brother. We'll get them back safe, and you..." He started to smile, but the expression seemed strained. "You'll have the whole pack around you, making sure no one can hurt any of you. Okay?"

Lindy swallowed hard. God, she wanted it to be like that. Wanted that world, where her family could be safe with protective wolves all around, ready to tear into the draugar and the Order and who knew what else if ever they were threatened.

Her chest ached. She wanted that so badly she could cry.

Even if she never lived to see it.

She nodded, looking away. "Is, um..." How the hell did she ask what she wanted to know without giving anything about herself away? "Is that common? The ulfhednar, you know... biting kids?"

"No." Wes was quiet for a second. "The one who attacked me... He was a sick bastard. I wasn't the first. Wouldn't have been the last. He'd been tearing kids apart up and down the Mississippi River, but everyone thought it was a human serial killer. Until me. I was the only one who, uh"—he cleared his throat—"lived through what he did and the change that came after it. But once the other wolves learned what was really going on, they tracked him down. Stopped him."

She blinked, at a loss for what to say.

He drew in a breath. "But the pack took me in. Gave me a place to stay." He gave her a smile. "They're my family. Best one I could have asked for."

Weakly, she struggled to return the expression.

"So what about you?" he continued.

She tensed.

"What are your dad and brother like?"

Turning back to the road, she struggled for words that wouldn't give anything away. "They're, um…" Her shoulder shrugged. "They're great. Frankie—my brother—he, um… he's just a kid, you know? Thirteen, but… still a kid." Her chuckle took her by surprise. "Not that I could tell him that, of course."

"Of course," Wes agreed, smiling.

She found a smile tugging at her lips too. "But yeah, he loves his Fortnite and Minecraft and anything like that. It's all he talks about. Well, that and the cello. He… he plays. A lot. He's *so* good at it, like he was born for it. He's going to a camp this summer and…"

Her words trailed off as the strangely cathartic feeling of talking about her family drained away. It was May now, almost June, and the world was encased in snow if not burned.

"Or he was," she finished.

"Sounds like a great kid."

She drew in a sharp breath, refocusing as she nodded. "He is."

"So if he plays the cello…" Wes began. "What about you?"

A sharp laugh escaped her. "Yeah, um, no. Not so much." She hesitated, her smile fading. "There wasn't much music when I was a kid. Frankie's lucky."

Wes was quiet for a second. "What kind do you like?"

She glanced at him.

"Music?" he prompted, his expression friendly, as if he wanted to help things be better somehow.

"Little bit of everything, really," she managed with a shrug. "Even country."

His brow climbed. "Seriously?"

"What?"

He grinned. "Nothing."

"It's not a disease, you know. There are some really good artists."

He held up his hands, still smiling.

"What about you, then?" she retorted, finding herself grinning too, in spite of everything.

"Not country."

She scoffed at the theatrically disdainful look on his face.

The conversation continued, meandering through music and movies and food. He liked anchovy pizza, which she couldn't believe, and the fact that she enjoyed sauerkraut made him shudder. He loved old comedy movies, same as her, though they disagreed on what was the best of the Mel Brooks canon.

And for a little while, she almost forgot how many things in her life had gone wrong.

GRADUALLY, THE LIGHT BEGAN TO GROW WEAKER AS THEY walked, hinting that evening was on the way. In fits and starts, their conversation stalled while they both kept an even warier eye on the terrain around them. Despite all the truck stops and assorted remnants of buildings they'd passed, nothing was left fully standing. The highways were dotted with burned vehicles, their occupants charred and motionless beneath the ice and snow.

And she'd thought Mariposa was hit badly by the flames...

But for all the destruction, one thing was missing, and

as much as that should have been a relief, she found herself getting more nervous by the moment.

"Have you, um, noticed..." she began in a quiet voice to Wes.

"No draugar."

She glanced at him. His jaw muscles jumped beneath the scruff on his cheeks, and his sharp eyes scanned the landscape with a focus that led her to think he saw more than even she could. In one hand, he adjusted his grip on a piece of metal he'd picked up a few miles back, the closest thing to a machete they had now that the last was stuck in a huldra.

"We need to find a place to get inside," he said.

"Or a car."

He glanced at her, not saying anything, and then returned his attention to studying their surroundings. Everything was reduced to rubble around the highway, offering nowhere to hide, and the flat land made it difficult to see anything too far in the distance beyond the destruction. "This way."

Leaving the highway, he started up the slope of an overpass, his boots slipping in the snow. Grimacing, she followed. A few abandoned cars dotted the road when they reached the rise, none of the vehicles appearing usable.

"Those look like buildings to you?" Wes asked, pointing to a spot on the horizon away from where the interstate curved.

Lindy squinted. In the distance beyond the charred and frozen terrain, she could just make out shapes like tall, narrow rectangles, what she would have obviously called architecture before she knew frost giants were in the world.

"I think so," she allowed.

"Come on." He headed toward a junction where the overpass met with another road leading toward the buildings in the distance.

She sighed. Structures still standing meant areas with less damage—hopefully, anyway. Maybe that would mean a car or another SUV they could use, rather than more walking through the exhausting snow.

And more time slipping away from her.

Even though she suspected they were heading into the city, the rubble of destroyed structures was still spread out along the road. A burned husk of a fast-food store here, the charred and bubbled remnants of a car dealership there, and swaths of snowy nothing in between. The long, straight road stretched out ahead of them, feeling endless with the distant buildings never growing closer, as if they were walking on a treadmill.

And overhead, the sky grew darker.

Lindy bit her lip. She still had a flashlight in her bag if worst came to worst, but she wasn't sure whether it'd be safe to use it. Yeah, it'd let her see, but in the great, dark world, that beam of light would also make them a target. And despite the fact the ruins of each structure were far apart compared to some towns she'd seen, after so long on the empty interstate, she felt like anything could be lying in wait, as if they were surrounded by countless traps waiting to be sprung.

"Son of a—" Wes stopped cold, his eyes locked on the distance to her right.

"What is it?" she asked.

"Draugar. I can't hear how many. Lots." He looked left. "More that way, I think. Fuck."

"Come on." She forced her tired legs to move faster,

and she could hear Wes take a ragged breath as he followed her.

She glanced at him, a new worry gnawing at the edge of her adrenaline. He had to be exhausted, even more than she was, given that he hadn't slept in nearly two days. The realization brought guilt, too. Sure, she hadn't forced him to stay awake like that, but he'd done it because of her all the same.

"There." He pointed, and she followed the gesture, her heart pounding.

A strip mall still stood about half a mile ahead. Other buildings waited beyond it, as if she and Wes had finally found the place the fires had stopped.

The shrieks of the draugar carried on the breeze.

Wes grabbed her arm. "Run."

They bolted down the road, her backpack bouncing on her spine. She could barely hear over the sound of her own breathing, and at any moment, she expected the draugar to come charging past the rubble, ready to tear them apart.

"This way." Wes pulled her with him as he ran for the back of the strip mall.

"Where are you—" she started.

"Can't break the glass doors in front." He dashed along the rear wall. "We won't have anything between us and them."

Skidding to a stop at a rusted metal door, he threw a look around fast and then jammed the sharper end of the metal beam he'd been carrying into the space between the door and its frame, wrenching the steel like a crowbar. "Come on... come on..."

The lock gave.

Looking around, he motioned for her to get inside. Slinging her backpack down, she fumbled around within it for a flashlight, clicking the device on quickly before hurrying through the doorway.

No draugar lunged at her. A small storage room barely larger than a glorified closet surrounded her. Metal shelving held everything from shoeboxes to clear garbage bags of what appeared to be clothes, and when she peered past the door on the other side of the tiny space, a disorganized thrift shop full of old toys, ragged clothes, and ancient electronics equipment waited.

She clicked off the flashlight while she inched past the storage room doorway, not wanting any light to pass through the windows at the front of the store and draw attention. The ambient light still outside was barely enough to see by, thinning the shadows of the store and picking out the shapes of clothing racks and glass cases. Warily, she crept farther in, checking carefully past the displays for any sign of bodies.

Nothing.

A breath left her, a puff of fog in the shadows. Whatever looters may have survived in this town clearly hadn't made it here yet, which would have been a relief if those types were the worst things the two of them had to worry about. Meanwhile, the light was fading fast outside, and the parking lot was empty. With the draugar somewhere in the distance, hunting a usable car right now might well be suicide.

Resignation settled over her, weighing heavy on her tired muscles. Guess they were staying here for the night.

She glanced back to see Wes carry a wooden chair from behind the register and wedge it under the door handle of the stockroom exit. Returning to the front of the shop, he checked around briefly and then took a box of old toys from the shelf, bringing it with him into the stockroom as well.

"Wes, what are you—"

"Alarm system." Carefully, he set the toys down on the floor in front of the rear exit and then in front of the storeroom door as well.

Her confusion faded. Right. Clever. Even if something got past the chair on the door, it'd make noise coming in, warning the two of them.

Taking another box from the shelves, he strode past her, heading for the metal-framed glass door at the front of the shop. The arrangement of the rudimentary alarm system done, he stayed by the windows, watching the darkening world outside.

Her eyes lingered on him. No way she was letting him be the one to stay up keeping watch tonight. The man hadn't slept in two days.

In the fading light, her eyes skimmed the racks around her, spotting what she needed a moment later. Careful not to make noise, she pulled down the quilts hanging on a display near the wall. The two of them were carrying blankets, sure, but more would always be welcome. Scanning the shop, she settled on a spot behind a display cabinet filled with costume jewelry. Tossing the heavy quilts down, she went and retrieved several more, along with a bundle of comforters hanging nearby.

Rough bed, but better than a hard floor, anyway.

Shedding her backpack and gloves, she sighed and then crossed the small store. In the shadows to one side of the front window, Wes stood, his tall form barely visible in the swiftly deepening darkness.

"Go ahead and get some sleep," she said. "I can take first watch."

He looked over at her, hesitating.

"I'm not going anywhere," she said, irritation in her voice. "Draugar and darkness and burned cars, right? Bad plan?"

Wes paused a moment longer before nodding. "Let's get some food first, eh?"

Her mouth tightened. "Okay, but I'm still taking first—"

His eyes snapped to the windows, alarm on his face. "Shit."

Moving fast, he pulled her deeper into the shadows of the corner and pushed her behind him. Her back hit the wall, and his firm grip held her there as he kept his focus on the glass. He was so close, she could feel every quick breath he took in the way his coat brushed against her, and his scent surrounded her in the tiny space, inexplicably tempting and yet distracting as hell.

Seconds crept by.

Shuffling forms staggered along the sidewalk only inches from the window of the thrift shop. Their rotted mouths dangled open, and one of them was missing a lower jaw entirely. Several looked as if they'd been dead for years, while others were clearly new additions. A draug at the front of the group wore a work uniform, blood and gore staining his khakis, and his name tag hung askew from his shredded polo shirt.

Bobby, the tag read.

Lindy trembled, the shadows stirring at the edge of her mind.

Keening and chittering noises came from the draugar as they stumbled along the pavement, their heads jerking left then right, as if they couldn't control their muscles well enough to move their skulls easily. Their foggy, rotting

86

eyes twitched in their sockets, seeming to focus on nothing but spasming wildly all the same. As they passed, one of them thudded a hand rhythmically against the window, the limb swinging from a dislocated joint and leaving smudges on the glass every time it struck.

Pressing her back harder against the wall, Lindy didn't dare to breathe. Would they hear her heart pounding? Pick up on the warmth of her body and Wes's here in the corner? How good was their vision, when their eyes were glazed so milky white?

In all her childhood, the Order never cared for what it would take to survive the draugar. They were only interested in the nightmarish damage the creatures could wreak.

The monsters staggered onward, passing beyond the store window. His hands still gripping Lindy, holding her behind him, Wes didn't move.

She swallowed hard, silently willing the creatures to keep going, not that it would do much good. For all she knew they were circling the building, making ready to come back again.

Shivers coursed through her. They wouldn't. They'd go away.

God, let them go away.

The light faded from the sky, gradually drowning the store in abyssal dark, and in the silence, their quiet breaths seemed inordinately loud without the noise of traffic or the hum of an air conditioner to disrupt them. She felt as if she might as well have her eyes closed, so dark were their surroundings, but the lack of sight proved the old wives' tale true, bringing every other sense into sharp focus.

The texture of the rough wall behind her. The chill of the winter air on her face. The warmth of Wes's proximity, like a delicious heater doing strange things to her insides, while his scent surrounded her, stealing away the dust and mothball smell of the thrift store, replacing it with spice and musk that tangled her mind like knotted string, making it hard to think.

"I can't hear them anymore," Wes whispered.

She inhaled sharply, startled by the sudden sound of his soft words.

His coat brushed against her as he turned. "You okay?"

"Yeah." Her response was quick.

But he didn't move.

The heat inside her grew, pooling low in her middle and somehow stealing command of her muscles. Dammit, he... he needed to go. He needed to step back right now because her body was wanting things that were stupid as hell, and she wasn't—

His fingers touched her own, and she clamped her lips shut on a needing whimper, only to hear his breath catch as if he'd picked up on the sound anyway. In the darkness, his weight shifted as he moved ever-so-slightly closer, and the flesh between her legs throbbed in mad, ludicrous hope.

Gently, he took her cheek, and she squeezed her eyes shut. No, this... this was absurd. This was insanity. Just because her mouth watered to taste him and her clit pulsed with desire, she... she shouldn't...

But God, she wanted to.

His lips brushed hers, and she couldn't restrain a gasp. Her hand moved like it had a mind of its own, gripping his side, keeping him from moving away.

A hungry noise escaped him, wild and not remotely human. Everything she should be running from, and somehow, it made her wet as hell instead. He moved forward quickly, pushing her to the wall as his lips crashed into hers, his tongue plundering her mouth. His hands raked into her hair, knocking her knit cap aside and holding her to him, while his body pressed against her own, the hard length of his cock pushing at his winter pants and her midsection alike, making her body beg for more.

Shoving past his layers of clothes, she slid her hands beneath his pants. As her fingers dug into his ass, holding him to her, he groaned against her lips.

But this wasn't enough. She wanted more. Wanted this to happen immediately because God help her, she'd lose her mind if she couldn't have him in her right now.

"Fuck me," she gasped. "Oh God, Wes, fuck me."

A desperate sound left him. Instantly, he hefted her up as if she weighed nothing, and her legs wrapped around him on instinct. As he carried her through the darkness, navigating by the sharpness of ulfhednar sight, she ground herself against his hardness, her body screaming for release, and a choked noise of desire left him.

Bending swiftly, he laid her on the makeshift bed behind the display cases, and immediately, she reached for him, drawing him down to her. His mouth found hers, one arm bracing him above her, while his free hand worked to tug her pants aside, not moving quickly enough for the irrational need heating her blood.

Releasing him for the moment, she twisted beneath him, grabbing at her laces and yanking the knots undone. Kicking off the boots, she shoved her pants away, her body throbbing and her impulses screaming to be rid of the fabric, to feel him, to have him in her this minute. The fact they had no protection was irrelevant—wolves couldn't get a human pregnant anyway, and there weren't any diseases that jumped species—which meant that even though he was stripping down beside her, pants and coat gone, sweater remaining, neither of them were moving remotely fast enough.

The scent of him surrounded her. The warmth of him was a banked fire only a few torturous inches away. And she was freezing. Drowning. Desperate for him to return in a way that made rational thought impossible.

Bitter cold gnawed at her bare legs, but in only a moment Wes snagged the blankets and hauled them over her, enveloping them both in the heavy coverings. In the dark, she reached down, her hand wrapping around his length. Moisture clung to the tip of him, and he groaned as she stroked his silken shaft. Her body throbbed for him as her legs fell to either side and her hips rose in a silent plea.

Kissing her ravenously for all of a heartbeat, he repositioned himself and guided his cock closer. As his mouth broke from hers, she clamped her lips shut against a moan, her clit aching. But for an eternal moment, he hovered at her slick entrance, not moving to enter her, and through his sweater, she could feel his muscles tense, his body hard as iron and utterly motionless except for his short, rapid breaths.

What...? Why wasn't he...?

A pleading whimper left her and she rocked toward him, and whatever cliff he'd been on, that tiny motion seemed enough to push him over the edge. With a growl like an animal, he impaled her with a spike of pain and pleasure so intermingled, it unraveled her thoughts, leaving only desperate craving. Inch by amazing inch, he drew himself out, only to drive himself deep into her again, over and over as her breasts tingled and her head lay back on the rough pile of blankets, her body lost to mindless need for him to never stop. Please, God, never stop.

Fighting not to moan too loudly, she slid her hands beneath his sweater and shirt, clutching his back, hanging on for dear life. Covered in a thin layer of sweat, his skin felt at first like hot granite, but then rough textures met her fingertips, gnarled but smooth, strange to the touch.

But she couldn't concentrate on it for long. His mouth came back to hers, devouring her while one of his hands slipped beneath her clothing, pushing her bra aside to embrace her breast, massaging it as he drove himself into her. His rough thumb played across her hardened nipple, pinching and rolling it with his fingertips, sending jolts of ecstasy down to her clit like electrical surges.

With everything she had, she tried to keep from crying out. The monsters were still out there. Who knew what else too. But... God...

Her breaths came hard and fast. The pain and pleasure and heat pulsing through her was building like a wave, rising higher with his every thrust. And it didn't matter if she drowned in it. Nothing mattered at all. All she wanted was his amazing body pounding into hers, hitting her so deep inside, she couldn't think beyond this moment.

"Harder," she gasped. "Please. Harder—"

Wes's fingers pinched down hard on her nipple, throwing her over the edge. The orgasm surged through her, obliterating everything in a blinding rush of ecstasy. Her muscles clenched around him, and her hands dug into his back as kaleidoscopic pleasure flooded through her, washing away all but his body and hers in this one white-hot moment. She felt him grip her tightly, and he let out a muffled growl as his own orgasm overtook him. Even as her muscles clutched him, he drove his cock into her desperately, emptying himself into her.

His motions slowed, his breaths coming in rapid gasps that matched her own. Beneath her ribs, her heart pounded so hard as if to break itself free, and she melted into the pile of blankets, her body sweaty and boneless in the afterglow.

Of sex.

With Wes.

She wetted her lips, blinking in the darkness. Holy shit, she… they…

Her clit tingled, ready for more.

Inhaling sharply, she shifted position beneath him, and he drew back, hesitating only a moment before pulling out of her. His motion sent a waft of cold air beneath the blankets covering them, and she tensed for a whole new reason, but quickly, he tugged them into place again, wrapping them both back in the warm cocoon.

For a moment, she couldn't move. Did she say something? Get up and go? One of them needed to keep watch after all, and even now, she could hear his ragged breaths slowing behind her. Making him stay awake would be cruel, given how he hadn't slept in two days, but getting up now might promote conversation.

And damn her if she didn't have a clue what to say.

Rolling to her side away from him, she bunched the blankets under her chin, trembling.

What the hell had she just done?

# 10

## WES

Wes opened his eyes. Morning. Gods, it was morning. Gray sunlight already poured through the store, lighting on the rough bed of blankets and quilts.

Which smelled of sex.

And Lindy.

And was empty.

Oh, gods.

He scrambled to his feet immediately, scanning the store, not giving a damn he was still half-naked. She wasn't in the bed, which meant she might have already left, and if he'd driven her away—

In a shadowed corner by the front window, she sat on the floor with her knees hugged to her chest and her knit cap firmly back on her head. She looked at him, her body language and expression radiating tension, and then her eyes flicked down toward his naked lower half.

"Would you put some clothes on, please?" she asked tightly.

Embarrassment flooded him, and he bent quickly and pulled on his pants even as the wolf inside him rumbled with confusion. This wasn't right, not to that beast. She'd opened for him, begged for him, clawed and clung to him as he'd driven himself into her hot depths. The wolf didn't want clothes. It wanted her back on this bed right now, moaning with pleasure as he worked her incredible body into orgasm after orgasm with everything from his tongue to his cock.

*My mate.*

Wes's hand stilled on his boot laces. That wasn't... *she* wasn't...

His heart began to pound. Everything in him was drawn to Lindy, and last night, he'd been too damn tired to resist. He'd tried. Gods help him, he'd tried, but the feeling of her amazing body, the smell of her arousal, and the way she'd moved to take him into her had just... He couldn't stop. Should have, probably. *Definitely*, considering the look on her face now. But she'd begged him to have her, and he'd craved her more than there were words to say.

And now the wolf thought she was his mate.

He wanted to throw up.

His mate couldn't be a human. It didn't matter that this particular human was a consummate badass or the most alluring thing he'd ever seen. It didn't matter how much he was intrigued by her, or amazed by her, or how fascinating and intoxicating it'd been to simply get to know her better on the road yesterday.

Lindy was human. Therefore, he could *never* have her, no matter what the wolf thought it wanted.

Damn that creature. Cardinal rule number one, and that bastard was breaking it.

Wes raked a hand through his hair. Gods, what if he'd

bitten her? He didn't remember doing that, but what if he'd done it all the same? The wolf wanted her, after all. Maybe it wanted her like *that*. And what about kissing her? Sure, that didn't break the skin and every study he'd ever read said saliva alone wasn't enough to force someone to turn—nor was coming inside them during sex, for that matter—but were the experts sure? *Really* sure? This was her life at stake.

The wolf inside him whined, straining at his skin. He needed to bring her back over here. Lay with her again and make her moan for him because it craved her.

Ruthlessly, he smacked the animal down, cursing internally. He'd never put much stock in the myth of wolves knowing their mates when they saw them, and given the fact the damned, rabid beast was pining after a human?

Yeah, that shot *that* fantasy straight to hell.

Holding his hands steady by force of will alone, he finished lacing up his boots and then rose to his feet. His body stiff with tension, he walked back toward her. "You all right?" he asked neutrally.

She looked up at him. "That can't happen again."

A slight shudder went through him. She was right. He knew she was right. But her voice was like iron, and the wolf inside him whined to hear it. He smacked the creature back a second time.

And nodded.

Echoing the motion tightly, she dropped her gaze from him and then climbed to her feet. Stepping back to give her room, he gritted his teeth against the tremor that shot through him as she passed, the air carrying her delicious scent in her wake. The whole shop smelled either of her or sex or both, and he didn't dare move toward her as she crouched beside the bed and rolled up several blankets to strap to the top of her backpack, for fear of what the wolf inside him wanted to do.

The beast whined, protesting that if not sex, at least he could bring her food for the morning or find her even more warm things to wear.

He turned away, heading for his own bag near the window. Food he could do, and not because the wolf wanted it, but because it was basic, and important, and she damn well needed to—

Lindy was already heading for the back door. "You coming?"

The ice in her tone was like a lock clicking shut against anything between them. Not that there *was* anything, nor could there ever be. As of yesterday, the best he could've hoped for would have been something resembling distant friendship, given that she was human.

But his wolf was a traitor, and insane besides, and even if by some miracle Wes hadn't bitten her, last night had still fucked everything up five ways from Sunday, so now...

Stabbing down the treacherous ache in his chest that had no right to be there, he shoved the can of food back into his bag. Best to just get going. Minneapolis was still a long ways off, and they could eat on the way.

In silence and barely looking at Lindy, he walked past her toward the rear of the shop. Pushing aside his rudimentary alarm system from the night before, he cautiously tugged the metal door open and peered outside, scanning the terrain for any hint of a threat. The early morning light through the dense clouds cast the world in gray, with all the soft shadows just thick enough to make him worry they would disguise movement. Beyond the back of the strip mall, small houses and trees dotted the next road, each building seeming ominous for how still they were.

He'd avoided the houses last night out of concern someone inside would have a gun, but the morning revealed an eerie quality to their stillness that somehow made him doubt anyone or anything was left alive inside.

His eyes caught on a streak of brownish-red, and he froze for a heartbeat. Wariness prickling through him, he eased from the doorway and down along the length of the strip mall.

Beyond a tree, a small white house stood, a symbol scrawled on its pale blue door.

His heart began to pound harder as he scanned the other homes. A few were nothing but scattered rubble and charred frames randomly placed among their still-standing neighbors, as if the houses had blown up rather than simply burned to the ground. But on every building that remained, there were more brownish-red symbols that had been lost to darkness the night before, now marking every front door he could see.

"Shit," Lindy whispered behind him. He threw a look over his shoulder to find her staring at the symbols too.

Marks of the Order.

Anger boiled in him. *Not* the Order. Not originally. Once upon a time, those had been sigils and runes belonging to ulfhednar history, marks meaning everything from the sun to the gods to all manner of things. They'd been *good* symbols, peaceful symbols from ancient ulfhednar faith, used the world-round by his people.

Instead of marks stolen by a group who had no right to them, who twisted them into signs of hate and terror, and claimed those signs from ulfhednar history represented the Order's vision of a "purified" world—one in which all his people were dead.

And now those bastards were painting them in blood

everywhere they went. The Order had scattered the marks across Mariposa after the city burned, and the gods only knew what they planned for them. Twisted or not, folks who used seidr said those symbols had power, and given what he'd seen of seidr thus far, he was inclined to believe it. But as for what *these* symbols were going to be used for...

Wes glanced around. He and Lindy were closer to the right side of the strip mall than the left, and houses surrounded them on all sides. Though his instincts demanded they find cover, there was no telling what wandering into the thick of houses painted with those runes would do. But if the two of them reached the main road, they might be able to find a vehicle and get the hell out this place.

The sooner the better.

He crept forward, moving as fast as silence would allow. Beyond the corner of the strip mall, an expanse of empty parking lot waited, enclosed on two sides by shops and sheltered from the road by some kind of family restaurant up ahead. The terrain around them was mostly flat, with trees and a few more houses, and almost no cover at all.

Dammit.

"Come on," he murmured. "Quick."

They ran for the relative shelter of the restaurant wall. Hurrying along it, he peered around the corner, scanning the road past the building. A car dealership stood about a city block's distance ahead on the opposite side of the street, numerous vehicles still standing untouched in its lot.

A breath left him. That'd work.

Checking around again swiftly, he started out from the

shelter of the restaurant. They'd need to break into the dealership itself to find keys, considering hot-wiring basically didn't exist the way Hollywood showed it. But with any luck, they'd have their pick of—

Rapid crunching sounds came from his right. He threw a fast look toward the sound just as a young woman with dark hair barreled from the neighborhood they'd just passed, running for her life.

Her eyes went wide at the sight of them. "Run!"

A dozen draugar charged out behind her. A man with a face like a skull strode after her, glowing green light twisting around him like a toxic aurora borealis.

Wes grabbed Lindy, shoving her ahead of him toward the road. "Go!"

She took off, and he bolted after her, racing toward the car dealership across the broad expanse of snowy road.

"No!" the dark-haired woman shouted. "Don't—"

Draugar poured around the cars at the dealership, shrieking and scrambling toward them across the icy lot. An Allegiant followed them, green auroras swirling around him. On the road, Wes skidded, grabbing for Lindy as he fought to change direction quickly. Catching her arm, he hauled her ahead of him again, pushing her toward the houses beyond the strip mall.

The Allegiant who'd chased the woman shouted a command in some bastardized form of old Norse. For one moment, nothing seemed to happen, and then shrieks rose from within the neighborhood ahead too, and corpses staggered out from between the houses.

Wes slid to a halt on the ice and snow. They were surrounded.

Cursing vehemently, he backed away from the draugar while his wolf stretched beneath his skin, ready to shift and rip through as many of the bastards as he could to protect Lindy. It'd cost him the winter gear he wore, but that was a small price compared to watching the draugar tear her apart.

*Kill them,* the wolf raged. *Kill them all.*

"When I say run," Wes snapped over his shoulder to Lindy. "You follow me, you hear me? I'll clear a path and you go."

She didn't move, her eyes on the draugar. Behind her, the dark-haired young woman stared at them both, confusion and terror in her eyes.

"Dammit, Lindy, do you hear me?"

Glass shattered and the dark-haired woman screamed. Draugar stumbled from the stores of the strip mall, their skin tearing on the shards of glass still clinging to the sides of the front windows.

His heart pounding, Wes scanned the area fast. The road away from the city would be a death trap. There was nothing that direction except burned buildings and ruined cars, leaving the three of them running for their lives until whenever the tireless draugar finally caught up to them. The neighborhood was likewise out, given the horde. That left running toward the city and hoping they could find some way to escape.

He rolled his shoulders, his wolf snarling inside him, ready to shift.

"Ulfhednar!" the nearest Allegiant shouted.

Wes's eyes snapped back toward the oncoming horde to find the bastard pointing at him. The man's skull-like face cracked into a garish smile as he walked toward them, anticipation glinting in the black pits of his eyes.

A derisive look on his face, the other Allegiant strode closer while the draugar parted around him. "Kill the wolf," he commanded idly. "Leave the women to convert or die."

Wes reached for Lindy. "Stay behind me."

Lindy stepped past him, avoiding his grasp. Her eyes never left the draugar.

"Dammit, Lindy," Wes cried. "Get—"

A blast of glowing green energy exploded from where she stood, shredding through the air like a sonic boom all around her. He staggered, the air burning as it passed him, and all around, the draugar toppled, their bodies collapsing into dust. Tumbling backward, the Allegiants crashed to the snow.

But she wasn't done. Racing forward, she flicked open a switchblade in her hand. With deadly precision, she threw the knife, impaling it in the nearest Allegiant's eye as the man tried to scramble to his feet. The other turned, attempting to run, and Lindy lunged, ripping the knife from the dead Order member and throwing it at the next with lightning speed.

The man flopped to the ground, the knife embedded in the base of his skull.

Wes stared as Lindy stopped, her expression unreadable while she regarded the dead Allegiants and the draugar in piles of dust. Her body didn't shimmer with toxic auroras like theirs, but when she turned to him, he could see a faint greenish cast on her skin, along with a hint of darkness that drifted over her face like cloud shadows. She watched him for a moment, something sorrowful passing through her eyes.

And then she collapsed like a rag doll to the ground.

# 11

## LINDY

Nervousness fluttered like a trapped bird in her chest and the hot autumn air made her sweat beneath her itchy black robes, but Lindy was determined to give no sign. This was it. The moment she'd been training for all twelve years of her entire life, and she couldn't risk any hint of a lack of discipline now. Only three other Initiates stood in line beside her and one—just one—of the four would be chosen for the greatest honor of all.

Dal Hegnar stepped onto the wooden stage. The Grand General of the Order of Nidhogg, his weathered face was pocked by old scars from battling the corrupt. Rumor had it he'd killed an entire clan of berserkers in the Grand Tetons—the very last of those bear shifters, even—and had single-handedly taken on a whole pack of ulfhednar in Michigan besides. His frame was short, stout, and only the most foolish would mistake that for weakness. He'd been her teacher since she was four years old, and he'd often said she was his prize pupil.

But favoritism meant nothing today. Only true worthiness mattered.

With a face of stone, he regarded the Initiates, and the trapped bird in Lindy's chest turned to a hive of bees. A thousand terrible scenarios raced through her mind—he'd found fault in her; she'd failed the training somehow—before Dal Hegnar ever opened his mouth.

"Your will has been tried. Your mettle has been tested. And today, you stand before us in claim that you are worthy. Who will vouch for these Initiates?"

Soft footsteps landed on the gravel behind her. A hand took her shoulder. "I vouch for Melinda."

Lindy fought to keep her face still at the sound of her mother's voice, for all that she wanted to beam with pride. Carolyn was Second to Dal Hegnar, next in line to lead the Order and nearly equal in worth to the general himself. To be claimed by her was a badge of honor all on its own.

But it was an obligation too. What would happen if he chose another today? All her mother wanted was for Lindy to achieve this, to prove their family worthy despite her father's reluctance to join their cause. If Lindy failed, how would she ever look her mother in the eye again?

Trembling, Lindy kept her back ramrod straight and didn't glance around as others stepped forward to claim the Initiates on either side of her.

"Today," Dal Hegnar continued. "We mark not only an initiation but a sacred rite passed down to us throughout the generations. The Scythe of Niorun is ready to leave this life, so another must be chosen. Thus, on this hallowed occasion, one of you will be selected to give your life in contribution to our cause. What say you? If chosen, will you accept? If not chosen, will you concede to the will of the Order?"

"Yes, sir!"

Her affirmative cry rang out in the autumn morning, and

she fancied for a moment that maybe, just maybe, Dal Hegnar's eyes landed on her with the barest hint of a smile.

"Then let us begin."

He looked to the side as a wizened old man stepped from behind the curtains. His body was gnarled by age, but it bore the scars of countless battles fought victoriously against the corrupt and his eyes were sharp as he scanned the Initiates.

Dal Hegnar turned back to them. "The mark shall pass from the former Scythe to the new, to be borne until the Great Awakening and the end of days."

The old man sank onto a small wooden stool, the only concession to his age.

"And now..." Dal Hegnar lifted his hands, his palms spread wide. "Step forward, Melinda."

Elation erupted in her. Just as she started to move, her mother's hand tightened on her shoulder, and Carolyn's voice whispered in her ear. "I'm so proud of you."

Lindy struggled to contain her smile. It wasn't fitting on the solemn occasion, she knew. But it rose up inside her like sunlight all the same.

As if on clouds, she walked toward the platform, scaled the three steps, and came up to Dal Hegnar's side. With determination, she put her palm in his, waiting as the old man took Dal Hegnar's other hand as well.

"This is the promise of your new birth," Dal Hegnar said to her. "Of the release of fear, of pain. When the day comes, you will not feel these. All doubt, all question will be gone. You will know only your purpose to serve as the Scythe of Niorun, and you will be pure." His hand tightened on hers slightly. "Do you accept this honor for which you have been chosen?"

Her smile quivered on her lips. "With all my heart, sir."

• • •

LINDY OPENED HER EYES.

Dim light thinned the shadows around her, and her back lay on something lumpy but soft. The smell of cleaning solution surrounded her, hanging heavy on air thick with damp and the nose-tickling feeling of mold.

She blinked, her gaze sliding around. The walls were unpainted concrete. There were pipes on the ceiling, and a ragged mobile of paper mâché planets dangled from one of them, lit by a blue-white light that didn't fully dispel the darkness.

Her brow furrowed. She felt... different. Emptier, just a little bit, and strange too. Not quite right, but she didn't know why. She was scared, she was sure of that, but the emotion seemed thinner than it probably should have been, like an image with the colors beginning to fade out.

And that scared her even more.

She was losing herself. There was no other explanation. To save Wes and that woman—hell, to save herself—she hadn't had an option.

Burn up her own spirit. Sacrifice her soul and become hollow like the Order, but far, far worse.

Or let the Order capture her in that parking lot.

She squeezed her eyes shut, pain passing through her like a fish below black water.

A rustling sound came from nearby. Her eyes flew open and she lifted her head. At the foot of the pile of cushions that formed her makeshift bed, Wes sat on a folding chair, his elbows propped on his knees.

Her leather bracelet dangled from his hand.

"Hope you don't mind I took your bracelet off," he said flatly.

She trembled, not taking her eyes from him.

"You're Order?"

Her head shook immediately. "No."

His brow twitched up. "Your wrist begs to differ."

Unsteadily, she drew a breath. "I was... once."

He didn't say a word.

"I was raised by them. My mother, she..." A chill crept through Lindy. "She's still part of it. I trained with them until I was fourteen, and then my dad... When he saw what it was doing to us, he worked to get us out. Break through the conditioning and the... mindfuck."

Wes eyed her. "But you didn't get the tattoo removed."

"Because the tattoo artist could be one of them. You know they're everywhere. They always have been." She shivered. "If I did that and they found out, they would've killed my dad."

Plus, it wouldn't have helped anything.

She swallowed hard. "Mom was content to leave us alone as long as she thought we'd come back to her someday. But now..."

"Apocalypse. All bets are off."

Lindy nodded. "I just have to know they're safe."

"And get them back to Mariposa." A cold note carried through his voice.

She hesitated. "If I can."

His eyes didn't leave her.

"Dad and Frankie aren't—" She cut off, revising. "Dad never got very deep into this. And Frankie was just a toddler. They started him on the training but... It was just games at that age. Not like... not like later."

The ice in his expression deepened.

"Listen," she said. "I'm not going to stay in Mariposa, okay? You can kick me out or do whatever you want once I've got them safe. But, please. They don't deserve what Mom would do to them."

He watched her for a long moment, and she swore the sound of her heart pounding was the only noise in the room.

A breath left him and he looked away. "Does Hayden know about you?"

She fidgeted uncomfortably on the cot. "Yeah."

He glanced back at her.

"The day that guy broke into our apartment, he…" She grimaced. "He said he'd recognized me in the flower shop. After he left, I kind of had to explain why."

Wes was quiet again. "I've heard rumors about their initiation process. What happens before you get one of those." He jerked his chin toward her wrist.

She couldn't meet his eyes.

"Who'd you kill?"

Her left hand twitched toward her right wrist as if to cover the damned mark, and she stopped herself. It wouldn't help anything. "I… I didn't. Not a wolf like you." The weight of the truth pressed on her chest. "I think."

Seconds crept by in silence.

"You saved my life."

Lindy looked up at him.

"Yasmeen's too." His head twitched toward the door. "But… it hurt you."

She didn't know what to say. The words were barely a question, and she knew the answer was obvious.

If lacking in detail.

"Can I have my bracelet back, please?" she asked instead.

He watched her for a moment and then extended the leather. She wrapped it around her wrist swiftly, some small measure of tension leaving her at having the mark out of her sight again. "Where are we?"

Wes hesitated as if debating whether to press for more, but finally he just sighed. "Subbasement of an elementary school. Yasmeen and I... After what you did, there weren't any more draugar around, so we got you out of there. The survivors have been hiding in this place." A nauseated look passed over his face. "The ones who are left, anyway."

She nodded, her gaze dropping away. "A-are they... Do they think I'm—"

"They won't touch you."

Wes's voice was uncompromising, like there wouldn't be an alternative no matter what he had to do.

Her eyes flicked back up to him, something hot stirring in her belly at the possessive promise in his tone. And at the intensity in his gaze, the heat grew, her body warming with a hungry desire for him to reach for her, touch her, kiss her, and do so much more. She was suddenly painfully aware of him sitting there, in the chair at her feet, where only a brief movement could bring him down onto the makeshift bed and on top of her.

And it was madness. Last night had been too much, and last night had to be it, forever. But, God, her body didn't want to listen. It wanted him on the pile of cushions right now, her mouth tasting him as his hands slid over her breasts, gripping her sides, his cock thrusting in her until she screamed.

Wes cleared his throat and looked away. "Come on." His voice was gruff. "We should get you some food."

She fidgeted uncomfortably, embarrassed at her own arousal, and then she hesitated, the hot desire fading like a receding dream. She wasn't hungry. Not even a little bit. If anything, the thought of food turned her stomach, though she couldn't understand why. But at the sensation, a flicker of terror passed through her, the kind that should bring tears to her eyes. Something had happened to her; she was sure of it. Something new and terrible, like a harbinger of unknown horrors to come. The details of the Scythe's transformation were sketchy, since for any regular Allegiant it would have been over swiftly, and they wouldn't have cared what it took from them anyway.

After all, a loyal Order member would have surrendered to the transformation immediately. They'd never cling by their fingernails to every last shred of their humanity, fighting like hell against the alterations.

Losing ground every day.

Darkness whispered on the edge of her mind, not fading this time, as if the clouds had finally rolled in to surround her on all sides. And in it, the feeling of shapes drifted, like ghostly specters in the fog. Some this way, more that way, hungry and snarling and ready to devour her whole.

But her eyes stayed dry and unaffected by the realization. Even as her heart raced, even as the pressure of a sob pushed at her chest, nothing changed, and her terror sank deeper into pure dread.

The Order had already taken away her ability to cry.

# 12

## WES

Order.

Lindy... was *Order*.

The thought had been banging around in his head for hours while she slept, her skin somehow more bloodless than he remembered. Within moments of getting her to this dingy subbasement, he'd taken off her bracelet, though what he'd sought to convince himself, he still wasn't sure. But there it was, the green-black tattoo of a snake wrapping her wrist, its fangs sunk deep into the roots of the World Tree. Sure, the mark was a little odd compared to other tattoos on the Order members he'd seen. The snake's body extended out farther across her inner wrist, and the World Tree's branches were twisted into runes he barely recognized. But there was no denying it. She was an Allegiant.

And she'd saved his life.

He couldn't understand it. From what he gathered from Hayden, she'd known Lindy for years. The Order *trained* to spot ulfhednar, learning everything down to the musculature and body language cues that most of his kind found impossible to hide. So Lindy must have known what her friend truly was, and thus by all rights should have killed her on the spot. Admittedly, Hayden was unbelievably good at hiding, but...

*Order.*

He felt like the world had flipped upside down.

Keeping an eye to her, he led Lindy across the small room. Old cushions filled the space, laid out like beds, though there were more of them here than survivors now.

It didn't take a genius to guess why, given the haunted looks he'd seen on the humans' faces.

But beyond the door on the far side of the tiny room, a larger space waited, a common area the survivors seemed to use for meals and gathering away from whoever happened to be trying to sleep. There were only four of the humans left now, a motley assortment of folks from all walks of life, hunkered down in a subbasement and only leaving to scrounge food. In the hours since Lindy passed out, he'd barely left her side to find out more from them, speaking to the humans only enough to establish that the group would be reasonably safe for Lindy—no one planned on running to the Order, and damn well no one was coming near her. But they'd seemed just as cagey about him as he was about them, and if nothing else, he couldn't leave Lindy unconscious and undefended.

Crises did strange things to people. Some shut down, some worked together, and some stabbed everything and anything in the back, just in case it'd help them survive.

The wolf paced, growling. He'd meant it when he told Lindy no one would touch her. He may not understand this—hell, if he'd possessed an iota of sense, he probably should have been running for the hills—but the idea of abandoning her now made the wolf inside him go even more insane. The damn beast was worried for her. Chew-through-the-walls worried over her, but really, so was the man.

She looked bloodless. Cold in a strange way that had nothing to do with the winter chill. The arousal coming off her a few moments ago had been the strongest flash of life, of *normal*, he'd seen from her since she woke up, and may the gods help him for how much he and the wolf wanted to take her up on *that*, ludicrous as it would be.

But when she'd first opened her eyes, she hadn't even appeared surprised she passed out. If anything, she seemed like she knew it would happen. Her expression had been resigned but pained, as if she'd lost a struggle but known she would. Yet, she'd helped him and Yasmeen despite that fact.

And despite the fact he'd bet money whatever happened was still hurting her now.

He turned back to the door, pulling it open. Something was still very wrong with Lindy. His gut was screaming it and his wolf wanted to tear it apart, even if he didn't have a clue what it was.

But, gods help him, she was Order. He'd say that was fucking wrong enough.

The survivors looked away from their quiet conversation at a folding table when he came in, and he could see the caution on their faces when they spotted Lindy. The wolf inside him growled instantly at the sight, and he bashed it down. They had every right to be nervous.

Whatever sane part of him remained was too.

"Lindy," he started. "This is Yasmeen, Anthony, Julia, and Eloise." He nodded toward the four people seated at the table.

"She safe to be in here?" Anthony eyed Lindy from beneath his stained baseball cap. A burly man with red splotches on his skin and a ragged beard, he sat with his thick arms crossed over his coat like he was passing cold judgment on the world from his folding chair.

Yasmeen cast him a tight look, but her dark eyes didn't leave Lindy for long. Like the others, she wore an assortment of mismatched clothes, whatever they each could find to keep them warm. Despite the heavy layers, though, everything about the young woman seemed hard and sharp, from her cheekbones to her clipped words when she spoke, as if everything in her had been honed down to iron determination just to survive. "She saved my life."

"Doesn't mean we should let her too close."

Wes's temper flared, but Eloise spoke before he could. "The girl obviously isn't one of them, Anthony." The thin, gray-haired woman braced herself on the table as she rose to her feet. "You can see it in her eyes."

Limping slightly, the woman crossed the room and reached out to take Lindy's hand.

Wincing, Lindy pulled back before Eloise could touch her. "I don't want to hurt you. I'm sorry."

Eloise nodded. "See?" She looked back at the others. "Now would one of the ghosts say that?"

Anthony frowned and adjusted his crossed arms with a discomfited shrug.

"Ghosts?" Lindy asked warily.

"That's what they call the Order," Wes wetted his lips, not sure how much to explain of what he'd gleaned from the humans. How much she obviously might already know. "They said they, um…"

"They take people," Yasmeen filled in.

Lindy looked over at her.

"They give everyone a choice. Swear your soul to their 'cause' or get turned into one of those zombie creatures." Yasmeen eyed Lindy like she was on the fence about having her here, despite what she'd said to Anthony. "My brother tried to join last week. He thought he'd survive it. Just tell them he was on their side to give me and my parents a chance to get away." Her jaw muscles jumped and when she spoke, her voice shook. "There wasn't anything *left* when they were done with him. That green power they have, somehow it *knew* he wasn't really with them, and it burned him alive. I managed to run when the rest came for us, but my parents..." She turned away, looking choked up.

"Out there now with the rest of them," Anthony muttered. "Just another body for the horde."

Near him, the teenage girl, Julia, whimpered and hugged her arms to her chest as if trying to hide inside herself. Her brown hair was a tangled mess, and an old bruise discolored her cheek green and yellow like an unripe strawberry. She couldn't have been more than fifteen years old, and Wes could only imagine what she'd seen. The entire time he'd been here, she hadn't taken her eyes from the floor and never said a word.

"Is that what they tried to do to you, dear?" Eloise asked, bending slightly to catch Lindy's eye.

Lindy swallowed hard. "Um..."

"She look burned up to you?" Anthony made an irritated noise, shoving up from his folding chair. "This was a mistake. We don't know what the hell this girl is. You never should have brought them back to—"

"We don't leave people to die!" Yasmeen snapped. "You agreed to that. You don't like it, *you* can get out."

Anthony's red splotches darkened, but for just a heart-beat, Wes caught a flicker of fear in his eyes.

"We won't hurt anybody," Wes said into the tense silence. "It's like I told you. We just need to get Lindy back on her feet and then find a car."

Anthony snorted. Wes's brow drew down.

"That's going to be a little difficult," Eloise said apologetically.

"Why?"

The older woman looked to the others.

"None of the cars work," Yasmeen said. "The, uh, 'Order' made sure of that. Messed up the engines or laid traps in all of them. They booby-trapped all the houses, too. Everything blows up if you're not careful. We were able to take some stuff from the kitchen at the Runza before they got it as well, but—"

"That's a fast-food place nearby," Eloise explained at his confused expression.

"But the markets are overrun with zombies," Yasmeen persisted. "Anywhere that doesn't stock food or supplies, they don't care much about, but grocery stores, houses, anything we need to actually stay alive..."

"But they haven't found this place?" Lindy asked, a wary note in her voice.

He understood the feeling. If things were as bad as they described, how was this place untouched? Surely the Order would have considered humans would hide out in this enormous brick building.

Yasmeen glanced at Anthony.

"School was built in the nineteen-twenties," he admitted grudgingly. "Had a couple renovations since. Old boiler room and some storage areas got sealed off till the school district could afford to haul all the old junk out, but no one ever did. And if you know your way in..." He shrugged a shoulder as if indicating the space the group now called home.

"He works here," Yasmeen added.

"*Used* to. Not like kids'll be starting class again anytime soon, will they?"

Yasmeen turned away, grimacing, while Eloise looked sick and Julia closed her eyes like she was trying to hide. Anthony shifted his weight, his sarcastic expression fading into a flicker of remorse.

"So there aren't any cars?" Lindy pressed.

Their discomfited expressions deepened.

"What?" Wes asked.

"There's downtown," Yasmeen admitted. "The place is practically made of parking garages, and we've seen a few cars driving out of there. But getting to them is impossible."

Lindy looked between them. "Why?"

"'Cause they've got the whole goddamn thing overrun, that's why," Anthony snapped. "Zombies everywhere. Ghosts too, patrolling every damn hour of the day. The bastards know we need a car to get far enough from here to stand a fucking chance, so we figure they're leaving the working ones there as bait, just so as we can get ourselves killed trying to reach them."

"Going there is suicide," Yasmeen agreed. "The road passes over two bridges, and while the first isn't so bad— just a little stretch across a frozen creek—the second one is long and has train tracks beneath it. There's no cover at all, so no matter which way you try to cross, you're totally exposed to the monsters on the other side." She shook her head. "We don't know how much longer we can make it here, but... downtown isn't an option. I'm sorry."

"Well, now, hang on a sec," Anthony countered as if something had just occurred to him. "If she claims she's not one of them, why not have her get us through?"

Wes's wolf was instantly on alert. "That's not—"

"I can't fight them," Lindy protested tightly.

"Why the hell not? You stopped them out there, right? You want a car or don't you?"

"I *can't*," Lindy insisted.

"Now how do you expect us to believe that, huh?" Anthony started toward her, pointing a finger at her face. "If you—"

Wes put himself between the big man and Lindy, and Anthony stopped. "That's enough." Wes could hear the growl in his own voice, and it was difficult to control. The wolf was snarling inside him, rabid with fury that this guy might try to touch her. "She *said* she couldn't."

"If she isn't working for them, then why—"

"Because it hurt her, you idiot," Yasmeen interrupted.

Anthony scoffed. "She's still standing. That's a damn sight better than your brother—"

Yasmeen shoved to her feet, her chair scraping loudly on the concrete. "Don't you dare bring him into this."

The big guy's mouth moved, frustration twisting over his face. "We're going to *die* here! She's the best damn shot we have at—"

Wes took a step forward. "She said no."

Anthony drew himself up, fury reddening his face to the shade of an apple. His nostrils flaring, he stared at Wes as if trying to figure out how to force them both to do what he wanted.

The wolf stretched under Wes's skin, even if his body didn't move a muscle. Without a word, he met the man's eyes, knowing what the blustering bastard would see.

Humans weren't that different from prey, not to his wolf. And prey knew when they were looking at a predator.

Fear flashed in Anthony's gaze.

"I-I think there's something I can do."

Lindy's voice was more tentative than anything Wes had heard from her before, and his wolf raged at the sound. Fuck this bastard for scaring her. Fuck the Order too. He'd kill the whole fucking lot of—

Wes made himself turn away from Anthony, though his ears still listened for any sound of the asshole trying to attack. If the man valued his life, he wouldn't push this.

Anthony didn't move.

"What are you thinking, dear?" Eloise asked carefully.

Lindy shifted her weight, her face so bloodlessly pale, it speared pain straight through his fury. "I..." She swallowed hard, and her eyes twitched toward the walls like she was seeing something through them. "I think... maybe... I can tell where they are." She looked back, her eyes meeting his, something heartbreakingly sad in her gaze, and his heart ached to hold her and take the pain away. "I think I can get us past them."

Anthony harrumphed. "Well then—"

Wes's eyes snapped back to him, a growl threatening to curl his lips. The man blanched and took a step back.

Drawing a breath and fighting to calm down, Wes looked back at Lindy. "You sure you can do this?"

She hesitated and then shrugged. "I'm not sure there's another choice."

He grimaced.

"Okay," Yasmeen said into the silence. "I guess we're following you, then."

## 13

## LINDY

S omewhere inside Lindy, fear fluttered like a moth lost in the darkness, but she couldn't tell if it was her own self-control or what the Order had done to her that kept her from reacting to it. Deep down, she knew she was probably panicking. Maybe even screaming in terror. But from the outside, she was pretty sure she didn't look like she was reacting at all.

And that only made the little moth flutter harder in the dark.

The others packed up quickly, loading what they could into a mismatched assortment of multicolored backpacks before pushing aside a wall panel and shining their flashlights out into the dark. Beyond the makeshift door, another room waited, this one clearly in better repair. Eggshell paint covered the cinderblock walls and cartoonish signs warned of the dangers of touching hot pipes. By the far wall, a metal stairway led up to a closed door.

She drew a slow breath of the cold air. Even though the

survivors didn't appear to have a heater, their body heat in that smaller space had kept it warmer than here. Warily, she glanced around, but somehow, she knew no one besides their small group was in the room with them.

The shadows whispering in her mind were sure of it.

A slight tremor rolled through her. She wasn't certain the figures shambling along the edges of her mind were the draugar. Nor was she convinced the lighter ones, the ones that slipped and slithered like electric eels through the darkness, were the Order. But as the others had been talking, she'd felt the figures moving in the distance, collecting here, leaving there, and she'd wondered.

Was it possible? Was she really picking up on them?

Her trembling grew worse, but no matter how her fear battered around inside, it couldn't bring to her eyes the tears she wanted to cry. But maybe the tears didn't matter anyway. She and Wes couldn't stay in that crowded collection of hidden rooms forever, and the survivors were clearly desperate. Hell, she was too.

Every second she waited was too long.

She climbed the stairs, watching the closed doorway above, but nothing burst out at her. No sound came but the soft clank of their footsteps, and when she reached the top and gingerly eased the door aside, only an empty hallway lined with mustard-brown lockers met her eyes. Dim light carried from the distant glass doors along the length of the corridor, reflecting dully from the speckled tile, and the smell of old smoke mingled with the scent of chalk dust on the chilly air.

Hoisting her bag a bit higher on her shoulders, she started down the hall. Empty classrooms lined the corridor, their desks arranged in neat little rows as if simply waiting for the students to arrive. Cheerful decorations dotted the walls, smiling suns and clouds and flowers, while posters exhorted students to do their best and be kind.

Swallowing hard, she locked her attention on the glass door ahead, feeling like a ghost herself, haunting a bizarre mirror world. And maybe, on the other side of that mirror, the kids were in their classrooms. Maybe, in some other reality, they were laughing and smiling and doing all the things the merry posters said.

Instead of lying dead in the frozen ruins or stumbling and snarling somewhere beyond these brick walls.

Shuddering, she continued on. When she reached the glass door, she took a moment to study the snowy street beyond the ash-covered panes, but nothing stirred in her mind. Cautiously, she inched the door open.

The world was as silent as ever.

"Which way?" Wes murmured behind her, and she cast a quick look back to see him regarding the burly asshole, Anthony.

The big guy eyed her with equal parts caution and satisfaction, and it made her skin crawl. "Left. Back to the main road, and then due east."

"Are you, um, sensing anything or... whatever?" Yasmeen asked her.

Lindy hesitated and then shook her head. Unable to meet the eyes of the others for long, she hurried down the steps.

The neighborhood was eerily still, and snow crunched beneath their feet as they walked away from the school. Keeping an eye to their surroundings, she avoided lumps in the snow that might have been bushes or corpses or something worse. The cold weather had thinned the smoke in the air, and it didn't seem to sting her eyes like it had in Mariposa.

Though maybe there was another reason for that.

She gripped the straps of the backpack and ordered herself to focus. Rust-red marks scored the doors and walls of the houses around them: runic commands for summoning the draugar, for controlling them, for setting alerts that would trigger if anything entered the buildings. Beside a blue bungalow, she spotted the wreckage of a car, its frame a warped mess of charred metal. Debris impaled the house walls. Twisted shapes that might have been corpses still sat inside.

"Booby-trapped," Yasmeen whispered behind her.

Lindy kept moving. The main road lay only a few blocks farther on, and at Anthony's muttered direction, she headed left again. Long stretches separated the buildings, as if the owners had all the space in the world and hadn't cared that dozens of yards of empty terrain lay between them and their neighbors. Fast-food restaurants and gas stations and car dealerships stood like islands in a snowy sea, some marked by symbols from the Order and others providing a final resting place to burned and abandoned cars.

But nothing provided much cover, and she found her feet moving faster and faster, trying to reach somewhere that at least would give them a place to hide.

Whispers carried from the edge of her mind, and her eyes snapped to the right. "Back. Back now." She motioned frantically toward an array of construction equipment lined up in a parking lot to her left, as if the vehicles had once been for sale. Frantically, the group rushed behind the large machines.

"What did you—" Anthony started.

"Shh." Wes's command was sharp. He peered past a nearby forklift, his eyes skimming the road in an unfocused way, as if sight wasn't the primary way he was surveying their surroundings.

Swallowing hard, Lindy didn't move from her crouch behind the wheels of an orange-painted bulldozer. Even with the bulk of the machine beside her, she felt painfully exposed on every other side. The cold seemed to seep deeper into her now that she wasn't moving, and all around them, the wind was the only sound.

Was she wrong? Maybe the whispers in her mind were only delusion. Maybe she was losing her mind, and now she'd dragged these innocent people out into the cold, when she couldn't help them at—

Groans and chittering sounds like bones clacking together carried on the breeze. Distant footsteps dragged through the snow.

Lindy froze. Behind a backhoe, the teenage girl, Julia, bundled a fist into her mouth like she was trying to keep from screaming, while Eloise closed her eyes, her mouth moving silently as if in rapid prayer.

Yasmeen stared at Lindy, expectation in her eyes, and Lindy looked away, the darkness at the edge of her mind stirring as if in anticipation of gaining more of a hold on her. Already, she could feel the mark on her arm tingling, waiting for her to call on the curse.

She dug her fingers into her thigh, barely daring to breathe. The shuffling sounds grew louder, and trembling, she risked a glance through a gap in the machine.

Half a dozen of draugar staggered out from behind a warehouse across the road, one of the dead still wearing a hard hat and another in a reflective vest stained in grime. Their heads lurched left, then right like guard dogs spasmodically sniffing the air, but they didn't rush at the construction equipment, continuing instead along the road until they disappeared into a neighborhood buried beneath the snow.

A slow breath left Lindy. No shapes drifted at the edges of her mind, and after another moment, she nodded to the others.

She could feel the group staring at her while she walked cautiously away from the bulldozer.

In silence, they continued through the snow, hiding twice more when draugar and the Order passed. But none of the creatures or their glowing green handlers came too close to the humans or the wolf hiding nearby.

But she wasn't reassured. Not when, as the minutes crept past, the shadows in her mind started to change. At first, it was only a tumbling feeling up ahead, like a little wave lapping onto a shore and then slipping away again. But the farther along the white stretch of snow and nothing the group walked, the larger it felt. There weren't any shambling figures ahead of them, nor any slippery eels darting from the shadows.

There was an ocean. A tidal storm rising on the horizon.

And they were heading right toward it.

She chewed her lip, her heart pounding. There was no going around it. The sensation stretched as far out on either side as she could feel. But the closer they walked, the more solid it felt, even as it kept roiling and churning in her mind.

The bridge came into view ahead. The broad stretch of cement had probably been pretty before the world went to hell, with green lamp posts and a matching metal railing with wide walkways on either side for pedestrians. Abandoned cars cluttered it now, most of them crashed into each other or hanging from the side of the bridge where they'd slammed into the fence. A tiny park waited to the left, right where the bridge began, with clusters of bushes, benches with the engraved names of whoever donated them, and an old-world lamppost like they'd all fallen back into Victorian England.

Lindy couldn't take her eyes from the space beyond the park. She couldn't see anything there yet, but it didn't matter.

She could feel it. The churning sea waited just past the greenery, along with a white-noise whine that made no sense off to her left. While the others glanced around worriedly, checking their surroundings, she crept forward, feeling like a kid in a nightmare who knew the monster was behind the closet door, but still had no choice but to look.

"Lindy?" Wes whispered, concern clear in his voice.

"Stay low." Her voice shook a little, and she didn't think it was her imagination when she saw fear flash across the others' faces from the corner of her eye.

In silence, they slipped into the park. Behind the bushes on the far side, she crouched and reached out carefully, pulling a few branches aside.

"Oh, Jesus have mercy," Eloise whispered.

Thousands of draugar filled the terrain below the bridge, continuing on either side as far as Lindy's eyes could see.

"Damn," Wes murmured.

Yasmeen made a desperate noise. "That... that's more than before."

"Bastards have been busy," Anthony muttered. "Fucking murderers."

Lindy stared. Underneath the bridge, a stretch of snowy field gave way to multiple train tracks with no shred of cover at all. A tall chain-link fence separated the field from what lay beyond, and one of the trains lay on its side where it had careened across the neighboring tracks, presumably derailed by the earthquakes that struck when the world fell. Past it all, a five-story parking garage beckoned like the promised land.

But the draugar were everywhere. Countless monsters ambled about the snowy field, a wandering, mindless mass that stumbled into one another only to rebound away like the decaying embodiment of staggering, aimless chaos.

Anthony was right. The Order were murderers. Nearly every corpse looked fresh. Some still had semi-wet blood glistening in their wounds. The Allegiants had taken a city full of survivors of the apocalypse, and if any refused to convert…

Ready-made army of the dead for the Order to control.

Somewhere inside her, she wanted to be sick.

Lindy glanced over her shoulder at the snowy expanse of parking lots and abandoned buildings behind them. Exploded wreckages of vehicles made evident where former survivors had tried using them to escape. But there was no guarantee the six of them would get over to the parking garage and find a usable car there either. Why wouldn't the Order have booby-trapped those vehicles too?

Except the Order had to be getting around somehow.

That didn't mean they'd put their vehicles *here*, out of all the city. And what about finding keys for the damn things *if* she and the others could even reach them?

Shit. There was no way this could work.

"So?" Anthony hissed, looking at her expectantly.

Lindy bit her lip, old lessons from tactics classes rising out of murky memory. It'd take a tremendous amount of power to hold a line like this around the whole town, though. Odds were the Allegiants wouldn't even try. The point of their apocalypse wasn't to barricade themselves inside random American cities like latter-day warlords laying claim to territory. The Order already thought they ruled the entire world. No, the point was conversion or annihilation. If they couldn't catch every surviving human in the city, then they wanted people to try for this place so the Order could gather more converts or create more draugar. Why else booby-trap every vehicle outside their perimeter, if not to force survivors to come here?

But to make that work, there had to be credible bait, and the four people behind her said they'd heard engines running. Chances were, besides placing that impenetrable horde of draugar and perhaps some alarm systems on the other side of this expanse, the Order hadn't wasted time or energy destroying much of downtown. After all, who was going to make it past those defenses? No, they'd most likely left the heart of their trap essentially untouched, barring killing or converting any humans who'd been in it.

One big, multicolored expanse of temptation meant to make desperate survivors kill themselves trying to reach it.

But that meant cars with keys in them might be over there. Maybe bodies who'd have keys in their pockets too, assuming the Allegiants hadn't managed to turn *every* corpse into a draug. Meanwhile, given the kinds of destruction behind her—burned cars, burned buildings— she suspected the booby traps on this side weren't solely made of seidr, which meant this weird ability of hers had precious little chance of picking them up if she tried to use these cars instead.

After all, C-4 would do just fine for wreaking bloody destruction, and God knew the Order trained its people in that too.

One wrong move and she'd blow herself and everyone else up.

So forward was the only option—though that still left the question of how to actually reach the parking garage and what to do once they got there.

"What now?" Eloise asked softly as if in echo of Lindy's thoughts. At her side, Julia clung to the older woman, visibly trembling.

Lindy shook her head, the white-noise whine in her head making it hard to think. Even what she'd done to destroy the draugar in the strip mall parking lot wouldn't be enough to get them across that stretch of land—and that wasn't even bringing into it the damage it'd do to *her*. There'd be nothing left of her if she tried to attack this head-on.

But then, there was what she'd done to leave the manor outside Mariposa...

She swallowed hard. God only knew if shielding them all with seidr would work against the draugar, let alone the Order members probably lurking in the buildings across the tracks.

"You *sure* there aren't any usable cars on this side of the bridge?" Wes asked the others.

Anthony snorted. "You're welcome to try finding one, big guy. Boom."

Rage erupted through Lindy in a violent, hungry wave. Her eyes snapped to the side, locking on the burly man with his sneering lips and his thick veins pumping fatty blood like a ruby-red milkshake waiting to spill onto the snow. He wanted to hurt Wes? Risk *Wes*? That contemptible bastard wouldn't take another step if he *dared*—

"Shut up, Anthony," Yasmeen hissed.

Shudders ran through Lindy, hungry and filled with anticipation. Yeah. Yeah, shutting him up was good. Shutting him up was what needed to happen right—

"Lindy?" Wes prompted softly.

His voice felt like hands pulling her back from a cliff. A ragged breath entered her lungs, the air cold like needles, and the wave of her rage receded only to have horror swell in its place. What the hell? Sweet God, she'd been about to—

"Hey." Wes took her arm and she gasped, fear spiking through her because it wasn't safe. He couldn't touch her or she might...

Her heart rate slowed. The panic ebbed like a tide slowly slipping back out to sea, and she no longer felt like she was going to drown in it. When he met her eyes, his expression so concerned, she didn't feel dangerous. Somehow, she just felt... steadied, as if she was held back by a force that wouldn't ever let her fall. The impulses and the darkness seemed to recede, even if the hissing noise in her head didn't change at all.

"You okay?" he asked.

Staring at him, she managed a nod.

"We can go back," he said. "We'll find another option that—"

The white-noise rush in her mind spiked higher, like someone had suddenly jacked up the volume tenfold. She flinched back, clasping a hand to her temple, and Wes's grip on her arm tightened as if to keep her from collapsing.

Around her, the others threw panicked looks between her and the bushes as if they'd suddenly heard something. But she hadn't felt a draug or an Allegiant in her mind.

That didn't mean this wasn't a threat.

A figure stepped from the shrubbery.

And it didn't even *kind of* look human.

Lindy stared. Tall and lithe, with skin that glistened like it was touched by moonlight and a cold, remote face made of sharp edges like chiseled granite, the creature seemed to shimmer even beneath the overcast day. Pointed ears stuck up through his tangled white hair, and the silken robes covering his body were thin and clearly meant for warmer climates, though now they were stained and ripped.

She winced with pain against the static roar in her mind. Oh God. This was an elf.

"Who are you?" the elf demanded, his deep and imperious tone undermined by the slight tremble in his voice. "What is this place?"

Wes glanced at Lindy and then stepped forward a bit, and she had the weirdest feeling he was putting himself between her and the creature. "Who are you?"

"I asked *you*, wolf."

Alarm shot through Lindy, and she could see Wes stiffen. She didn't dare glance back at the others, for fear of them asking questions.

Or panicking.

"Though," the creature continued, "if you are here, I assume I am in Midgard." His eyes slid to Lindy, a disdainful expression crossing his face. "Even if I have not heard of *that* one's like inhabiting these lands before."

She hesitated, not sure what to make of that. The creature sounded like she was a particularly repellent bug.

But the pain in her head was lessening, though she had

the feeling it wasn't the elf's doing. More like she was adjusting to the white-noise roar of his presence.

Or the *curse* was adjusting.

Chills ran through her.

The elf drew himself up. "I command you to tell me, wolf. I was in my home in Elfhame when the sky split and the ensuing destruction cast me here. I do not choose to endure Ragnarok in this... *place*, so speak now and say where I shall find the nearest path back to—"

Lindy gasped even as the elf's eyes suddenly widened. As the white-noise rush faded, whispers came clear in her mind, originating from behind the group.

And practically on top of them.

Panic surged through her again, and on instinct, she reached out, taking Wes's wrist. Beyond him, the survivors stared, clearly terrified, and she didn't have another option. There was nowhere close enough to hide, not from the number of monsters she felt coming.

Seidr was the only hope.

"Grab on to each other," she hissed.

Their confusion only froze them for a heartbeat, and then they did as she asked. She turned to the elf.

Damn, damn, damn.

"Take my hand." She reached for him. "Hurry!"

The elf recoiled like she'd offered him a dirty diaper. "And what in *all* the realms makes you think I would—"

Shrieks carried on the breeze. In the stretch of land below the bridge, the draugar there began to shriek too, charging up the slope toward the park.

"Now!" Lindy cried at the elf.

He ignored her. Horror on his face, the creature backed away from Lindy and the rest, casting a look around quickly as if seeking somewhere to go and then racing back the way he'd come and shoving past the shrubbery there.

The shrieking got closer.

"Dammit." She drew in a sharp breath. This was going to cost her. *God*, this was going to cost her.

Gritting her teeth, she willed the seidr to rise and spread across the others. All around her, the air seemed to grow colder while the tattoo on her wrist tingled and then bit at her skin like the snake it was designed to imitate. She winced, fighting not to cry out as the feeling carried along her forearm like needles stabbing into her skin.

Draugar charged into the park, two Allegiants right behind them.

Lindy and the others froze. She barely dared to breathe, and she felt Wes's grip clench down on her hand, his eyes locked on the draugar. The monsters spread out through the park, snarling and shrieking, while the Allegiants paused at the edge, their eyes narrowing.

But they didn't point or shout, and as the draugar staggered around, the monsters didn't come close to Lindy and the rest.

"*Something* was here," the taller of the two Allegiants insisted.

"Indeed," the shorter said.

"You doubt me?" the taller snapped. "You saw the footprints in the snow too, for the Abyss's sake."

Lindy's stomach sank. Footprints. Of course they'd left footprints. Why the hell hadn't she thought—

Like there was anything she could have done about it?

The shorter guy held up his hands as if to deny any doubt, though his humored expression wasn't nearly so appeasing. She didn't recognize the two men, though given the extent of the Order's reach, she knew that didn't mean much.

Or that they wouldn't recognize her if this defense failed.

Irritation flashed over the taller man's face. "Search everywhere!" he shouted at the draugar.

Snarling, the creatures raced past Lindy and the others, flowing around them as if they were an invisible rock in a river.

The shorter Allegiant's brow furrowed at the sight. "Wait. Do you see—"

A cry came from the far edge of the park, and Lindy's heart hit her throat. That wasn't a draug.

The monsters hauled the elf from the bushes.

Thrashing and shouting what sounded like curses in a language she'd never heard, the elf struggled to break free, failing miserably when the draugar didn't react to him in the least. Under his blows, the monsters' flesh shredded and fell away, but still they dragged him forward until they reached the Allegiants.

"Told you," the taller Allegiant commented to the shorter.

"Yes, I see that. Though those footprints were more numerous than this *one*."

The taller threw him a dirty look and then turned his attention to the elf. "Well, aren't *you* a long way from home?"

Fury rendered the granite lines of the elf's face in vicious relief as he glared at the Allegiants. Snarling, he spat out incomprehensible words that made the fine hairs on Lindy's arms stand on end.

"Oh, no, no." The Allegiant's hand snapped up, grabbing the elf by the throat. "None of that."

Seidr grew stronger in the air and Lindy cringed, fighting to hold on to the power around the six of them while the darkness roiled inside her mind and her skin burned.

But it was nothing compared to what was happening to the elf.

In horror, she watched as green smoke rose from the Allegiant to wrap around the elf. Where it touched, the creature's moonlit skin turned gray. The leeching of color spread like he was a photograph losing all saturation. His mouth opened in a scream, but no sound emerged as the flesh of his face drew in, turning gaunt, and his cheekbones became like knife blades beneath paper-thin skin.

And then even that began to crumble. In flakes like ash, the elf's flesh fell away and his hair did too, and as the Allegiant released him, his body toppled to the ground, where it burst apart like colorless leaves scattering across the snow.

The shorter Allegiant made a disgusted noise, throwing an irritated look to his taller companion as he stepped back, brushing at his robes as if to rid them of debris.

"Shall we?" the taller man said, ignoring the glare as he gestured to the bridge.

"There may be others out here."

"They've undoubtedly run by now. Let the southern and northern patrols catch them."

The shorter man's brow arched. "Tired already?"

Anger crossed his companion's face. "I didn't see you attending to that... *thing*."

His eyes narrowing, the smaller man didn't respond.

The tall guy smirked. "On we go, then."

Without another word, he strode toward the bridge, motioning to the draugar to accompany him as he went.

The shorter man looked back at where Lindy and the others hid behind the seidr she'd wrapped around them. His eyes narrowing, he walked closer. Lindy didn't dare to breathe.

"You coming?" the other Allegiant called.

The guy stopped. Muttering heated insults under his breath, he eyed the space where Lindy and the others hid for another heartbeat, and then turned and followed his companion. The draugar trailed after him in a staggering, chittering entourage.

Lindy trembled, her eyes tracking them as the monsters made their way onto the bridge. She couldn't follow them directly. That bastard had been inches from discovering them. But if the draugar made a space around them, that would be a giveaway too.

Her gaze dropped. Unless they stayed under the bridge, that was. He wouldn't notice them from up there, and maybe, just maybe, anyone on the other side of the expanse wouldn't either.

She drew a steadying breath, trying not to think about the darkness chewing at the sides of her mind, devouring more of her with every heartbeat, or the way her entire arm was burning now. She didn't dare release the seidr, though, for fear that the next time she reached for it, she wouldn't be able to stop the magic from simply swallowing her whole.

But... this she could manage.

Maybe.

She cast a quick look to the others. The humans looked like they were hanging on by willpower alone. Wes appeared worried, but strange. Like it wasn't just the monsters and the Order that had him concerned.

It was her too.

Tightening her grip on his hand, she returned her eyes to the draugar on the snowy terrain ahead. "Okay, follow me."

IF SHE'D EXPECTED TO SURVIVE THE NEXT FEW WEEKS, LINDY would have worried this would haunt her dreams.

Because this was the stuff nightmares were made of.

Barely daring to breathe, she led the way down the slope away from the park, her hand gripping Wes's so tightly, she suspected she was cutting off his circulation. Rotted mouths gaped around her, some with jaws missing and others with remnants of whatever they'd last devoured hanging from their teeth. Milky eyes rolled toward her, and she braced herself until the opaque gazes drifted onward. Groans rose intermittently and decaying limbs swung haphazardly, passing within inches of her. The monsters were on either side, and more ahead, milling about like sleepwalkers at a rave.

The parking garage felt farther away with every second.

Her eyes twitched toward the bridge above her, and she swallowed hard at the sight of a body dangling in a gap between the girders and the concrete pillars. Someone had tried scaling the side to escape the draugar, and from the damage to their corpse, they'd failed horribly.

Apparently, the draugar could climb.

She couldn't see the Allegiants above the bridge, though, which would have been a relief, except it meant nothing for any Order members on the other side of the expanse. At least the erratic paths of the draugar meant her group's footprints were lost amid the trampled snow, and that anyone watching might not notice the gap their passage left in the horde.

But that was the only bright side. The rest was nothing but hell.

A faint whimper came from behind her. She threw a look back to find Eloise glancing around frantically as two draugar closed in on either side. They weren't shrieking. Didn't seem to be reaching for her. But they were on an ambling collision course with her at the center.

Anthony tugged Eloise forward, thrusting her ahead of him as the two creatures ran into each other and then staggered away like groaning billiard balls.

Lindy drew a shaky breath and kept moving.

Nervous sweat collected on her back as shadows snarled and writhed on the edges of her mind, drawing ever closer. Her right side burned now along with her wrist and arm, like fiery barbed wire was being pulled through her veins, radiating out from her tattoo. As the group reached the chain-link fence separating the snowy terrain from the train tracks, she stumbled from the pain, nearly falling before Wes's hold on her other wrist pulled her back.

A worried sound left him, barely more than a murmur at the edge of hearing. Not looking back, she waved the concern away with her free hand. There was nothing he could do. Nothing anyone could.

They just had to keep going.

A choked sound came from behind her. She looked back again to find Yasmeen staring at two draugar stumbling along several yards off.

Lindy's chest ached. Minus the decay, the family resemblance was obvious.

Fear on her face, Julia tugged on the young woman's hand, trying to draw Yasmeen's attention from the corpses of her parents. Her mouth working in a silent sob, Yasmeen didn't move.

Anthony stepped in front of her, not releasing his grip on Eloise. Yasmeen flinched as he blocked her view, and for a moment, she just stared at the ruddy-faced man.

His brow rose. Unsteadily, she nodded and turned away.

Lindy let out a slow breath, returning her attention to the fence. At some point, a car had careened from the highway above, toppling over itself to land wheels-up across part of the barrier about twenty feet to her left. Heading toward it would mean leaving the shelter of the bridge itself, and yet the only alternative was scaling the chain-link fence and hoping no draugar or Allegiants noticed.

Not a good option.

Carefully, she led the others toward the gap. Draugar bumped into the fence and then rebounded away, but she couldn't see any sign of the Allegiants on the bridge above. Inside the vehicle, a motionless body was pinned by crushed metal and a mangled seat belt, and she held her breath as she struggled through the gap between the car and the barrier.

The corpse didn't move.

Adrenaline pumping through her, she scanned the area while the others slipped past the fence. The derailed train had not only taken out the fence on the opposite side of the tracks, but also several cars and a chunk of the concrete road itself. The street beyond was swarmed by draugar, but after that lay only the garage, inside which nothing seemed to be moving.

She wished she could believe it would be that easy.

Keeping an eye to the bridge and the multistory garage alike, she started across the tracks, wincing at every little crunch of ice and gravel beneath her feet. Needlelike pain crept over her chest and back, and the darkness in her mind now felt like an ocean all around her, rushing and teeming with monsters waiting to devour her whole. Her pulse drummed in her throat, evidence of panic that her body felt even if her mind couldn't quite access it.

But with every step, her vision drew in, as if the shadows were rising to swallow her at last. The world narrowed, becoming a long tunnel with the garage at the end. Faces of the draugar swam in and out of focus around her, and she grit her teeth, clinging to the seidr surrounding the survivors. It was getting harder to hang on, though. She couldn't even hear them anymore. Just the whispers roaring around her like a hurricane.

Lindy's grip tightened on Wes's hand, and she locked her focus on the ground in front of her and the feel of his wrist beneath her palm. He was real. Not this noise in her head. Not the nightmare trying to claim her. This wolf, this *man*, somehow holding her back even now from falling, falling, falling into the dark.

For him, for these people, she had to hang on.

Her feet stumbled and a sharp breath entered her lungs as a brick wall suddenly reared up in front of her. Blinking, she looked around, trying to see clearly.

She'd reached the garage.

Dazedly, she looked back. The survivors were there. Wes too. With worry painted clearly across his features, the beautiful ulfhednar man studied her for a moment and then drew her with him toward the entrance.

Static tingled across her skin. "Wait," she gasped, pulling him back.

He stopped. Struggling to concentrate, she studied the dark brick walls ahead of her and the cement of the upper levels. A steel overhang sheltered the entrance while an enormous blue sign bearing only the numeral three hung above it, dangling from only two of its multiple supports like a guillotine waiting to drop.

There were no bloody markings. Nothing to signal a trap.

But she could feel it.

Warily, she walked past Wes, not letting go of his hand. The tingling on her skin grew worse, and instantly, the darkness in her rose up to meet it.

She gasped, her steps faltering.

The static sensation faded.

Her eyes slid around, and she trembled at the sudden suspicion that the one power had recognized the other and so it let her through.

"Come on," she whispered.

She crept inside, the others following her. The cement all around somehow made the air feel colder, and the overcast light outside faded to twilight the farther from the entrance she walked. But none of the vehicles around them were destroyed, and some even had snow on their tires as if they'd been driven more recently than the end of the world. Biting her lip, she waited as Wes crept closer to one and peered inside, searching for keys.

He glanced back, shaking his head. Nothing.

She grimaced, her vision still swimming. It'd take forever to search if they had to all hold hands like schoolkids on a field trip. But the draugar were just outside the building, and once she dropped the defenses around them all, those monsters would almost certainly come running.

But if she stood at the entrance... if she kept the seidr around her while the others searched... would that provide a barrier?

Her chest burned like acid was etching her skin. She didn't know what was happening to her, but she was afraid to look. Besides, it would take too much time.

The sooner they found a car, the sooner she could stop this.

"Search fast," she breathed, releasing Wes's wrist.

He made a choked sound of protest, but she couldn't take the time to assure him.

"Go," she begged, concentrating with all she had on holding back the darkness inside while keeping the defense around her alive.

The ground wavered. She braced herself on the wall, the rough brick like jagged glass beneath her palm. She felt so... *wrong*, and yet the darkness was making even that feeling hard to focus on. Somewhere inside, she was afraid the nightmares were just toying with her, hanging back to make her think she still stood a chance, when really, they'd already won. It was just a matter of time, really. A game they were playing, because why not? The curse was coming whether she liked it or not, and every passing minute brought it closer, relentless. She'd just been fooling herself to think she'd make it to Minneapolis. To think she stood a chance at all.

A strangled cry of panic came from behind her even as the whispers in her mind shifted, and unsteadily, she turned. The two Allegiants from the other side of the bridge now stood at the far entry to the garage. Grins split their skull-like faces. Green smoke rose up around them like spirits summoned from an emerald hell. The power coalesced at the speed of thought and then surged forward like spears.

Aimed at Wes.

Lindy's world blurred, a sensation of speed passing around her, and then she was in front of the spears, the twin blades of ethereal smoke slamming into her. Her eyes flew wide, her mouth opening in a silent gasp. The weapons sank into her deeper, deeper, driving into her chest with the strangest feeling of falling even as she stood still.

But the blades didn't come out the other side of her body. Into her, they plummeted, as if her body were a sea and the blades were anchors.

Tying her to the Allegiants.

The burning on her skin flared higher, scorching deeper down, biting into her muscles. She could feel the Allegiants. She knew their will. The darkness inside her pulsed with it, attuning itself fully to them, until their desire for death and destruction became its own. Dark sensations like icy fingers danced across her skin, rising to wrap her throat, choking away all of her own will. The transformation was not yet complete, but the potential was still there, and that was enough.

In her mind, the whispers became a singular command, reverberating in her skull. The Allegiants wished to kill these people.

And so she would.

"Lindy!" Wes cried.

His voice shot through her like lightning, and inside her mind, she screamed. Seidr erupted from her in a smoky wave driven totally by her own terror. The power slammed into the Allegiants, throwing them back, and their hold on her shattered as they collided with the wall, their bodies smashing against the bricks with a sickening squelch.

Her legs gave out beneath her, and she barely caught herself as she dropped to the ground. In her mind, the darkness halted its encroachment, not attacking but not ceding what it had gained either.

Hands grabbed her, and she whirled, terrified the draugar were here.

Wes was on his knees beside her. His wide eyes swept over her as if confirming she was still alive, and then he threw a fast look to the others. "Check for keys on those guys."

Footsteps hurried past. She struggled to rise. "The... the draugar."

Wes didn't say anything. Pulling her to her feet, he kept an arm around her as he followed Yasmeen toward the flash of a car's taillights.

Lindy swung her eyes toward the street, and her brow furrowed. There were still draugar, but not close. Not even near the train tracks. In fact, there didn't seem to be any on this side of the fence around the field.

Though the rest were coming, their shrieks carrying on the breeze.

"Here." Yasmeen shoved a set of keys at him. "They each had one."

Lindy struggled to keep her feet. Of course the Allegiants had. Those two hadn't sounded like they trusted each other an inch. They'd never leave one or the other of them with sole control over their way out of here.

Wes thumbed the key fob. Lights flashed on a black pickup truck nearby. "Follow us." He told the others. "Get over the bridge and then head for the highway."

Yasmeen nodded while the rest piled into a bright-orange compact SUV that looked more like a sporty sedan.

"Come on." Wes kept his arm around Lindy as he hurried toward the pickup and tugged open the door.

"You... you shouldn't..." Lindy swallowed hard, catching herself on the door. "You shouldn't stay with me."

Wes ignored her, bending fast and scooping her up like she was weightless before placing her in the passenger seat. Slamming the door, he ran to the other side and swung behind the wheel.

She stared out the windshield at the oncoming draugar while the engine turned over and Wes threw the truck into reverse.

"Wes..." She forced the words out as the pickup flew backward. "You should go. Please."

He shoved the gear shift into drive and floored it, charging for the exit while the orange SUV came racing after him. "Not going to happen."

The truck shattered the gate arm and barreled onto the street. Whipping a tight turn while the tires struggled for purchase on the snow, Wes sent the pickup flying down the curving road away from the parking garage.

Lindy gripped the armrest on the door. Her entire body was shaking, and even though the burning sensation had faded from her skin and the darkness seemed content to swirl at the edges of her mind, she felt far from okay. Emptier. Hollow, somehow, like parts of her that she couldn't even remember were now gone.

She glanced down and cautiously drew aside her sleeve with a trembling hand.

Her wrist band was surrounded by the tattoo. Tangles of green-black ink glinted metallically in the overcast daylight, extending like jagged vines up her forearm to disappear beneath her coat.

A quivering breath left her, and she bit her lip. No tears came. Some part of her couldn't even summon up the impulse to cry. And the rest of her ached somewhere inside, not just for herself, but for the wish that Wes would have listened and left.

If only so he'd be safe from her.

14

# WES

I f he didn't do something, his wolf was going to take a bite from the steering wheel.

Maneuvering the truck around the turn to the bridge, Wes couldn't stop himself from throwing yet another glance at Lindy. With her body pressed to the passenger side door and her legs drawn up, she looked fragile and small in the large truck, and his wolf snarled, damn near rabid with the need to attack whatever the hell was frightening her.

Except the threat was inside her.

And it scared the hell out of him too.

He pushed the pedal down harder, sending the truck roaring past a cluster of draugar surrounding an abandoned car on the bridge. She'd moved like lightning, one minute standing by the west entrance of the garage and the next standing in its center while the power those Allegiant bastards had been throwing at him hit *her* instead. And just as he'd been about to shift and tear those murderous fucks limb from limb, she'd...

What the hell had she done? Slammed them into a wall so hard they damn near became pancakes?

Gods.

And it hurt her. *Everything* hurt her. The Allegiants and what they'd tried. Getting across that field full of draugar like the six of them were invisible. It hurt her and it was impossible and if he didn't figure out how to help her...

He raced the truck through a narrow gap between two destroyed vehicles, silently cursing the obstacle course of the bridge. Maybe he was making a mistake. Maybe he should insist they head back to Mariposa rather than continue on to Minneapolis. After all, what the hell did he know about seidr? In Mariposa there was the seer, Ingrid, with all her expertise, not to mention Hayden and all she could do. They could help Lindy better than he ever could.

Except... she'd never agree.

His eyes twitched to her again. She'd barely been able to stand after everything that happened in the garage. What happened if she had to do that again?

*What happened?* He didn't even know what the fuck was happening at *all*.

The end of the bridge passed and he threw a look into the rearview mirror, checking on the orange SUV. The humans were right behind him, and when he sped up on the open stretch of snowy road, they did the same, sticking to the treads left by his tires and following him as he raced toward the interstate.

No draugar charged the vehicles, and whatever other Allegiants remained in the area, the bastards didn't show their faces.

When the on-ramp finally appeared, he slowed, checking around carefully before coming to a stop. Putting the truck into park, he hesitated a heartbeat before taking the keys from the ignition as well.

"Stay here for a sec, okay?" he said.

She didn't respond.

Guilt gnawing at him, he climbed out. Leaving the keys would have been foolish. He wasn't trying to trap her, but she seemed back to wanting to go off on her own. And she could. She really could. This wasn't a hostage situation.

But he was scared for her, and the thought of her being out here alone, barely able to stand while the gods knew *what* was happening to her inside?

If he'd been in wolf form, he would have howled.

Yasmeen climbed from the small SUV. After their passage through the field of draugar—and seeing her parents—she still looked shaken, but the determination was creeping back into her bearing. "Everything okay?" she called.

Wes nodded. "Yeah." Not even close. "Just wanted to say, unless you all have somewhere else you're planning on going, you should head to southern Colorado."

The woman's eyebrow twitched up, curious.

"Mariposa. It's, um—" He threw a quick look back to the truck. "It's where we're from. It's safe there."

Yasmeen nodded. "That's where we'll go, then."

"One thing, though?"

She paused.

"There are some folks there who are, uh… different. Not like her—" He nodded to the truck. "But different. They won't hurt you if you don't try to hurt them, though. Just tell them Wes sent you."

After a heartbeat, she nodded again, thoughtfully. "Okay." She drew a breath, giving him a smile. "Thanks for… everything."

He smiled back.

She started back to the SUV and then paused. "Tell her that, too, please?" She glanced toward the pickup. "Thank you?"

"Will do."

Her smile returned. Without another word, she climbed into the vehicle. Anthony steered the SUV past him a moment later, and in the back seat, Eloise waved while Julia managed a shy smile.

He exhaled, his breath puffing out in the frigid air, and walked back to the truck.

"Yasmeen says thank you," he told Lindy when he got in.

Lindy gave a small nod, not looking at him. "You tell them to head for Mariposa?"

"Yeah."

She nodded again.

He braced himself. "Don't suppose you'd consider also—"

"I'm not going back yet." Her voice was hard.

He sighed. Of course not.

Unsure what to say, he started the truck up again and headed toward the on-ramp.

Lincoln fell behind them, and then Omaha and the border of Nebraska did too. Snow growled beneath the tires, slowing them down, but the sandbags piled in the back of the pickup helped keep them on the road. A collection of gas containers was back there too, letting him refuel after a while. If nothing else, those Allegiant bastards had clearly been prepared for the bad weather, though there didn't seem to be any food in the truck.

He tried not to think about why.

After a few hours, snowy signs told him they were

nearing Des Moines. From what he'd been able to tell from an atlas he'd found tucked in the pocket behind his seat—along with a stuffed pig that made him wonder who the Allegiants stole this truck from and whether that person was still alive—after Des Moines, it was just a straight shot up the interstate for a few hours and then they'd be in Minneapolis.

He eyed the sky. Under normal conditions, he'd believe they could make it in a day, easy. But the sun would be going down in not too much longer, and that would put an end to driving for the time being.

The last thing he wanted was for them to crash again and lose use of this vehicle too.

His hands adjusted on the wheel, and he blinked tiredly, trying to drive the snow glare from his eyes as signs for the turn toward Minneapolis came into view. Des Moines seemed surprisingly intact, based on the buildings he could see from the highway. Businesses and hotels were still standing, as if the fires hadn't come near this place and the earthquakes hadn't managed to tear anything down.

But, intact or not, staying overnight in the city probably wouldn't be the best plan. Something just didn't feel right about this place, though damn if he knew what. There wasn't much of it to see, so far. But if the Order were there and Lindy needed to do *anything* to stop them again, he'd never forgive himself. Better to head a bit beyond the city. Maybe get off the road entirely, if he was honest. Get away from here and find somewhere remote so they could—

"Holy shit!" He slammed on the brakes as the reason for his discomfort suddenly registered. The truck fishtailed on the snow and ice, sliding onward while details that hadn't penetrated his mind before now pelted him in rapid-fire horror.

The gray horizon, too close. The gray *everything*.

Skidding sideways, the truck slid to a stop. Staring, his mouth open in a silent cry, Wes couldn't move for a moment. They were alive. They'd stopped.

And the road... was gone.

His hands shook as he forced himself to release the wheel, and it wasn't until he'd jammed the gear shift into park and waited a moment in case the truck decided to move anyway that he could make his foot ease away from the brake.

"What the *hell?*" Lindy whispered.

His eyes twitched to her, finding her staring too, and then his attention returned to the nonexistent road. Still shaking, he jammed the emergency brake into place for good measure before fumbling for the handle and pushing the door open.

Cold wind swirled around them as they climbed from the truck. Twenty feet ahead, the snowy interstate became rubble, as if the world's biggest jackhammer had broken it to bits, but only for a small distance.

Beyond that lay an abyss so wide, he had to strain to see any trace of the other edge.

Cautiously, he walked closer. The destruction stretched out on either side, tearing through an apartment complex to his left and a hotel to his right. The buildings clung to the cliff's edge, pipes sticking out like bent twigs from their sides while pieces of concrete and cinderblock crumbled from their walls as if gradually succumbing to gravity. To the side of the highway, an off-ramp led to nothing, the overpass gone. In the distance, he thought he could make out the opposite side of the abyss, but in the weak gray light, he couldn't be sure it wasn't just a trick of the overcast sky.

He paused several feet from the edge, his legs and insides quivering with the irrational fear that the ground between him and the chasm would suddenly vanish and send him plunging down. Heights had never been his favorite, and the cliff was a sheer drop with shattered pipes and ripped cables dangling from the sides where once they'd been buried in the earth. He craned his neck, but the bottom of the ravine was lost in shadow and darkness, too deep to see.

"Fenrir," Lindy whispered.

He backed away from the edge. "What?"

She dropped her attention from the ever-present black gashes torn in the sky, and when she glanced at him, she hesitated, her expression unreadable.

"Fenrir," she said again, as if admitting something to him. "His teeth. In the myths I learned growing up, when Ragnarok begins, he runs through the realms, his top jaw scraping the heavens and his lower ripping into the earth, devouring..." Her eyes slid along the abyss, and she drew a shaky breath. "Devouring everything in his path."

Wes followed her gaze. The chasm carved nearly a straight line north.

Right toward Minneapolis.

"They'll be okay," he said, willing the words to be true for her sake as well as her family's. "You'll see."

She nodded.

He hesitated, not sure what else to say, but then, there probably wasn't anything. They just needed to get going and prove him right.

Or deal with the alternative.

His eyes strayed to the canyon, a shudder rolling through him. Quickly, he strode back to the pickup truck and climbed in.

Lindy didn't say a word when she joined him.

Putting the vehicle into gear—and checking three times it was in reverse, just to assuage his sudden anxiety about getting that wrong—he backed away from the ravine and then made a swift turn, speeding back the way they'd come. "You want to dig that atlas out?" he asked Lindy, casting quick glances at the chasm in the rearview mirror. "Find us a state road going north?"

"Sure."

Her voice was quiet and he couldn't read her tone, but she twisted around, reaching behind the seats and drawing out the map all the same. A few miles later found them headed north along snowy roads through the gently rolling countryside, and the only way he could tell they were staying on the road was by steering between the ditches and occasional trees on either side. From where they were, he couldn't see any trace of the impossible gash torn through the land to the east of them, but that didn't stop him from taking it slow, just in case they crested a hill to find the earth ahead of them gone.

His palms felt sweaty beneath his gloves. As if draugar and the Order and creatures from other realms weren't enough, now the damned *ground* had gone missing.

The sooner they got back to Mariposa, the better.

Light gradually began fading from the sky as time ticked onward. Vast swaths of farmland surrounded them, and houses were few and far between. At a small house surrounded by trees with a For Sale sign near its driveway, he turned off the road. "Just, um... stay put a sec, okay?" he suggested when he came to a stop.

Lindy glanced at him and then pushed open the door.

"Dammit." He scrambled out and rounded the truck. "It's not safe."

"Neither am I." Bracing herself on the side of the pickup, she scanned the area and then headed toward the house, her legs seeming barely stable.

Snarling a curse under his breath, he followed her.

The windows of the house were dark and curtains were drawn across most of them. Keeping an eye to them and the surrounding area alike, he headed up to the door, staying to one side in case someone tried to shoot through it.

His knocking produced nothing. Easing down behind the bushes, he inched toward the front window to peer past the glass.

Covered furniture lurked in the gloomy twilight of the living room, and cardboard boxes were stacked against the far wall. Cautiously, he made his way back to the front porch, debating how to get the door open. Kicking it down would be a great way to get shot if someone *was* hiding inside, but he didn't exactly have lock-picking tools here.

The windows were pretty old, though.

"Mind if I borrow your knife?" he asked.

Lindy handed it over without a word.

He returned to the old window frame and jimmied the latch. "Hello?" he called when he pried the window open.

Silence answered him.

Hoisting himself over the sill, he waited a moment for anyone to shout before turning to reach back for Lindy.

She was already climbing inside.

He moved quickly to help her, and she froze. "Don't," she ordered, her voice tight.

Grimacing, he stepped back. She was shaking when she straightened, and he couldn't help but note how bloodless she looked. Keeping distance from him, she walked farther into the house, seeming to look anywhere but at him.

Cursing internally, he followed her.

Everything in the house seemed at least forty years out of date, from the threadbare sofa to the ancient kitchen appliances. The bed was missing, but the moving boxes were new. Adult children relocating their parent to a rest home, maybe? That was the best answer, he suspected, and possibly not the correct one, but at least the entire place seemed empty.

He hauled cushions from the sofa and gathered blankets from a closet to make two beds near the fireplace. Lindy searched the kitchen drawers, returning a few minutes later with matches, and in only a few minutes, they had a fire going as well.

Seated on the cushions several feet away from her, Wes tried to ignore the way his damnable wolf paced inside his head, urging him to go closer to her. Lindy had her arms wrapped around her knees, her eyes on the flames, and barring brief yes or no answers, she hadn't spoken a word.

So he said the only thing he could think to say. "How can I help?"

Her head moved slightly in his direction, and for a long moment, he wasn't sure she'd answer him. "I don't know."

"Can you tell me what's happening?"

She didn't respond.

He risked bending a little to catch her eye. "I'm not leaving you, Lindy."

She turned toward him, something so certain in her eyes. "You should."

His mouth moved, wordless. Her gaze returned to the flames.

Consternation gnawed at him. Why the hell was she *so* damn determined to get him to go away? Was it because of what she could do? She'd had multiple opportunities to hurt him. Countless ones, in fact, and she never did. Even when she'd barely been hanging on, damn near collapse, she'd only ever lashed out at those seeking to harm him, her, and anyone they were with.

And she had to know he wasn't going anywhere, anyway. How the hell could he face Connor and Hayden if he went back alone? Not to mention the fact his conscience wouldn't let him get away with that, regardless. Insisting he leave didn't make sense.

He sighed. Arguing with her over it wouldn't help, though. He could tell she was scared. Attacking would only put her even more on the defensive.

Dammit.

Rising to his feet, he headed into the kitchen and set to digging through the cabinets, returning a few moments later with a collection of cans, spices, a suitable pot, and a can opener. In silence, he set to work over the fire, mixing the canned beef, broth, and vegetables into a stew flavored by the spices. After letting it simmer a while, he dished up dinner into bowls he'd retrieved from the kitchen as well.

Murmuring thanks, Lindy took the bowl, only to pause with it in her hands.

"What's wrong?" he asked.

She shook her head, not looking at him. "Nothing." Taking up a spoon, she drew up a bite of the stew. A grimace ghosted over her face as she forced herself to swallow.

"Look, if you don't like it, I can make—"

"It's fine."

Frowning, he sank onto the cushions across from her and took a bite of the meal. It wasn't French cuisine, but for a makeshift dinner in the middle of nowhere, the stew wasn't terrible. He'd eaten far worse in Alaska during the year and a half he and his friends spent training in the wilderness at Connor's father's command.

"Sorry."

Lindy's quiet voice was rueful. He glanced over at her.

"I'm just…" Her brow shrugged. "Not feeling well."

The wolf inside him whined. He pushed the feeling aside. "Anything I can do?"

She shook her head. "Thank you, though."

He nodded, not sure what to say. She wasn't even looking at him, and after a heartbeat, she set the bowl down in front of the fire, the food barely half eaten.

The skin of her wrist flashed between her glove and coat when she moved. He froze.

Lindy glanced over as if noticing his sudden tension. When she saw where he was looking, she blanched and swiftly tucked her wrist beneath her coat sleeve again.

He measured his words carefully. "That, um… that wasn't like that before."

She hugged her wrist to her middle, not looking at him.

His alarm warred with his concern, leaving him at a loss. "May I see?"

She closed her eyes, turning her face away, and frustration surged inside him. Dammit, the woman was a brick wall, and nothing he did made her trust him an inch. One night of sex aside, she seemed determined to keep him locked out. She looked lost in a world of pain—emotional for sure, and for all he knew, physical too—and because he didn't even know what the hell was going on, he was helpless to do anything about it.

A breath left Lindy, and he looked back at her again. One finger at a time, she pulled the glove from her hand.

Black ink twisted across her skin like a jagged vine, tangling over her fingers, thumb, and palm. The lines almost reminded him of Norse art or old ulfhednar draw-ings, and when she moved, the dark markings reflected the firelight with a metallic green sheen.

"What is it?" he asked softly.

"A curse."

He looked up at her in alarm.

Her eyes on the flames, she continued. "Did you know the Order has some of the greatest magical storehouses in the world? Possibly *the* greatest?"

Wordless, he shook his head.

"They've been collecting things for millennia. Ancient spells. Old artifacts. Things they probably stole from the wolves or someone else. Things humans"—her lip twitched, cold certainty in the expression—"*never* should've touched. Some of the spells you've seen. The ones that let them control the draugar. The ones that killed that elf. But others…" She held up her hand, the tattoo catching the firelight. "Others let them do things like this."

"What does that mean?"

"It means you're not safe. No one is."

She tugged the sleeve back down and started to put her gloves on.

He put a hand to her leg, and she froze. "Why?" he asked.

She looked up at him. "Because I'm a monster."

His chest ached at the painful certainty in her voice.

"Or I will be." She wrapped her arms around her legs as if drawing in on herself. "Soon. When this takes hold and I…" Her face tightened like she was struggling with the words. "I'm not like the other Allegiants, Wes. I'll be so much worse. What they did to themselves was as far as they got on the global scale, but… there are darker magics. Older. A mantle passed down through the generations, even if it was only symbolic"—an ironic look twisted across her face—"before now, anyway. And that's what they gave me. *Made* me." She shivered. "The Scythe of Niorun."

He hesitated. The last word was familiar, but he couldn't place why until foggy memories of mythology classes returned to him, filled with countless hours of memorizing old stories and reciting them back. Niorun was... a goddess, maybe. But not much was known about her. She hid her face in darkness. She lived in a different realm from the other gods, a dangerous one, obscuring herself in rainbow mist and deep shadow. But some worshipers believed she was a goddess of dreams.

And nightmares.

He forced his focus back. "What does that mean? What will you do if you... become that?"

"Hurt people." She shifted uncomfortably. "Kill them. That much I know. But mostly... I'll drive people mad. Get into their minds and make them turn on each other, murder each other." Her eyes went to him, pained. "The ulfhednar packs would tear each other apart. As the Scythe, I could make you kill your best friends with your bare hands if..." Her hand rubbed at the front of her neck as if she could feel something tight there. "If the one controlling me wanted it."

"*Controlling* you?"

She nodded.

Inside him, the wolf paced, snarling. Like hell. Like bloody, *gods-damned* hell. "That won't happen," he promised.

A tiny laugh left her, humorless, defeated.

"Lindy, you're not a monster. I saw you. You helped people with this... whatever this power is. You won't—"

"It won't matter."

"Why?"

"Because I'm fading. I can feel it inside. It's taking me. I don't even know everything of what's coming or what this is going to do. All I know is that someday, maybe really soon, whatever makes me, me? It'll stop."

He stared at her.

"This thing they turned me into, it's a power too strong for one person to possess and control at the same time. It'd be like asking the engine of a car to steer itself." She hugged her legs tighter. "I'm the weapon. And when this takes over, they'll control me. I won't be me anymore. I'll just be a monster, even worse than the Allegiants you've seen. Nothing more than the Order's weapon." She looked back at the flames, bitterness flashing across her face. "Just like Mom always wanted me to be."

WHEN IT WAS HIS TURN FOR REST, SLEEP BARELY CAME, A BLUR of tossing and turning to fitful dreams of Allegiants dragging Lindy away while she screamed and he couldn't do a thing to stop them. By the time dawn finally arrived, he was almost grateful for the excuse to abandon the tangle of blankets and do something—anything—useful to get them on their way.

Because that's all he could do. That, and get her to Minneapolis and hope to the gods that her family had answers to help her.

He shoved food and bottles of water into his bag. She'd be okay. He didn't care what it took. They'd find a solution for this because like *hell* those Order bastards would use her. Erase her.

*Control* her.

Striding out of the kitchen, he headed deeper into the house, raiding every drawer and closet he could find for matches and rope and any other damn thing he thought they might need. Guilt lurked in the background—he was stealing, after all—but they had to survive.

Hopefully whoever owned this place would understand, assuming they were still alive.

More snow had fallen in the night, forming a thick cover on the truck and making the road even harder to find. With his hands clenching the wheel, he drove them north again, praying the tires stayed on the road and that nothing else went wrong.

Lindy barely said a word.

Wes watched her from the corner of his eye. He couldn't see her tattoo anymore. She'd put the gloves back on last night and hadn't taken them off since. But how the hell could the thing *change* like that? Grow like it was some disease spreading through her? How far did it go? Could it be reversed?

He steered the truck through a bank of snow, hoping the road was beneath it. His own tattoos chronicled the new life he'd gained as much as anything. And hers?

They chronicled everything she was losing.

Burying a grimace, he struggled to push the thought aside. They'd fix this, whether by finding the answers with her family or somewhere else, they'd fix this.

He just had to get them to Minneapolis first.

Beneath the tires, the snow growled and grumbled. Chunks of ice hit the undercarriage and thudded on the floor of the truck. He felt ironically grateful to that Allegiant asshole for choosing a vehicle capable of maneuvering through this mess, but gods, it was slow going. They'd crossed the Minnesota border a while ago, as evidenced by a small sign protruding from a snowbank, and they'd passed through several towns since. He'd gathered gas and a few more supplies, but with every mile the road grew worse, the tires spinning as often as they caught traction and the engine grumbling toward overheating from all the effort. The world was an endless expanse of white, buried so deep that now he was only guessing where the road might be.

On a good day, Minneapolis should have only been a few hours distance from where they'd stayed the night. Now, it might as well be Tokyo.

The tires lost purchase again, spinning while the truck suddenly sank into snow past the doors.

Fuck.

He closed his eyes. Well, that had been nice while it lasted, having a vehicle and all.

Now what?

Avoiding Lindy's eyes, he glanced around. Last he'd seen a sign, they weren't actually all that far from Minneapolis, though if the monochromatic wasteland around him was any indication, they certainly weren't there yet. And given that digging out the truck would only be useful for the twenty or so feet it took for it to sink into a snowdrift a second time, there was really only one option. They had to walk.

Again.

But on what road? The snow in Nebraska had been bad, but this was absurd.

He eyed a tree about fifty feet away. That might work.

"May I borrow your knife again?"

Lindy gave him a skeptical look, but she drew out her knife and handed it to him all the same.

"Thanks. Back in a sec."

Shoving at the door was useless, so he climbed from the window instead. Slogging through the snowdrifts took forever, and it took longer still to cut off the branches, but dammit, this *would* work.

His training up in Alaska hadn't been for nothing.

He returned to the truck and climbed into the back, needing the space. Through the rear window, Lindy watched him, curiosity clear in her eyes. Tapping a gloved knuckle to the glass, he waited until she slid the pane open.

"Could you hand me the rope? It's in my bag."

She did as he asked.

Working as quickly as possible, he fashioned snow-shoes using the rope and branches, and a pair of ski poles too, and then turned back to Lindy.

Did she look impressed? A warm feeling spread in his chest at the thought, though of course that was ridiculous. What should it matter what she thought of him?

Something in him wanted to grin like a schoolboy, anyway.

He cleared his throat, keeping his voice as neutral as he could. "You want to try these on?"

She nodded. Climbing out the passenger window, she waded through the snow and jumped into the back of the truck too. She lifted her foot, and he took it, lashing each boot to the snowshoes he'd made.

"Try it out, eh?" he suggested.

She hesitated. "What about you?"

Her voice was wary. She already knew the answer, he could tell.

"It, uh… it'll be easier if I travel another way."

The fear that flashed across her face was painful.

But that was ridiculous too. Of course she was uncomfortable with what he was. She should be. Human? Wolf? Lindy was no fool.

Unlike a certain ulfhednar. Namely *him.*

He dusted the bark from his gloves to cover his discomfort. "If you want to—"

"I'll wait over there." She said the words quickly and scrambled from the back of the truck before he could even agree.

He buried a grimace. Glancing around, he tried to figure out a better way to do this than the frigid option before him, but couldn't think of much. The doors were blocked. Getting back in the truck only to get back out would be ridiculous, not to mention extremely awkward to accomplish.

But gods, this was going to be *cold.*

He stripped down quickly, his body protesting the bitter breeze and the snow, and he shoved everything into a bag as fast as he could. With a sharp breath, he braced himself, snarling an order at the wolf to keep itself damn well under control.

Because this was Lindy, and that fool beast wanted her, and he'd throw himself into that fucking ravine before he let the creature harm her.

Warm fur engulfed him as he shifted, but his skin still burned with the aftereffects of being exposed to the open air. The wolf's stronger senses flooded his mind, and instantly the beast wanted to head for Lindy, to smell her, to feel her hands on his fur.

To taste her.

Inside his mind, he cursed at the wolf, ruthlessly

beating the bastard back with all of his might. Like hell that sick fucking side of him would touch her. He wasn't going *near* her in this form, and the rabid beast either accepted that, or they'd damn well stay here in this truck while he sent her away.

His wolf side paused.

The impulses faded.

Damn straight.

A breath left him. Gathering the handle of the bag into his mouth, he turned to jump down from the truck.

He stopped at the edge of the truck bed. Lindy was staring at him, but quickly, she ducked her face away.

How long had she been watching him?

Eyeing her, he leapt down into the snow. The thought she'd watched him strip down was... flattering? Definitely arousing. But it took second place to the concern thrumming through him. As a wolf, he could see shadows around her where his human eyes had seen nothing. Darkness pooled in the hollows of her cheeks and drifted across her face like sinister ghosts. But they weren't the same as the Allegiants with their skull-like faces and black-hollow eyes. On her, the shadows were everywhere, as if they were working up to devouring her whole.

And at their core stood a beautiful woman, her eyes filled with sorrow and a fear of him she was desperately trying to hide.

His heart ached. He would never harm her. No matter what the wolf thought she was—his mate or any other impossible thing—he never would. Whatever Lindy became, she would be safe from him. Now. Always.

He'd die before he would ever hurt her.

# 15

## LINDY

Wes was breathtaking.

And every instinct screamed for her to run. Not daring to move, she waited as he jumped down from the truck, muscles rolling beneath his fur. He wasn't what she'd expected—although, really, she didn't know what that would've been. His fur was the color of dark ash, of storm clouds and smoke, though lighter shades interspersed it here and there like wisps of daylight. His paws were enormous, splayed out on the snow as if they were snowshoes all on their own. Pale-gray eyes locked on her when he turned back, as if questioning whether she was going to follow, and all the while his ears twitched like he was catching sounds beyond anything she could hear.

And he was huge. Most ulfhednar were large, surpassing the size of any ordinary wolf.

But God help her, up close like this, he seemed *really* huge.

He regarded her for a moment, and she braced herself, waiting for him to attack. She was Order, after all—or had been. Would his wolf side be as understanding as his human side had been? How did that work, anyway? The Order taught that all ulfhednar were beasts no matter their form. Wily crafty beasts, sure, with heightened intelligence that made them dangerous as hell, but without a trace of anything resembling a soul. When they shifted, nothing of their human "facades" remained. Just animal instincts. Just hunger and bloodlust and violence.

Their *real* selves, the Order said.

Lindy had never really put the Order's description to the test. Her best friend, Hayden, disappeared every month right around the full moon, always with one excuse or another, so Lindy never had the opportunity to prove to herself how wrong the Order had been—and it wasn't like she'd gone hunting for any other ulfhednar to find out for sure.

Years of putting their bullshit out of her head evaporated in the face of a wolf that maybe, just maybe, would show her the one thing the Order *hadn't* been wrong about.

But would Wes really have suggested this if he knew he was going to be a danger to her?

He nodded to the side, the motion almost like a request for her to go on.

She swallowed hard. Was he still in there? Was this a trap? "Y-you go ahead."

The wolf watched her for a moment, and something flashed through his eyes that almost looked... hurt?

How could she know that?

Wes bobbed his head as if in agreement to her request. He started across the snow ahead of her.

For a moment, she hesitated, glancing around at the truck, the snow, and the utter lack of alternatives. If she didn't move, he wouldn't keep going. He'd just come back here, and then they'd both be stuck standing next to a truck they couldn't drive, miles from the destination she'd insisted they try to reach.

Forward was the only option.

She took a step out onto the snow. The rough snow-shoes he'd made her held up beneath her feet surprisingly well, and the two longer branches like walking sticks helped her stay steady. Though his head turned back toward her slightly, Wes didn't stop or slow down, continuing on several yards ahead of her as if he wasn't inclined to come too close.

Wait... was Wes-as-a-wolf scared of her?

Something in her chest twisted at the thought. She wouldn't blame him if that were true. She was scared of herself. Terrified, really. She could feel the fear deep down somewhere, thin and distant, like a person at the bottom of a canyon, screaming. But if he was afraid, he wasn't attacking. He reacted to her when she spoke, too, which meant he must understand human speech.

The Order was wrong. They had to be.

She hoped.

Even with the snowshoes, forging through the drifts was exhausting, and she was grateful when finally they stopped in the shelter of a cluster of evergreen trees where the snow hadn't managed to pile very high. Awkwardly lowering herself onto a relatively cleared patch of ground, she rolled her tense neck and tried not to do the math on how many miles they still had to go.

From a couple of yards away, Wes watched her and

then maneuvered open the bag with his teeth and paws. She watched, obscurely impressed, only to freeze when he drew out two cans of food and nosed them toward her.

Her stomach rolled. Last night's dinner had tasted like ash, though it wasn't Wes's fault. She saw what he put in the pot. It'd seemed like a nice stew, and she felt terrible for possibly making him believe it wasn't.

But the thought of food was nauseating, even if she didn't want to think about possible reasons why. What the hell did the Order intend for her to do? They'd never mentioned not needing *food*.

Wes nosed them toward her again with a small yipping sound.

She fought off a grimace. Maybe she was just nervous. Every scrap of logic in the universe dictated she needed to eat. She hadn't touched a bite this morning and they'd been slogging through snow for an eternity, with another eternity to go.

It wouldn't do anyone a damn bit of good if she passed out from hunger.

With a tense nod to Wes, she took the cans and pried them open by their pull-tops before setting one back down where he could reach. Retrieving a spoon from her bag, she scooped out the cold SpaghettiOs and gulped them down fast, each bite hitting her stomach like lead.

She could feel him watching her when she was done. Not meeting his eyes, she tucked the cans away beneath a tree, hoping some small creature could finish up the scraps, and then climbed back to her feet. "Ready?"

Soundlessly, he turned and headed past the evergreen trees. Her stomach tumbling, she followed.

Time crept by, though God knew the world around her

didn't show it. The overcast gray light continued unabated, casting scarcely a shadow while she and Wes trekked onward through endless snow, and slowly, a new fear spread through her. How did she know they were heading the right way? There were barely any landmarks. No signs. Just distant houses and lonely trees like stalwart blots of color amid the endless white, along with the occasional top of a bush nearly buried in the snow. Had she seen any of them before? She couldn't tell. What if they came across their own footprints? Or, worse yet, the truck?

Her stomach churned worse. Maybe she'd seen that bush already. Or those trees. That house might be familiar. There wasn't a damn other thing around them to let her know for sure, besides empty fields of white and two black dots on the horizon that maybe were birds.

Those wouldn't help.

Her heart began pounding harder, her insides twisting into knots. All these hours couldn't be for nothing. They *had* to be going the right way, but she couldn't even ask Wes. And how would he know any better than she could? To be so close and yet lost was almost more than she could bear, but there wasn't...

Wasn't...

Nausea rushed up her throat, and she turned, stumbling behind a bush just in time. Everything she'd eaten came back up, her insides heaving as if to flee her body too. On her hands and knees, she huddled next to the bush, her gloved palms sinking into the snow.

She couldn't even feel the cold.

Trembling shook her as she swiped her mouth with the back of her wrist. She could still move. She wasn't numb.

But she felt nothing of the chilled surface beneath her.

A rustling sound came from the bush at her side, and instantly her hand snapped out. In her grip, a half-starved rabbit squealed when she yanked it from beneath the branches. The creature squirmed and thrashed, its little heart racing beneath her thumb and its sides heaving with fear.

Everything in her wanted to take a bite.

A whisper came on the snow. Her head snapped up, her teeth baring in a snarl.

Wes was staring at her.

Lindy blinked, reality returning. What the hell was she...

Oh, sweet God.

She dropped the rabbit like it was on fire, and frantically, the creature bolted away. Shoving to her feet, Lindy took off too, striding across the snow as quickly as her legs could carry her.

SHE DIDN'T STOP WALKING WHEN THE LIGHT BEGAN TO FADE from the sky. Or when the horizon started to vanish in the encroaching night. Or when one of her walking sticks snapped.

But then Wes tried to block her path.

Slamming to a stop, she stared at him. "Go." Her voice shook. "Get away from me."

He didn't move.

"Dammit, go!" She flung the remaining stick, the branch flopping far short of hitting him.

Never taking his gray eyes from her, he took a step forward. She flinched back.

A huff left him. Her lips pressed together, though even now her eyes were totally dry.

But maybe she was just trying not to scream.

A shudder racked her body. Closing her eyes, she sank down into a crouch, her arms wrapping around her head as if to block out the whole damn world. Her entire body was trembling, whether from exhaustion or hunger or God knew what else, she didn't know. But with everything in her, she wanted to teleport straight to her father and brother, grab them, and race to Mariposa.

Except it may already be too late.

Soft sounds came on the snow. Gently, Wes nudged her hand with his snout.

She recoiled. "No, please. I don't—"

He gave a quiet whine, and it hurt to hear. Squeezing her eyes shut for a moment, she shoved to her feet to start out across the snow.

He blocked her path again.

Quivering, she stared at him. His head twitched to the side, and she glanced over to see a small house sitting atop a snowy rise.

A breath pressed from her chest. She didn't want to stop for the night. She wanted to run like hell.

Wes made a gruff sound, harsh and insistent, and jerked his head again.

He'd just keep this up until she agreed.

"Goddammit." She started toward the house.

Scaling the slope up to the house was like climbing a hill of ice. At the top, the little brown house appeared lifeless with snow piled high in front of the door.

The *open* door.

Beside her, Wes slowed, his head moving like he was carefully sniffing the wintry air. Trepidation quivered through her, and hesitantly, she felt for the shadows along the edges of her mind.

Nothing. No draugar. No Order. Not a hint of the white-noise rush she'd picked up from that elf.

That left a lot of categories that could kill them, the foremost of which was human.

Wes paced closer, and with a flicker of apprehension, Lindy followed. The entrance was almost entirely swallowed by a snowdrift, as if the door had been closed at some point but then finally given way. Several windows were likewise semi-covered, but she could see through one near the entryway.

The house seemed utterly still.

"Hello?" she called through the open doorway.

The wind twisted around her, carrying no hint of sound.

Glancing around, Wes seemed to debate for a moment before pacing over and attempting to scale the snowdrift, finally succeeding in a cascade of powdery white and chunks of ice. Using the doorframe for balance, Lindy climbed after him. The snow blocked most of the remaining weak sunlight, and keeping an eye on the dark space around her, she retrieved a flashlight from her bag.

The beam shone blue-white on a living room with overstuffed furniture and family pictures on the walls. The air was cold on her skin while she walked farther inside, but no sound besides her own breathing reached her ears. To the right of the living room, she could see a dining area that opened into the kitchen, both of which seemed empty, while straight ahead lay a hallway with what looked like bedroom doors along the sides.

If there were going to be any monsters or dead bodies in the house…

She took a sharp breath and headed for the hall. The bathroom was empty, as was the child's room to her right. Lions on wallpaper patterned with tall grass smiled back at her in cartoonish glee, while big block letters of wood spelled out JEFFREY on the wall. The room next to it was an office, empty, cold, with an open filing cabinet and a cleared desk, while at the end of the corridor, the master bedroom was a staunch mixture of gray and navy, with throw pillows patterned in silver on the bed.

If not for the front door standing open and the bitter cold in the air, it'd seem just like any other house waiting for its people to return after their workday.

Feeling more like an intruder by the moment, Lindy turned to find Wes watching her from the doorway, almost as if he'd been keeping an eye on her. She shivered. She hadn't even heard him standing there.

Without a sound, the wolf turned and walked back down the hall.

Shifting her shoulders with discomfort, she glanced at the bed again. It'd be so nice to sleep in a bed, but somehow here it felt… wrong. Like stepping on someone's grave, except of course, maybe no one was dead.

But out by the fireplace would be warmer anyway.

She crossed the room to the closet, hoping maybe extra blankets would be in there, only to hesitate. If someone had tried to hide… if they'd frozen or turned into a draug and she hadn't picked up on them…

Seidr rose in her, lapping black shadows at the edge of her mind like dark water in which she'd drown.

Swiftly, she yanked open the closet.

Clothes on hangers swung gently in the sudden disturbance of the air.

A breath left her. She tugged them aside for good

measure, checking behind the clothes, and then yanked down the blankets stacked on the shelf above. Bundling them in her arms, she retreated to the living room.

In the kitchen, Wes made a small yipping noise.

Alarm shot through her. She dropped the blankets and ran, rounding the corner to find him standing in the kitchen, his eyes on the refrigerator.

Her heart pounding, she looked around. "What is it?"

He jerked his head toward the refrigerator door. Cautiously, she walked closer, gripping her flashlight like a weapon.

A piece of paper was pinned to the fridge by a magnet shaped like an ear of corn.

*Uncle Bill,*

*If you find this, Alan and I took Jeffrey and we're heading south. The power's gone and the radio is too. We haven't been able to reach anyone for days. Don't worry about us. We've got what food we had left, and the Suburban should be able to handle the snow. We're heading for Granddad's place outside Des Moines. I hope we'll find you there.*

*Love, Marjorie.*

Lindy looked down at Wes. Something sad in his eyes, he turned away with a sigh.

Nodding to herself as much as anything, she headed back for the living room. Maybe the family made it. Maybe their granddad missed what happened in Des Moines too.

Retrieving the blankets from the floor, she set them on a chair and went to gather couch cushions while Wes disappeared into the bathroom, emerging a minute later in human form with his winter gear in place again. She gave him a small nod, avoiding his eyes with sudden discomfort. Him as a wolf was one thing, scary all on its own. But now that he was back looking like a human, that was a whole other issue. She'd watched him get undressed when he shifted, and though of course she knew from the other night that he was sexy as almighty hell...

She hadn't seen him fully naked in daylight before.

The man was nothing but muscle, sinewed and chiseled like some kind of tattooed biker god. His naked body took away every question she'd had over how far those tattoos went, because the answer?

Damn near everywhere, and God help her for how her hands had twitched with the urge to trace them across his flesh, exploring every inch of his amazing body.

Her insides heated at the memory, and she ducked her face away, bashing the arousal down hard. With a tight smile, she hurried back to the bedrooms, ostensibly for more blankets because of course that was practical. Craving this man?

That was just idiocy.

She snagged a stack of quilts from the back of the closet, listening hard in case he followed her again. Watching him shift had been... amazing, in a way. Logically, she'd known what was happening, but her eyes hadn't seemed able to track the change, like what she saw simply couldn't be processed by the human mind. Seidr had crackled out through the air, tingling over her skin, and somehow, the man became the wolf right in front of her, but without the stretching and bending of some Hollywood portrayal.

He *was* human, and then, he *was* a wolf, as if both had existed in the same space, blurring one into the other until the latter took precedence.

The Order described the process as revolting.

The Order didn't understand what beauty was.

Working quickly, she piled the blankets on the

makeshift beds, not looking toward him while he managed to get the front door closed and then went to search for firewood. When he returned and set to making a fire, she headed to the kitchen, checking for any remaining food—for him more than her—but there was nothing except an empty box of crackers and a half-empty container of salt.

And that brought an end to all her ways of avoiding him.

She returned to the simple bed of cushions, looking anywhere but at him when he sank down across from her. His attention was like a magnet determined to draw her gaze no matter how she fought it, and from the corner of her eye, she could see him watching her, never looking away.

Because, of course, he was going to have questions too —and not about anything she'd seen when he shifted.

Discomfort seeped into the space between them like water soaking everything with its icy-cold touch.

"Are you hungry?" Wes said softly, breaking the quiet.

A shudder ran through her. She was starving, but not for anything that made sense. The moment she started paying attention to it, her body began clamoring for horrible things. Blood. Raw meat. She shook her head as flashes of the rabbit in her grasp played behind her eyes, making her stomach growl. "No."

He was silent.

She cleared her throat, straightening the blankets. "I can keep watch if you want to, um…"

"What was that with the rabbit today, Lindy?"

Her hands stilled. He knew the answer; she'd told him. She was a monster. He really wanted her to repeat that?

She moved to get up. "I'm going to just—"

He caught her wrist and she stopped.

"I promise," he said softly. "Whatever it is, I'm here. I'm not going to run. Just talk to me."

Her eyes slid up, finding his in the firelight, and indecision tore at her. She wanted to retreat. Wanted to draw him closer. Fear gripped her for him, for herself, for the whole damn world and yet this…

This was contact and warmth when everything inside her felt so unbelievably cold. Despite all the reasons she should be retreating, she found herself sinking back onto the cushions across from him, making no move to push his hand away.

His brow rose again in silent repetition of his question.

"I don't know," she admitted.

He sighed. Taking off his gloves, he reached up, cupping his hand against her cheek. A shuddering breath left her, and she leaned into him in spite of herself. He felt real. Solid when all of her life had become unstable, and his gentle touch made her stomach get butterflies, however tiny and lost in the dark they were.

"I'm scared, Wes," she whispered.

He rose a bit, shifting around and coming to sit down next to her. His hands moved carefully, pulling away her gloves while she tensed, afraid of what he'd see.

But he only wrapped his fingers around hers. "You're still you."

She couldn't take her eyes from his tattooed hands in the firelight. "I'm not sure. I… I feel this inside of myself, and I don't want to hurt you, but I—" Her eyes prickled, hot tears slipping down her cheeks.

And her breath caught. Trembling, her hand rose, her fingertips touching the moisture on her skin. A tiny gasp left her, and she looked back to him, eyes wide.

Curiosity passed across his face at whatever expression

she wore, but she couldn't explain. Somehow, some *magical* how, pain and joy were rising up inside her, more vibrant and real than they'd felt all day. The numbness in her flesh seemed to fade, the heat of the fire beside her taking precedence, and a veil felt as if it was slipping from everything, like the color was gradually returning to the world.

Barely breathing for fear the sudden wash of emotions would vanish, she reached up gingerly, taking his cheek. His skin was warm to the touch, and the scruff of his growing beard prickled at her fingertips. "How are you doing this?" she whispered.

His brow flickered down in confusion. "Doing what?"

"Making me feel alive."

A breath left him, a smile crossing his face like her words stole all of his. He leaned in closer, and she met him, closing her eyes as he kissed her.

Tension eased from her even as desire began a drumbeat of need through her body. Her lips parted, and he took the invitation immediately, deepening the kiss. Gripping him tightly, she moved to lie back on the makeshift bed, and her leg wrapped his when he joined her, holding him closer as she grinded herself against him.

Breathless, he pulled back. "Are you sure?"

She lifted herself up on one elbow to reach him, kissing him again briefly. "Yeah."

The corner of his lips rose. Swiftly, he unzipped his coat, tossing it aside, only to hesitate for a moment before stripping off his sweater and shirt too.

Her eyes roamed over him. The firelight played across his skin, the glow touching on intricate artistry of interwoven tattoos over powerful muscle. The skin beneath the marks wasn't entirely smooth, however. Now that she was closer to him than when he'd undressed in the back of the truck, she could see a knotted and gnarled tangle-work of scarring crisscrossing his chest and midsection like an interwoven map all its own.

Surprise flickered through her. She'd felt roughened skin beneath her fingertips in the darkness days before. But she'd never imagined...

He didn't move to come closer, and something inside her ached. Was he worried about this?

She sat up, kissing him before swiftly shedding her own coat. Later, she'd ask him. Later, if he wanted to talk about it at all. But now, she only wanted this.

Something in his eyes made her think maybe he did too.

Heat from the fire warmed the air around her as she lifted her sweater and shirt. Snow barricaded the windows and door alike, nearly covering them, and in her mind, she couldn't feel a trace of the Order or the draugar anywhere. They were safe as they could be, here alone together, and swiftly, she tugged her sweater and shirt off, tossing them aside.

And then she froze.

The tattoo wasn't just on her wrist anymore.

A breathless sound of panic escaped her, horror shattering her anticipation. Jet black vines tangled up her right arm and across half her chest, each one carving a jagged path along her flesh and ending in a narrow point as if it were a claw tearing into her body. As her chest rose and fell in short gasps, the firelight glinted from the markings, throwing back shimmers of metallic green.

"Hey."

Her eyes flew up to Wes for a heartbeat and then returned to the tattoos. How was this possible? How could they just *grow* like—

"Hey, Lindy, look at me."

She dragged her gaze up to his with effort, and he caught her chin when she started to look down again.

"You're still you. These don't change that."

She clamped her lips shut, a sob rising in her throat.

Compassion filled his eyes. Never looking away from her, he reached out carefully toward one of the jagged vines.

She tensed, flinching back. "Don't—"

"Does it hurt?"

Her head shook.

He nodded in response. "Then let me try?"

"I don't want to hurt you, either."

He was silent for a moment. "Let me try. Please."

"Why?" She pulled back, finding her sweater and hugging it to her chest.

"Because you're not a monster."

Protests rose up in her, sobs that surely she was becoming one; couldn't he see that? But even as she tensed all over, he reached out, gently brushing a fingertip along one of the jagged vines while she held her breath.

A shiver went through her to feel him touching her.

But nothing else happened.

A smile touched his face. "See? It's not hurting me, either."

Quiet assurance filled his voice while his expression urged her to believe him. And she wanted to. God, she wanted to.

His fingertips drifted up her arm, sending tingles through her that had everything to do with magic and nothing to do with the darkness inside. "You're beautiful." His hand traced along her bra strap. "Do you still want this?"

Her heart ached. "I think so. Do you?"

A smile crossed his face. Gently, his hand slipped behind her, unclasping her bra. The silken fabric fell away, revealing interwoven vines tangled thick across her right breast.

His hand took her breast as if the marks weren't even there, and she looked up at him in alarm.

"I'm okay," he assured her. "Are you?"

Desire and need tangled in her belly, steadily draining her surge of adrenaline. She managed a nod. "Yeah."

The corner of his lips rose, calm certainty in his gaze while he massaged her soft flesh, pinching and playing at her hardened nipple, and a pleased grin crossed his face when she gasped beneath his ministrations. Still watching her, he moved his hands down her body, featherlight, and her breath caught, her breasts tingling and her core turning molten. How could he be doing this to her when he was barely even touching her?

Carefully, he drew her winter pants away. Relief flickered through her to find her legs still clear of the jet-black markings.

His own clothes joined hers on the floor in only a moment, and despite all her fear, despite all the worry, hot desire welled up to wash it all aside. Firelight played across his powerful body, dancing shadows and vibrant glow across sheer muscle and tattooed skin. As she traced her gaze all the way down to his large cock, her lips parted, her body throbbing.

"You want this?" he asked, teasing threading through his voice.

Her eyes flicked up to his, challenge rising in her, and his smile grew wider. Taking his shoulder, she pulled him to her again, her hips rising toward him.

A hungry noise left him, sending an irrational thrill through her. She should be scared of him—hell, he should be scared of her—yet that primal sound excited some deep part of her like nothing she'd heard. He lowered himself down, penetrating her even as his lips claimed hers. Slowly, he pulled away and then entered her again, as if trying to draw out every second of this, building the pleasure between them.

She closed her eyes with a groan of need, and his lips caught it. His tongue tangled with hers, their breath mingling as he rocked in and out of her. But it wasn't enough. Slow left her mind still racing. Still *thinking*, and right now, that only caused pain.

Shifting around on the bed, she pushed him back and then rose with him when he pulled away. "Harder," she whispered.

His apparent confusion vanished into anticipation and dark desire as she straddled him, taking his cock deep inside her and rocking against him. A deep sound left him, like a growl mixed with a groan, and his hands gripped her ass hard, moving her on him.

The firelight caught on her tattoos, and she tensed.

His hand came up, his fingers taking her cheek and drawing her face toward him. Without a word, he captured her mouth in a deep kiss, his tongue tangling with her own and his motions so intent, it was like he was trying to draw every bit of her focus to him, to this.

Gratitude swelled in her even as her body thrummed to feel his cock hitting her so deep. Here in this moment, she was still her, as he said. She was just Lindy, not a monster, and everywhere he touched seemed to come alive. Even as his lips broke from hers to trace a scorching line down her throat, she was safe. When his grip returned to her ass, grinding her against him, she was secure. Sweat clung to her impossibly marked skin, hot and cold by turns in the firelight and chilled air, but none of it could take this moment.

Her hands held his lips to hers as she rode him, wishing she could pour every ounce of her gratitude from her body into his. She was herself now, not a monster or a curse or any mistakes she'd once made. The darkness was missing, and only pure ecstasy remained, and it was because of him, only him, magically and impossibly driving it all away.

White-hot pleasure built inside her, drawing her focus down to the sensations he wrought in her body. Harder and harder, she drove herself onto his cock, gripping him tightly, and desperate sounds of desire and need escaped him. Her heart raced, thrilled by the cries, and when his hand clenched down on her ass, the jolt of pleasure that shot through her seemed to fly straight into her core.

The orgasm erupted in a surge of white light racing through every limb. She cried out, everything in the world vanishing for a beautiful moment where there was only pleasure, only him, and even as he thrust into her harder, pounding his own orgasm out into her sensitized flesh, she could only ride the wave of ecstasy, safe and secure in his arms.

His motions slowed, and his hands tightened on her, holding her tired body to his. Before she could even look around, he drew her to him, kissing her deeply and then gently lowering her back to the bed. The firelight barely had a chance to touch her before he was pulling the blankets over them again, wrapping them in thick fabric and hiding every impossible mark on her body away.

Warmth surrounded her as he pulled her close, and she

nestled against his side. "You're still you," he whispered like a blessing.

She closed her eyes, tears stinging from gratitude that overwhelmed distant pain. The words were a kindness, and more than that, they felt true.

As long as she was with him.

# 16

## WES

The world may have been hell, but lying here with Lindy in his arms felt like a slice of heaven all the same.

One arm crooked behind his head, he lay motionless, relishing the soft sensation of her breast brushing against his chest with each gentle breath. Her comforting scent surrounded him, a delicious mixture of sex and sweat and spice, and sleep tugged at him, trying to draw his eyes closed. At his side, the fire was burning down to embers, letting the winter chill seep back into the room, but beneath the pile of blankets, with her at his side, warmth filled him like the flames had never died.

On some level, he knew this was still dangerous. The wolf inside him could never be trusted. But also, he knew he hadn't bitten her, hadn't done more than give her every ounce of pleasure he could, and the mere thought of harming her made even the wolf inside him pace and whine.

He wasn't safe and never would be, but in this

moment, he was determined to be as close to it as he could come.

For her. For now. Because this was wonderful.

She stirred next to him, her fingers trailing across his chest. A smile crossed his face. It tickled, ever so slightly, but the delicate feeling of her there was soothing too.

Her touch paused when she reached one of his scars.

He waited, knowing what she'd probably ask.

"Did I hurt you?" she whispered.

He blinked. That wasn't what he expected. "Not at all."

A breath left her as if she was relieved.

"What about you?" he asked gently.

She shook her head against his chest and chuckled. "No."

In the fireplace, a burnt log cracked, falling in darkening embers to the ashes below. Carefully, he stretched over, grabbing another from the pile nearby and tossing it onto the dying flames, trying not to disturb her with the movement.

She sighed. "Wes?"

"Yeah?"

"May I ask, um…"

He glanced down at her. "What?"

"Are these from the wolf?" Her fingers traced along the mottled path of a scar. "The one who… you know."

He weighed how to answer, but there was only really the truth. "Mostly."

She glanced up toward him.

"Exorcism got a bit rough. When my parents…" He shrugged rather than get into the ugly details of how they'd thought it took blood and pain to reclaim his soul from being "possessed." How they hadn't stopped until he ran, weak and barely conscious, and escaped into the

woods, where he survived for a blur of days before one of
the Thorsen clan smelled the blood and found him.

"My God," she whispered.

"Not the best parents." He kept his tone light, but she
looked up toward him again all the same.

"I'm so sorry."

He shook his head. "Over a long time ago."

Seeming thoughtful, she lay her head back down
against him. "And the, um, tattoos?"

He chuckled. "Something better to look at."

Her fingers strayed over his chest again. "They're beautiful." She hesitated. "Not to make you uncomfortable. If
calling them that does, I mean. Is 'handsome' better? I
just—"

He grinned at her sudden rush of anxious words.
"Thank you."

She was silent for a long moment. "You're going to
change back again, aren't you? When we leave here, I
mean."

He hesitated. "Does it bother you?"

Discomfort spread through him when she didn't
answer. He'd seen the fear in her eyes yesterday. The way
she'd watched him as if waiting for the wolf to attack.

"I just…" She hesitated. "It's awfully quiet."

He paused, a strangely warm-but-confused feeling
rising in his chest. That was her concern? "I can understand you when I'm in that form, if that helps?"

Thoughtfully, she nodded. "A bit, yeah."

A breath left her, and she looked back toward the
windows. He followed her gaze. The snow was piled high
against the windows, and in the darkness, he couldn't tell
if any more was falling. He only hoped it wouldn't be too
hard to manage in the morning.

"Do you, um..." she started. "Do you know if we're going the right way?"

He glanced back down at her. "We are."

"How can you be sure?"

"I've got a pretty good sense of direction, especially as... you know."

"A wolf."

"Yeah."

She nodded like maybe she was relieved and then nestled her cheek into his chest. In the fireplace, a log cracked and sent sparks drifting up with the renewed flames.

A sigh left her. "I don't want move."

Inside his mind, the wolf rumbled contentedly to itself. He pushed the feeling aside, though warmth still blossomed in his chest. "You don't have to. I can take first watch."

She hesitated. "That's okay, I can—"

"Really."

She drew a breath that turned almost immediately into a yawn. "You sure?"

He smiled. "Yeah."

Kissing her lightly, he shifted position to let her lie back on the pillows while he sat on the edge of their makeshift bed. The chilled air stole the residual warmth of the blankets from his skin while he retrieved his pants and then glanced around for his sweater.

A fingertip slid down his spine. He looked over his shoulder to find Lindy watching him, her cheek propped on her palm.

"What?" he asked.

Her light touch traced a sinuous path along his skin. "Just enjoying the view."

The wolf inside him made a hungry sound. "You do much more of that, I'm not going to leave."

She regarded him with feigned innocence. "Remind me how that's a bad thing?"

His cock hardened all over again at the heat in her eyes and the wicked edge to her smile. Gods, he loved her confidence, and this teasing side of her too. And when she'd asked him to fuck her harder... when she'd clutched him so tightly, her nails digging into his skin...

He turned, coming back toward her. "I can't think of a single reason."

THEY SCARCELY LEFT THE BED ALL NIGHT.

"If you need anything," he said as she pulled on her boots the next morning. "I can understand every word, okay?"

She glanced over her shoulder at him, nervousness tightening her face. But she nodded.

He echoed the motion, hesitating a moment longer while reluctance to lose the ability to speak to her gnawed at him. Among the pack, body language cues and their bond was sufficient communication. But with her, the silence was deafening, and she wasn't the only one bothered by it.

But there was nothing for it. They were burning daylight.

Drawing in a sharp breath, he shifted into his wolf form and then padded over to her. Trepidation flickered over her face, but still she reached out, brushing a hand along his fur.

The wolf tried to rumble with pleasure, and he shoved it down hard. No need to scare her.

She looked worried enough.

Apprehension tangled inside his gut as he watched her rise and walk toward the door. Beneath the ghostly shadows on her face—visible only in his wolf form—she looked paler than yesterday. Less steady too, and guilt colored the observation. They'd spent hours together in bed, bringing her to orgasm over and over. But she'd barely slept as a result, and she hadn't eaten anything without throwing it up in over a day.

She must be starving.

Glancing around briefly, he headed for his bag, nudging it open with his nose and paws. Chances were, she'd decline the food, but he still had to try. Surely, Lindy had to eat or she'd collapse.

He picked up a can carefully and brought it over to her.

She grimaced at the sight, like her stomach wanted to heave just at the can's proximity.

A sigh left him. He returned the food to where he found it and picked the bag up in his teeth. Together, they made their way through the blockade of snow at the front door out into the cold morning. A renewed layer of white obscured everything, swallowing their footprints from the day before. Without pause, he turned north and Lindy followed him, trekking down the slope to the snow-covered road.

But as the minutes turned to hours, her movements grew ever more unsteady, her footsteps stumbling in the snow. She waved him away whenever he came near, but that didn't stop worry from building inside him like a howl.

This couldn't go on.

Inside his mind, he paced. He had to help her, but the only thing that presented itself was bound to terrify her—or make her hate him forever. But he'd seen the look on her face yesterday when she held that rabbit in her hands. Ravenous. Chillingly so. Wild too, like a starved animal defending its catch.

Like someone looking at food.

It wasn't logical, if he thought about this from a human perspective, but whatever was happening to her wasn't exactly human anyway.

His eyes slid around the terrain. He couldn't be sure this was a good move—with her, if nothing else. But then, continuing on like this... Hell, that was making it worse too.

She stumbled a bit, almost as if proving his thoughts accurate. He yipped with worry, and as always, she motioned as if to reassure him, not looking his way.

Dammit. If small game was what she needed, then by the gods, he'd get it for her.

Especially if it was that or watch her collapse.

Intently, he scanned the world of endless white all around them. He'd caught glimpses of small creatures here and there, so surely this wouldn't take long. With so many humans all undertaking their own personal versions of "anywhere but here," animals large and small had begun moving into terrain they normally would have avoided. And out where there was nothing but Lindy and him...

A rustle in a nearby bush caught his ear, and he was moving before the rabbit completed its hop. Tearing past the branches, he sank his teeth into the small creature's fur, thinking a quick apology and a thanks to the animal as he bit down.

Lindy stared at him as he emerged, but in only a

moment, the alarm in her eyes turned to a terrified, crazed sort of hunger when she saw what he held. Her body twitched, and her face did too, and she turned away, as if trying and failing to make herself retreat.

Pacing toward her carefully, he never took his eyes from her as he laid the creature down at the tip of her snowshoes and nudged it closer with his nose.

Lindy's whole body quaked, and she locked her eyes on him like she was fighting not to look anywhere else. Her gloved hands twitched, her mouth moving like she was struggling not to gasp or scream.

A soft whine left him. Gods, what he wouldn't give to be able to tell her this was all right—as much as it could be, anyway. She wasn't a monster. Wasn't anything but a beautiful woman who needed to eat or she'd die.

Her head shook, a tight and quick motion. Her mouth tightened like she was holding in a gasp. But then her gaze sank down to the rabbit, and a tiny whimper left her, the battle on her face turning to agony.

With lightning speed, she dropped to a crouch, her hands snagging the creature and bringing it to her mouth before he'd even managed to blink. Tearing into the rabbit with her teeth, she gulped the meat and blood and fur down like she was starving.

Conflicted pain twisted inside his chest at the sight. The wolf side of him was brimming with satisfaction over feeding his mate, while the man was at a loss for anything else to do. She really might hate him for this. Probably would, honestly. But she had to eat, and if this was what it took to keep her going, then it's what had to happen.

He'd do whatever it took to keep her alive.

After only a moment, though, her frantic motions slowed. Blood coated her gloves and the lower half of her face alike, but her flesh had more color than even a few minutes before.

With burgeoning horror, she drew the remains of the rabbit away from her. "What's wrong with me?" she whispered, staring around wide eyes. "Oh God, what's wrong with me?"

Her voice was terrified, almost like she was begging someone to explain. On impulse, he started toward her.

She recoiled, dropping the rabbit and shoving to her feet, her bloody gloves leaving red smears on the white snow. For a moment, she stood frozen, her arms out from her sides and her entire body shaking.

And then her eyes rose to him, pained betrayal consuming her expression.

Without a word, she spun and fled from him as quickly as the snow would let her.

# 17

## LINDY

S he had to make this stop.

Lindy strode across the snow, her body feeling better than it had in days and her mind reeling. That hadn't been human. Hadn't been normal. Hell, it hadn't even been *sane*. How could she have done that? Torn into that poor little rabbit like it was a sirloin steak?

She swiped a hand over her face, and her palm came away covered in blood. A shriek built within her, and frantically she wiped at her face over and over, the blood smearing across her sleeves and gloves alike.

A scream ripped from her. Tearing at her coat, she tried to throw it aside too, if only to get the blood away.

Wes circled in front of her quickly, barking at her, and she could hear the alarm in his voice. Without a coat, she'd freeze to death out here.

With a coat covered in blood, she felt like she'd go insane.

He barked at her again, a pleading note in the sound.

Unable to bring herself to even look at him, she stood

motionless for a moment before drawing the zipper back up again with shaking hands. Trembling like a leaf in a hurricane, she started off again.

Covered in blood.

Panic throbbed like a drum beat in her chest. She couldn't do this. Live like this. *Eat* like that. She'd known the changes were going to be bad, but this...

*Do you accept this honor for which you have been chosen?*

*With all my heart, sir.*

Her breaths came faster, fear giving away to something hot boiling within her, burning out through her core and limbs like she'd cracked the shell of a volcano. What the hell had been *wrong* with her as a child? What the fuck had she been *thinking*? Agreeing to this. Thinking giving up her *soul* would be a such a wonderful, amazing thing. Some high honor, instead of the depths of fucking hell. And all for what? To serve a bunch of apocalyptic psychos who just wanted to watch the world burn so they could rule over the ashes?

Soft footsteps came from behind her, and her head snapped around, her teeth bared in a snarl.

Wes watched her from twenty feet away.

She stared, trembling. Seidr quivered through her body like an electric current just beneath her skin. God help her, she could have hurt him. Killed him, even.

But how the hell had she even *heard* him?

Whirling fast, she kept walking, more sounds making themselves known now that hunger wasn't beating a migraine rhythm against her skull. Rustling in the bushes. The call of birds so far away she couldn't even see them against the sky. Every noise was amplified, every sensation like a dial turned to eleven.

What the hell *was* this?

Her snowshoed feet stomped through the drifts while her distant fear whined like a mosquito in her head. Wes should have let her starve. What had he been thinking, bringing her raw dead meat? That she was some fucking animal? Dammit. Damn *him*. She no sooner told him she was scared she was a monster than... what? His answer was to agree?

*Goddamn* that reckless idiot. For all he knew, she could have attacked *him*!

An ache pressed her chest like a sob trapped inside. She could have hurt him, that moron. She could have ripped into him and torn him to shreds, no matter how the mere thought made her insides clench like she'd been punched a hundred times. His beautiful body could be the one lying bloody on the snow right now, not some innocent animal that had only needed to die because Lindy was a fool who'd sold her soul to a doomsday cult.

Tears wanted to rise in her eyes but couldn't, and it only made her feet pound into the ground harder. Maybe he'd leave now. That'd be the smart move—not that he was making those. Sleeping with her like she might not have driven him insane just by accident. Being so... so goddamn *kind* when it could have cost him everything. But maybe this would be enough. Maybe when she looked back, he'd be gone, having finally seen enough to get it through his thick head she wasn't someone he wanted to be near.

Or be with.

She bit back a pained snarl. There wasn't any "be with." There wasn't anything at all. Having sex in the apocalypse because they were the only two people for God knew how many miles didn't qualify as a relationship, never mind how there couldn't be any future for the two of them anyway. And yeah, sure, he was amazing. Gentle but strong. Funny. Caring and seemingly smart—current evidence notwithstanding. And fine, so he'd given her some of the best sex of her life, considering most of the guys she'd slept with before the world ended had thought the mere sight of their dick was enough to constitute foreplay. Wes was attentive. Compassionate. Basically everything she would have dreamed of, if the world had been different.

And thus he was an absolute fucking *idiot* for risking himself to stay near her.

She threw a glance over her shoulder and found him there, still pacing along twenty feet back with his pale-gray eyes locked on her.

"*Why?*" she shouted at him. "Why are you— Why won't you just—"

His head cocked, questioning. He started to walk toward her.

"No!" She took a step back but he kept coming. "Dammit, Wes. Why the hell couldn't you leave when you — I said stop, goddammit!"

He paused.

Tears spilled from her eyes, searing and impossible and freezing to her cheeks in tiny rivulets of ice. He shouldn't be this worried about her. Shouldn't for a thousand reasons. After all, she wasn't the victim here. She'd agreed to this. *Wanted* it back then. Hell or not, she'd brought it on herself.

Carefully, he walked toward her.

The ache in her chest grew worse, and she gasped against it. "Don't," she sobbed.

He gave a soft whine, worry and care somehow so clear in the sound, and it stabbed her heart like a knife.

"Please," she begged. "I don't want to hurt you."

Turning, she made herself walk away from him and refused to look back when she heard his footsteps following even closer than before.

Time crept on, the world passing around them in endless white and gray. Occasionally, she came across vehicles abandoned in snowdrifts, the owners frozen inside or else long since gone, and every so often she saw a house with smoke still rising from the chimney. A motley assortment of starving dogs crossed their path when the two of them circled the frozen expanse of a lake, the animals baring their teeth but continuing onward when they laid eyes on Wes in wolf form.

Though, to her great discomfort, they'd whined and scurried away even faster at the sight of her.

Gradually, signs the two of them might be nearing the city began to appear: more houses, businesses, and dead stoplights over intersections. She didn't recognize the street names, but that didn't mean much. Dad and Frankie moved to Minnesota around the time she started college, and though she'd flown into Minneapolis a few times, she hadn't explored everything around the city itself.

But her family lived over an hour's drive north, out beyond the city where it turned to rural land again, and she had no idea how long a walk that would be.

Or what she'd find when she got there.

Her feet slowed as they reached a bridge over what might have been a frozen river beneath the snow, and heaviness settled over her as she looked to the east. Far in the distance, the horizon seemed to stop short of where it should have been, as if the ground fell away, taking every-thing down with it.

She swallowed hard, nausea rolling her stomach. So

much for hoping Fenrir's destruction hadn't reached this far.

Wes came up beside her, bumping her gloved hand lightly.

A sharp breath entered her lungs, and she tensed with the warring urges to reach out to him and yet retreat.

Not looking at him, she started walking again.

Hours slid by in a blur of aching muscles and far-off sounds she couldn't understand how she could hear. She knew she should have been more tired than she was—snowshoeing was laborious in the best of times—but still her body continued on. In the distance, amid the darkness encroaching on her mind, she could sense the draugar and the Order deeper inside Minneapolis. Whether that group had made it out this far was anyone's guess, though from the broken-in doors and occasional bodies lying in the snow, it seemed likely. People were still around, though, that much she could tell. She'd seen more than a few curtains twitch closed when they passed, and murmurs of low voices reached her ears, muffled though they were by walls.

And it worried her. If the house they'd stayed in last night was any indication, food was scarce, and whatever these people had left after so long buried in snow couldn't be much.

There was every chance they'd attack her for supplies, or Wes in order to make him into dinner.

She cast a quick glance at him. The two of them needed somewhere safe before night fell, for both their sakes and the sake of the humans who probably wouldn't survive the error of trying to hurt them.

Wes met her eyes. Somehow, she got the impression he worried about the same thing.

Chewing her lip, she kept going, and as the last light began fading from the overcast sky, she spotted somewhere that could be an option. The restaurant's windows were still intact, though the door was busted in. Snow filled the entryway, and when she climbed past it to see inside, it was clear the food had been taken as well. But the door was still usable, and all that snow was better than a deadbolt, in some ways. And best of all, a fireplace stood in the center of the room, with a few wooden chairs still present to give them a fire, at least for a little while.

It was undoubtedly the best they were going to find that night.

Swiftly, she set to spreading blankets near the fireplace while Wes went into the back and shifted. When he returned, he broke down the chairs without a word and then started the fire before finally sitting down next to her.

Silence hung between them, and he seemed in no hurry to break it.

Even if someone had to, eventually.

"I think it'd be best if we went our separate ways," she said, not looking at him.

From the corner of her eye, she saw him turn to her. "What?"

"Because of today."

Wes gave a small chuckle. "Come on, I've eaten my fair share of rabbit over the years."

"In human form?"

His humor seemed to drain at the flat tone of her voice, and he sat quietly for a moment. "It's okay." His voice was soft and so heartbreakingly kind that it brought those impossible tears to her eyes. "It doesn't make you a monster, and if it's what you need to survive, then so be it."

She looked away, hugging her knees to her chest. She *felt* more when she was with him, though she had no idea why.

But it hurt.

Silence fell between them, broken only by the crackle of the fire.

"I asked for this, Wes," she said softly.

He was silent.

She didn't take her eyes from the flames, the truth pressing at her. She had to tell him. He had to know.

Maybe then he'd understand why he should leave.

"I was trained by the best the Order had to offer. Grand General Dal Hegnar, slayer of…" Closing her eyes, she shook her head. "*So* many wolves. He taught me everything. How to fight." Pain throbbed in her chest. "How to kill. And when the day came and they were ready to pass on the mantle of their weapon, he chose me out of all the Initiates. Mom was so proud."

Disgust twisted her lip, though for herself or her mother, she wasn't sure.

No, she admitted to herself. For both.

Because God knew she'd been proud too.

"How old were you?" Wes asked.

"Twelve."

A breath left him.

"The Order was all I'd known." Guilt tugged at her because it wasn't an excuse. Not really. She'd still signed up to kill the enemy and never once questioned who that truly was.

Wes took her hand, and her breath caught. She looked over at him, alarmed at the risk, but she couldn't quite make herself pull away.

She felt so much more alive with him.

Even if she knew it couldn't last.

His other hand came up, brushing back her hair beside the knit cap on her head. "It's not your fault."

"I agreed to it. Wanted it. How is it not my fault?"

He appeared pained, like he wasn't sure what to say.

She turned back to the small fire, watching the broken pieces of a chair crackle and decay in the flames. The darkness in her mind churned in the distance, hungry, waiting.

"Would you blame Frankie?"

At Wes's quiet words, she looked back. "What?"

"Frankie. He's thirteen, right? Just a year older than you were. And if it was him instead of you, would you be this hard on him? Hold him responsible for what grown-ass adults in the Order convinced him to do?"

Discomfort made her shift slightly.

"You were a kid, Lindy. And you didn't know any better. And for what it's worth—" He shrugged. "Maybe you need to let yourself off the hook."

Her brow furrowed as she looked at the flames, a weird ache passing through her like a chain loosening around her chest. So many years, and she'd never once thought about it like that. Looked at her brother and imagined if the Scythe of Niorun was him instead. Mostly, she'd just been grateful it wasn't. That he'd escaped before the Order could sink their hooks too deep into him. She'd spent years feeling relieved that Frankie, at least, got the chance to be a kid instead of a weapon-in-training, sworn to a bloody cause and taught to despise any life but the brutal one with which he'd been charged.

But she'd never wondered.

And she knew the answer.

A breath left her, ragged, harsh. Of course she wouldn't hold Frankie responsible. Of course she'd blame the goddamn adults who'd talked a kid into sacrificing more than that child could ever understand. And why had the Order chosen a kid anyway? If it was such an honor, why hadn't Dal Hegnar and all the rest been clamoring for the mantle?

Because it wasn't. Because they wanted to be the ones holding the reins while they stripped another human being of their soul. The other Allegiants, the *grown* Allegiants... they didn't want to give up who they were. No, they'd just brainwash a kid into doing it instead.

Bastards. *Cowards*. Doomsday scum.

Her fingers curled into fists as her heart pounded. All these years, she'd blamed herself. Cursed *herself* for how much she'd once wanted this so-called honor. But was it really her fault? Yes, she'd agreed, but by God, what child didn't want to please their parents? What kid didn't want the approval of their favorite teacher, the one whose praise was like gold only because it was so rare?

But Dal Hegnar and her mother... they'd used that. Yes, she'd been a damn good student. Best weapon they had in training, so caught up in trying to prove her worth, it'd never occurred to her it was a bad thing that all the Order saw in her was a tool. And if her position and Frankie's were reversed, she never would have blamed him for that. She would have hated the adults.

And ached with sorrow for her baby brother instead.

Pain tangled with her rage, throbbing in her chest. Drawing her knees up tighter, she hugged them while in her mind, the darkness churned, uncaring about her pain. Waiting to devour it all.

The Order took so much from her, back when she was young. Things she hadn't understood. Things she would have wanted—a life, friends, a future—if only she'd known what they were. And now it was on her to make sure the Order didn't take everything that was left. Now all she could do was cling by her fingernails to her self and her sanity, determined to keep them from one last victory of making her their weapon and killing everyone she loved.

If she could hold on.

Chills crept through her. "Wes?"

"Yeah?"

"I need to ask you to do something for me."

He hesitated. "Okay…"

She drew a breath. It was the only answer. The backup. He may be an idiot for staying with her, but if it all came down to it, maybe he was also her only hope.

"If—" She cleared her throat. "If I can't hold out against this or if it starts making me do… terrible things, and I can't stop myself…" Resolutely, she turned to him. "I want you to kill me and take my family back to Mariposa."

His eyes went wide.

"Please, Wes. Your wolf could—"

He pulled away sharply. "I'm not going to—"

"What if that had been you today instead of a rabbit? What if next time it is? If I have to use seidr again and that one time is the last straw, I could—" Her breath hitched. "This was always the plan, Wes. *My* plan. I've been running out of time since…" She sniffled sharply. "Since I was twelve years old, and—"

"Lindy, we'll find an answer. Either from your dad or someone else, but we'll find one. You don't—"

"There *isn't* an answer. Not besides this. I don't want to become their monster. I don't want to do the things that are waiting for me when I lose this fight. But if I can't get to my family in time, or if I can't stop myself before

I..." She shook her head, pain throbbing in her chest. "Please."

He looked agonized.

"I'm begging you, Wes."

Without a word, he drew her to him, and after a day of fighting it, she let herself fall into his arms.

"Please." She gripped his coat as he held her close, hanging on his warmth as if it could drive away the world. "I'd rather die."

# 18

## WES

I f ever he met this Dal Hegnar bastard, Wes was fairly certain his wolf would rip the man's throat out.

And Wes wouldn't give a damn.

In the restaurant lit only by the waning embers of the fire at their side, he lay with his arms around Lindy, wishing it could be enough to protect her. Hell, wishing someone *had* protected her all those years ago when she was just a kid.

And didn't he know that feeling?

Gods above, he wanted to get his hands on the bastards who'd brainwashed her into giving up more than she could ever understand she was sacrificing. Who'd offered up a *child* to their own selfish worldview, to hell with all it would cost her.

And now...

He drew her closer, nestling her deeper into his arms. He couldn't do what she asked. He simply *couldn't*. Everything in him recoiled from the sheer thought, like someone was asking him to rip his own lungs out.

She planned to die.

His wolf wanted to die at the thought.

He didn't know what she was to him, really. Not beyond the delusion the beast inside him believed, some mad claim that she was his mate, of all things. But that didn't mean he could *ever* do this.

She was so sure there was no hope. How did he argue with that when he didn't even know what was going on?

His brow furrowed as he squeezed his eyes shut. He *couldn't* argue with her about it, but maybe he could prove there was an alternative. Someone had to have answers for this, whether it was her family or the bastards who forced this on her.

Resolve settled in his chest, and he drew her closer. Even if he had to hunt down the Order himself, he'd find a way to save Lindy.

Rest didn't come easily as the night slowly passed. Every little shift and noise she made when it was her turn to keep watch brought him back to consciousness, and when the next morning finally arrived, exhaustion weighed heavy on him. Lindy didn't say much before he shifted back into wolf form, and they left the restaurant in silence after making sure the fire was out.

She didn't eat, and he didn't ask, but he kept his eyes peeled. The neighborhood around them was eerily still, without so much as a mouse huddling beneath the frozen bushes. Only a pair of ravens watched from a steepled rooftop, and even they didn't make a sound. It wasn't until he and Lindy reached another neighborhood around a small lake that he spotted a squirrel and took off after it, bringing it to her only a moment later.

Immediately, she shook her head.

A gruff growl left him, and she looked at him in alarm,

but he simply began ripping meat from the small creature and then nudging it toward her.

Pain twisted her face, and it hurt to see. He wished so badly that he could communicate with her the way he did with his pack. That somehow he could let her know this was okay, and it didn't make her a monster. The farthest thing from, really, considering how desperately she was fighting to remain human in spite of everything against her.

He made a short huffing sound, nudging the meat. The pain on her face only deepened, but after a moment she closed her eyes, reached out, and took some of it all the same. Never opening her eyes, she stuck it in her mouth and swallowed, shudders rolling through her. But her hand went back quickly, grabbing more, shoving it in her mouth, and gulping it down like she couldn't devour it fast enough.

His heart aching, he sank onto his haunches, watching her. If nothing else, she wouldn't starve.

After a few bites, she got up and walked away as fast as she could. He swallowed down the rest of the food in one bite and then followed her, keeping up as she moved along the roads through the city. He tried not to think the worst about how she paused from time to time, looking around as if picking up on things even he couldn't hear, only to veer off along another road like she was avoiding something.

But it worried him. Was that ability chewing away at her… her *soul*, or whatever it was she thought this power was consuming? And what would happen if she *stopped* using it—if she even could? Stumbling upon the Order wasn't a better option, though at least with the draugar he could kill them in wolf form.

Not a hundred of them, though. A thousand. However many might be lurking deeper within the streets of Minneapolis.

Anguish throbbed through him. If she stopped using whatever this was, and he didn't hear the draugar or the Order in time, she'd have to use even *more* power to eliminate them. Gods above, what he wouldn't give for his pack around them both now, helping protect her from this.

The day passed, and they spent the night camped in the looted remnants of a store, where he made love to Lindy and then held her as she fell asleep in his arms. When the next morning dawned, they continued on in silence beneath the overcast sky.

Time passed with only brief stops and small meals of whatever he could catch. Midway through the second day, they found a ransacked sporting goods store with a few mismatched snowshoes that fit Lindy still clinging to a display on the wall, along with replacements for her gloves and coat now stiff with blood. They spent the fourth day backtracking when every other road seemed to empty into dead ends they couldn't cross, and the fifth day was a serpentine mess of avoiding the hungry packs of wild dogs or the coyotes now roaming the area. At long last, they left the metro area behind entirely, continuing north and knocking snow from road signs in an attempt to find their way.

He'd always liked GPS, but by the gods, he never thought he'd miss it this much. Locating a specific house in all of Minnesota was entirely different than his own sense of general direction.

As they walked down a stretch that once had been a state road, he scanned the trees and abandoned cars. From what he could tell of the overcast sky, they were only a few hours from nightfall, if not less, and he hadn't seen a decent place to spend the night in a while. Worse yet, they were heading east again, meaning at any moment they could run into the fissure torn through the earth.

With her family possibly at the bottom of it.

Lindy's feet stopped. "Oh, thank God."

She took off through the snow, moving as fast as she could for a turnoff on the opposite side of the road.

He gave a small yip at her.

"This way," she called over her shoulder.

She hurried down a stretch that may have been a gravel road, given the rocks turning up in the deep snow. There were no tracks or sign that anyone had come this way in a while, but after a small eternity of slogging onward, the path finally came to an end in a little brown ranch house half buried in white.

Lindy stopped when she saw it, her entire body becoming still, and he got the strangest feeling from her body language that she was checking something, even if she didn't move at all.

Worried prickled through him, the feeling familiar after so many days.

And then she took off again.

He raced after her. Had something gone wrong? The door was sheltered from the deepest snowdrifts by the porch and the trees around it, leaving it practically bare but still closed. Without a word, she fished for a key inside her pocket and then jammed it in the lock, turning it quickly. Shoving the door open, she strode inside, her snowshoes thumping on the tile floor.

"Dad?" she called. "Frankie?"

Dread sank into Wes's stomach. He couldn't hear a damn thing. No movement, no voices. Nothing.

Oh gods…

Lindy unfastened her snowshoes swiftly and then hurried deeper into the house, calling out as she went. He stayed with her, sniffing for any hint where her family might be. But the smells were old and the silence didn't change. No one was in the bedrooms, nor the living room or the garage. But the car was still there.

Shit, this couldn't be good.

He followed her into the kitchen, torn about taking the time to shift back. In human form, he could talk to her. But if a draug was nearby, he could only kill it as a wolf.

The silence was killing him.

Air escaped Lindy at the sight of a cell phone lying on the kitchen island, and when she spoke, her voice was thin. "Dad's." She crossed to the phone, clicking it on and then cursing to discover the battery was dead.

Short breaths left her and she turned away, clutching the cell as she leaned on the kitchen island. He walked closer, rubbing up against her, and her hand dropped to him, stroking his fur distantly.

A shiver went through him. He loved that sensation. He only hoped it was helping her somehow.

"Frankie's cello is gone," Lindy said, her voice tight but matter of fact. "But his phone is here too. Mom thought music was a waste of time, so if she'd found them already, she wouldn't take the—"

He glanced up as she cut off.

Pushing away from the kitchen island, she strode toward the refrigerator, her body language tense. But he couldn't understand what she was seeing. There was just a collection of random magnets in a row. Some pictures. A grocery list for bread, milk, and cheese.

But Lindy turned to him with a relieved smile. "I know

where they are. Dad, he..." She swiped a stained glove over her face as if trying to focus. "He made up codes in case Mom..." She shook her head. "Just in case. Milk is north, cheese is east, bread is south. But eggs are missing, so that means they headed west. The magnets in a row are miles." Grinning, she turned back to him. "They're okay. Come on."

Racing back to the front door, she retrieved her snow-shoes and strapped them on with speed born of days of practice. Without another word, she tromped through the house and out the back door.

Hope pounding through him, he followed her.

Hurrying across the yard, Lindy headed into the forest behind the house. When she reached the tree line, her eyes darted around, and then her grin widened. Moving fast, she took off at an angle through the forest as if following some kind of trail, though he'd be damned if he could see it. The tree cover was thick, and the undergrowth was too, a tangle of frozen woods that seemed to go nowhere.

And that didn't change while the minutes ticked on.

Wes glanced around, worried. The sky was getting darker, and beneath the trees, the shadows were thick. Sure, Lindy could detect the draugar, but that left all kinds of predators to contend with—not the least of which were humans.

He paced after her through the deepening shadows, his wolf sight helping him pick out the shapes of their surroundings more than any light now. Maybe he should shift back, nudity and cold be damned, to tell her they needed to find some place safe for the night. They'd locate her family, but this wasn't—

The distant sound of a cello carried on the breeze, so faint his ears could barely catch it.

Lindy stopped.

Wes glanced at her, alarmed. Human ears shouldn't be able to pick up on that faint of a noise, and yet from her body language, he knew she could hear it.

Trepidation moved through him. Craving raw meat. Possessing strong senses. Those were ulfhednar traits, except all in the wrong combination. Wes's human body didn't need to eat those things. He didn't throw up when he consumed a regular meal.

She started through the trees, and he paced after her quickly. What the hell had the Order tried to make her into?

The music strengthened in the forest as they followed the sound, the melody beautiful and haunting, sad and uplifting in turns. The notes seemed to twist among the trees, like the woods itself was singing, drawing the two of them onward through the darkening shadows and deepening night.

If that was Frankie, then gods above, the kid was incredible.

The trees parted at long last, revealing a sprawling, one-story log cabin that blended naturally with the trees around it. A green roof was peaked sharply above a covered porch that sheltered a dark-brown door and windows with red shutters. Light glowed from beyond the curtained windows, beaming gold out into the snowy night. Amid it all, the sound of the cello never faltered, mesmerizing with its beauty.

Lindy slowed, her body language suddenly nervous. For the thousandth time, he wished he'd shifted, if only to provide some kind of comfort. But he nudged her side all the same, and she nodded distantly, her eyes still on the house. Drawing a steadying breath, she walked toward the door.

A faint sound came behind them, nearly lost beneath the cello music.

Wes whirled. A large man stood there, bundled in a dark-green coat with heavy winter pants to match. He wore a deer hunter cap on his head, the flaps tucked down over his ears, and held a bundle of chopped firewood in his arms.

He was also seven feet tall if he was an inch and built like a solid block of muscle.

Wes risked a fast glance at Lindy. Did she know this guy? Was this her dad?

The alarm on her face was enough of an answer.

His lips curled back in a snarl.

The guy's eyebrow twitched up, not a shred of fear in his expression. "Well, you're a long way from home."

Wes moved ahead of Lindy, blocking her from the man. Something was off about this guy, though the gods help him if he knew what. But that didn't matter either, because Lindy couldn't use seidr. Not with what it would cost her.

A low growl filtered out from him, daring the man to try coming closer.

"Where's my family?" Lindy demanded.

The man cocked his head at her. "What's your name?"

"Answer the question."

Wes growled louder, seconding the command.

The guy chuckled.

At their back, the door opened. Immediately, Wes backed up, trying to keep the guy and the opening door both in view.

A middle-aged man stood there. Dressed in jeans with

a sweater and flannel shirt layered beneath, the man was stock-still as if frozen in shock.

Alarm threaded through Wes. He was also missing his left hand.

The man took a step forward. "Lindy?"

Turning, she gasped. "Dad!" She hurried toward him.

Wes stayed put, eyeing the other guy who simply grinned wider.

"Looks like your girl made an interesting friend on the way here," the big man commented.

Her father didn't react to the comment. For a moment, he held Lindy close and then stepped back, looking her over swiftly. "Come inside, please. Thank you for keeping an eye out, Henry."

The big guy nodded.

Her father motioned quickly, stepping back to give them room. Lindy headed in immediately while Wes hesitated, staying between her and the large man and fighting the urge to growl again.

Still grinning, Henry motioned as if to say "after you."

Wes backed toward the door and slipped inside. The entryway emptied into a spacious room with hallways stretching off on either side and an open door to what appeared to be a den on the far end. The smell of cooking meat and warm spices filled the air, reminding his stomach of just how long it had been since he'd eaten anything but small game and cold meals from a can. The cello music continued, wafting down the hallway to the right, though when Henry shut the door behind them, Lindy's father called out over the sound of it.

"Frankie? Could you come out here a minute, please?"

The music stopped. A boy came running from the hallway, and at a glance, Wes could instantly see the relation. He had Lindy's same dark eyes, same chin and nose.

"Lindy?" The boy rushed to her, and Wes heard Lindy take a sharp breath like she was bracing herself before the kid threw his arms around her.

Tension seeped from Lindy's shoulders as she hugged him back.

But then the boy caught sight of Wes, and he froze, his eyes going wide with fear.

"It's okay, Frankie," she said.

"But that's a—"

"I said it's okay." Lindy's voice took on a hard edge.

Henry chuckled at them. "Your friend here have any clothes?"

Wes looked up in alarm while Lindy stared at the man.

The guy smiled. "Come on, I can tell an ulfhednar when I see one too."

Lindy looked between her father and Henry. "Dad, who is this?"

Her father shifted his weight apprehensively, and Wes caught the way the man eyed him, his body turning ever so slightly toward Henry as if intending to ask the big man for assistance somehow.

Which made no sense.

"Honey, how about you ask your friend to do whatever he needs to do, and we'll talk more after that?" her father offered carefully.

What the hell was this?

Lindy didn't say anything more, though, and in wolf form, Wes was stuck in silence. With a small jerk of his head toward her, he waited, watching the others carefully while she lowered the bag from her shoulders and drew out his clothes.

"Bathroom down the hall, third door on the left," Henry said, nodding over his shoulder.

Wes didn't budge.

"It's okay," Lindy said softly.

Only then did he take the clothes in his mouth and go.

# 19

## LINDY

L indy watched Wes pad away, wishing irrationally that she could have gone with him. "Are you guys okay?" she asked, forcing herself to refocus on her dad and Frankie. "No... problems?"

Andrew nodded. "Yeah, honey." He gripped Frankie's shoulder with a smile. "No problems at all."

Relief pushed a breath from her chest, and her legs felt shaky. After so long worrying that she'd reach her family only to find something terrible had happened to her brother or dad, some part of her just wanted to collapse.

But there was a stranger here, and she couldn't risk fully letting down her guard.

She glanced at the man warily. Henry was huge. World Wrestling Federation huge, and this whole time, he'd never stopped grinning like this was all some great joke, only no one else knew the punchline.

"So..." Andrew cast a quick look to the hall. "That isn't Hayden."

Lindy hesitated, not sure how to begin to explain. Her

family hid from the ulfhednar as much as the Order, and for her to show up with one...

With a *male* one, no less...

Anxiety knotted in her stomach. She suddenly felt like a teenager bringing a boy home for the first time.

"He's, um, one of Hayden's... pack." The word sounded strange to her even now. For so long, her friend had seemed like such a loner, which was part of the reason Lindy felt safer around her than she ever would have around another ulfhednar. But now Hayden was part of a group of her own kind—and in a relationship with their alpha for that matter. But by extension, it also meant Lindy now knew half a dozen of the wolves, even if they hadn't known anything about her.

At least until now.

Wes came back out of the bathroom, his focus going immediately to her as if checking she was still okay. She gave him a tight smile, gripped by the sudden impulse to reach out to him and bring him closer for moral support.

Even if that was absurd.

"Dad. Frankie. This is Wes."

Her father extended his hand, which Wes shook carefully. "Andrew," her father said by way of introduction.

Wes nodded in greeting.

Frankie stuck his hand out too, the look on his face pure challenge. Taking it, Wes shook his hand as well with a solemn expression, only the slightest crinkling around his eyes hinting at a suppressed smile.

"And this is Henry Blackburn, a good friend of mine," Andrew continued. "We've been his guests for about two weeks now."

"You never mentioned him," Lindy managed.

Andrew glanced at the big guy. "Yeah, well, Henry

likes to keep a low profile. But after the power and radio went out, I thought staying at our house probably wasn't the best plan. Henry's something of a prepper, though—"

The large man chuckled at the description.

"—and he graciously didn't mind sharing his supplies," her father continued, echoing the chuckle. "So he offered to let us room here for a while."

Lindy hesitated. There was so much left out of that explanation, she didn't know where to begin. "Any sign of Mom?"

"No."

A shuddering breath left her.

"Hey, uh, Frankie?" Henry offered into the silence. "How about you show me some of that Fork Night stuff?"

The kid gave him a dry look. "*Fort*night."

"Ah, Fork Night sounds more my style, but okay. We can check that out too."

Frankie rolled his eyes, but as Henry headed for the hall, the kid still hesitated, glancing at Andrew and Lindy.

"I'll come see you in a bit," she said to him. "Okay?"

Her brother nodded and followed Henry down the hall, the large man teasing him the whole way.

The door closed.

"Perhaps we should continue this conversation, um..." Andrew glanced toward the den and then at Wes, his mouth tightening. Ulfhednar hearing was incredible. Even if he asked Wes to stay in the foyer, the wolf would probably still hear everything.

And Lindy didn't want him to go, regardless. Yeah, this was her dad, so it made no sense to be uncomfortable. For that matter, her father probably knew what was happening to her—if not the details—so it wasn't like there was anything to hide.

But still.

"Let's all talk back here," Andrew finished, nodding toward the rear of the house.

Lindy followed him. At the door, her father paused, letting her and Wes walk past him down the short steps into the sunken den. The room seemed built for comfort, with an oversized sofa and armchairs ringing the space and a huge television on the far wall. To her left, the windows were nearly snow-covered, while a massive fireplace stood below the television, flames crackling merrily inside.

She studied the framed images on the mantle. Henry and a woman, three boys with them, all pictured in countless activities on bright and cheerful days. The woman laughed at a park or grinned over a Christmas present. The boys played sports or wore silly costumes for Halloween. In picture upon picture, years of family life played out over and over again, and it took her a moment to catch what was wrong.

A cold feeling stole over her. In every image, Henry was younger and everyone's clothes were out of date.

Her eyes slid back to the door. The house was so still, with only the distant sound of Frankie's video game breaking the quiet.

Andrew pulled the sliding door shut, sealing them in the den. "How bad is it?" he asked immediately.

Lindy cast an aborted glance at Wes. "Bad."

Andrew drew a breath, the sound slightly shaky. "How far along?"

She could feel Wes watching her. Reaching up, she pulled aside the neck of her sweater to reveal what they both knew was there.

Her father's breath caught. "God…" Running his hand

over his face, he swallowed hard. "But you're still... I mean..."

"I'm still me," she said quietly. "For now."

Her father nodded. "Good. That's good." His brow furrowing, he threw a glance toward the rest of the house. "Listen, would it be okay with you if I brought Henry in here?"

Lindy gave him a confused look. "Why?"

"I'd just like him to hear this, please."

"But—"

"Please."

Warily, she nodded.

Andrew pulled open the door and hurried out of the room. At a loss, she looked to Wes, who came over immediately, taking her hand.

Drawing a steadying breath, she closed her eyes, and he squeezed her hand, not saying a word. A smile crossed her face and she squeezed back, something inside her chest loosening at the feeling of him here. Whatever else he was to her, right now he felt like a rock holding her stable.

And that was something she sorely needed.

Footsteps came from beyond the den. Wes squeezed her hand once more, gently, and then stepped back again.

Gratitude filled her chest, and she gave him a small smile as her father walked back in.

Henry followed him, his size suddenly making the enormous furniture seem ordinary by comparison. His jovial attitude was replaced by a solemnity that left her wanting to retreat.

"May I see?" Henry asked, twitching his chin toward her neck.

Lindy looked between her father and the big man. "Dad, what—"

"It's okay, honey."

She shook her head. "Who is this guy?"

Andrew sighed. "A researcher. One who specializes in the occult and the paranormal. We met when Frankie and I moved to the area, and about a year ago, I asked him to start looking into a few things for me." He nodded toward her. "Things about this."

Lindy blinked. "Why didn't you tell me?"

"Because I hoped it wouldn't be needed." Her father splayed his arms helplessly. "Why bring up something that might be another one of your mother's delusions? You were finishing up college. You were moving on with your life. I didn't want to worry you, especially when it may never have mattered."

She nodded. "So… what did you find out, then?"

Her dad glanced at Henry.

"It would help if I could see it," the big guy said.

She hesitated before pulling the sweater neck aside again. It was harder to do it this time in front of stranger, and of their own accord, her eyes went to Wes to find him watching her with so much care and concern, it felt like a lifeline.

Henry moved toward her, bending a bit as if studying her neck, and she recoiled, tugging her sweater into place.

"What other aspects have you seen so far?" Henry asked as if nothing had happened.

Lindy looked up at him, alarmed. "What?"

"Traits. Changes in personality. Compulsions."

"I-I don't—"

"Lindy, it's okay," her father said.

She trembled, her eyes finding Wes. Concern on his face, he hesitated and then twitched his chin in an encouraging motion.

Wetting her lips, she shoved her hands into her pockets. "I can't eat. I just throw up. But I can tell where the Order and the draugar are, even from a mile away. Maybe more." Her shoulders shifted uncomfortably. "And I feel numb, like I'm going away inside."

Henry and Andrew shared a look she couldn't read.

"I want you to come meet some friends of mine," Henry said. "Tomorrow morning, we can—"

"No," Lindy protested. "No, Dad, we need to go. I have a place where you and Frankie will be safe, but we need to head there as soon as we can."

A frown crossed Andrew's face. "What about you, sweetheart?"

"This is too important. There was an Allegiant on the way here. She said Mom was coming for you, and when she does..." A lump filled her throat. "Dad, she'll kill you. To get to me and Frankie, you know she will. So, please, let me take you back to Mariposa first thing tomorrow morning. Hayden and her pack are there, and they can—"

"I understand," her father interrupted.

"Okay. So let's just—"

"But I also know what's going to happen to you."

A shiver ran through her. "Dad, that... Please. Just let me get you back to—"

"I'm not going anywhere, Lindy."

She flinched at the iron in her father's voice.

"We think we can help," Henry offered into the silence.

Lindy looked between them, baffled.

"How?" Wes demanded.

"I've had friends of mine researching Lindy's situation," Henry said. "At her father's request and because... let's just say it matters to us too. To the world, really. Or wouldn't you agree, given what you know about what's happening to you?" His brow rose pointedly.

Lindy trembled.

"My friends will be the best ones to explain, though, which is why we need to see them first thing tomorrow. I —" He chuckled, glancing between her and Wes for some reason. "I don't want to misrepresent the details here, so I'd ask that you wait. I've got the generator out back and plenty of room, along with supplies in the basement too, so there's no need to worry. Just come meet them tomorrow; let us do what we can, and hopefully you and your family will be on the road to this—what was it? Mariposa?—as soon as possible."

Lindy exhaled, wanting so badly to press for more.

"Come on, sweetheart," her father said. "You've traveled a long way. Get some rest and with any luck, Henry and his friends will fix this in the morning."

# 20

## WES

I n a guest room, Wes lay beneath the thick covers without a clue what to think. There was hope—*real* hope—for Lindy, just as he'd wanted. And he was happy about it. Truly, he was.

But worry still gnawed at him, and the wolf wouldn't quit pacing in his mind.

Lindy was somewhere on the other side of the sprawling house in one of the guest rooms, and the lack of having her in his arms felt... strange. After only a few days of sleeping with her, of traveling with her, he found he couldn't close his eyes when he didn't know for certain she was all right.

As much as she could be, anyway.

He adjusted his arm behind his head. He knew he was being ridiculous. Tonight had been the closest thing to normal they'd had in a while. Warm house, soft beds, even a rudimentary shower—and gods, how he'd missed that. And no, they hadn't eaten dinner because Lindy looked terrified at the thought, but her father put her in a room right next to Frankie's and his own, and surely, if anything were to go wrong, they'd shout and Wes would hear it.

Not that anything would.

Or really, that the distance was even the problem.

Closing his eyes, he willed the wolf to stop pacing so he could get some damn sleep. Lindy hadn't told her father they were lovers, let alone anything more, because of course she hadn't. And probably they weren't. Their time together could have just been meaningless sex as far as she was concerned. But for him...

He punched the pillow under his head, trying to get the damn thing to be comfortable.

*Hello, sir. I've been fucking your daughter every chance I get from Colorado to here, and my wolf is certain she's my mate for life. Mind if we share a room?*

He scowled. Dammit, he hated being this far from her. Hated how his wolf wouldn't stop wearing a goddamn groove on the inside of his skull about it, either. The beast was half-crazed being apart from her when she was struggling.

But these people tomorrow would be able to help. Even if Wes didn't have details, he had to trust her father would never risk her.

Parents being so trustworthy and all.

He rolled to the side, punching the pillow again to get it into position. Andrew wasn't like Wes's own parents. The man obviously loved his daughter, and not in the shitty way his mom and dad "loved" him through nearly fatal torture. No, Andrew wanted her safe, so he must know this Henry guy wouldn't harm her.

Unless Andrew was wrong.

Wes rolled to his back again with a groan. Henry's friends were the best option. Hell, they were the *only* option, considering the alternative was a race between Lindy killing herself and the Order's curse taking hold. So Henry's plan had to work. Whatever it was, it had to work, which meant with any luck, Lindy would be back to her normal self by tomorrow.

Though the gods only knew what that meant for anything to do with the two of them.

He threw an arm over his face, swearing at himself. Gods, he was selfish. Foolish too. There *was* no "two of them." Neither of them had made any promises. They'd shared nothing but a bed and a few days of trekking through snowy oblivion.

But damn him, he hated being this far from her.

A small click came from across the room. His head snapped up, his eyes locking on the door as it slowly opened.

Lindy peered through the narrow gap, her face cast in silver from the way his eyesight compensated for the dark.

"Wes?" she whispered, her voice barely a breath in the silence.

He sat up. "What is it?"

She hesitated and then pushed the door open just wide enough to slip inside. "I, um... Listen, do you mind if I just... I mean..." Her mouth moved as if she was giving up on various explanations before they could make it past her lips, and when she finally spoke, her words came out in a rush. "I'm scared I'll hurt Frankie. Or my dad. And I don't want to risk you either, of course. I can get blankets and sleep on the floor. I just don't want to be where I might—"

She cut off as he threw the quilts aside and crossed the room. Tensing, she wouldn't meet his eyes while he put a hand to the door, pushing it closed behind her.

"Like hell," he said softly.

Taking her hand, he led her back to the bed, not letting go until she sank down onto the spot he'd vacated. Circling around the other side, he climbed in.

"Come here," he offered.

She shifted around, curling up beside him, and he wrapped her in his arms.

Tension melted from him like ice on a summer's day. And maybe it was just the past several nights of her sleeping in his arms that made him feel this way, some nonsensical muscle memory he'd eventually have to shake, but...

Gods, he'd missed her.

On impulse, he kissed the top of her head. "How are you doing?"

A sigh left her. "Worried."

Gently, he brushed a hair away from her cheek, and she reached up, catching his hand. Lifting it to her lips, she kissed the back of his fingers.

His heart felt like it swelled in his chest. "What do you need?"

In the darkness, she looked up at him. "You."

Warmth filled him. He shifted around on the bed, mounting her as his lips met her own. She opened to him immediately, the minty remnants of her toothpaste mingling with the taste he knew only as her. His hands slid up through her hair, holding her to him as he breathed in her scent and relished the feel of her beneath him.

He'd more than missed her. Everything in him felt like it'd craved her, like even in this dark room, somehow her presence brought back the light.

Her body arched up against him, grinding at him, and the wolf inside him growled. But he pushed the beast back.

They had to be quiet. Couldn't risk waking anyone. But for the first time, they were in a warm bed and damn if he didn't want to take his time with it.

"More," she murmured, pressing herself against him.

He pulled back, smiling down at her in the darkness. "Not yet."

A noise of equal parts protest and confusion left her, and she writhed beneath him with a pouting look on her face.

His pulse pounded. Gods, he loved her teasing side, the one she hid except when they were in bed.

Pulling back, he slid down her body, his hands slipping over her sides and then drawing her flannel pajama pants down with him. She lifted her legs, helping him pull them free, and then tugged her shirt over her head as well.

His eyes flicked up, finding her beautiful breasts—one free of any markings, the other covered in twisted tattooed lines—and his hands itched to take them now.

But one step at a time.

He wanted to taste all of her first.

Slowly, he slid his hands along her thighs, easing her legs apart, and was rewarded with Lindy's quiet gasp. A smile tugging at his lips, he massaged her for a moment and then delved between her legs.

Her hips lifted toward him, the motion seeming involuntary, and as he licked between the soft folds of her flesh, she gave a stifled moan. His tongue twisted over her, playing at her clit, tasting her while she writhed and made tiny noises as if trying not to cry out. Her scent filled his head like an aphrodisiac, and her taste was like a fine wine. He couldn't get enough. With one hand, he reached up, taking her breast, teasing at her nipple while he worked her over and over, licking and sucking at her clit while she pled with him in ragged whispers not to stop.

Not that he would.

He kept up his motions, devouring her. There were so many things he wanted to do with her. So much pleasure he wanted to explore giving to her.

If only they had the chance.

He shoved the worried thoughts aside. Somehow, Lindy would be okay, and everything else could be figured out later. But here, in this moment, her pleasure mattered more than any doubt.

Beneath his hand on her breast, he could feel her heart racing. Breathing fast, she clenched her fists on the bedsheets, her hips pushing at him as if she could never get enough, and a choked noise left her as she came.

Satisfaction swelled in him. As she rode out the orgasm, he eased back, not fully stopping until she sank onto the bed, her chest rising and falling rapidly.

"*God*, Wes..."

Pride filled him. He loved giving this to her.

"More?" he whispered.

An incredulous, pleading noise was his answer.

His smile grew. Returning to her soft folds, he slipped his fingers inside her, massaging firmly as his tongue laved her. Mouth opening in a silent cry, she arched her back, writhing against him as he worked her to another orgasm. A gasp left her as she came harder in only moments, her body pulsing wet and hot around his fingers. Breathing fast, she melted against the mattress, little aftershocks still radiating around his touch.

In the darkness, her eyes found his. "I need you inside me," she whispered. "Now."

Red-hot desire fired his blood. Sliding his hands along

the planes and curves of her beautiful body, he kissed and nipped and licked at her as he moved back on top of her. Meeting his eyes with a slightly dazed look, she spread her legs wider for him and smiled as if in invitation.

His heart swelled. Fire could break out and all the world could fall again, and he wouldn't even notice. All he wanted was to be inside her, to feel her.

Forever.

Her hand ghosted over his chest and up to his neck, pulling him to her as the tip of his cock found her slick entrance. The scent of sex and Lindy surrounded him, more overwhelming and beautiful than any he'd encountered in his life. Kissing her deeply, he pushed into her only to groan against her lips as she rocked into him, taking all of him to the hilt.

His pulse raced. He was so hard, so ready, even this felt as if it would send him over the edge.

But he'd resist, for her.

In the darkness, he looked down at her, his night vision tracing her gorgeous face in silver. Her eyes locked on him as if there was nowhere she'd rather be.

"Make love to me, Wes," she whispered.

The strangest feeling suffused his chest, as if everything inside him had filled with light and yet didn't hurt at all. He met her lips again, his tongue twisting with hers as he drew himself out and thrust into her over and over. His hand massaged her breast and then slipped down, pulling her ass to him while she moaned quietly, biting her lip to keep from making too much noise.

What he wouldn't give for more nights of this. *Every* night of this, his body pounding into hers while her nails dug into his skin, clutching her to him, claiming him until they were far more than just two people who, a week ago, had been barely more than strangers.

Until they were truly lovers and so much more.

His hand fisted the bedsheet as he fought to continue thrusting his throbbing cock deep into her wet channel. Tightness built inside him, making him grunt and growl into the pillows as he penetrated her, and when her orgasm overtook her, clenching her pulsing muscles around him, every trace of restraint fell and blinding ecstasy washed all but Lindy away.

Heart pounding, he lay still for a moment, his cock pumping out every last trace of him into her. Gods, he hoped they'd been quiet enough, here at the far end of this sprawling house, but right now, he could scarcely remember. Carefully, he withdrew from her and then pulled her close, breathing deep her beautiful scent while she curled perfectly into his arms.

"Thanks," she whispered.

A chuckle left him, utter relaxation stealing through his muscles, draining everything but this quiet moment from his world. Gently, he tightened his arms around her, smiling in the dark. "Anything for you."

# 21

## LINDY

Morning light peeked past the thick curtains on the windows, and beneath her, an actual bed supported every inch of her body. Wes lay sleeping at her side, his slow breaths peaceful, and somewhere down the hall, her family was sleeping too, not dead at her mother's hand or stolen away by the Order.

It wasn't perfection, but God, it was so close.

Blinking the sleep from her eyes, Lindy looked up at Wes, his face relaxed and softened by sleep. What would it have been like if this was her normal? If the two of them were together, really together, and had come up to visit her family for the weekend or something ordinary like that? What might have been, if she'd had her whole future and life ahead of her, and they could have been together for... what?

Forever?

She nestled her cheek against his chest. It was silly, really. They'd spent so many hours together and been through so much that it felt like longer than the few days they'd only actually known one another. And neither of them had made any guarantees or had any *real* conversations about how they felt, because why would they? She'd spent the past weeks thinking she was going to die. What would the point of long-term discussions have been?

And she still might not make it anyway.

She breathed in the smell of him, trying to push the dark thoughts aside, if only for the moment. But what *would* it have been like if things were normal? Would he have noticed her? Would she have noticed him?

Her eyes strayed across his chest, tracing the lines of his tattoos and scars.

God, yes. She'd be in heaven right now, having him with her. Everything physical was only the start. To be with someone so loving, so attentive and compassionate, who treated her the way he did...

It would have been amazing.

Except... it still wouldn't have worked out.

A pained feeling rose in her chest. Wes was ulfhednar. His kind had ancient beliefs about finding their true mate and being with them forever. And, if there was even a *shred* of truth to that, what did it mean for her? Yeah, she was drawn to him, and yes, she enjoyed being with him, but... she was human. Or would be again soon, hopefully. And he'd always be a wolf. A beautiful, amazing, breathtaking wolf. But she couldn't ever share that world with him.

So where did that leave them?

She closed her eyes, focusing on breathing in the warm, spicy scent of him. If nothing else, she could remember this. Even if there never would have been a happily ever after with her and Wes, whether or not she made it past the next few days or weeks, at least she had this now.

He stirred next to her, and she blinked fast, driving any

trace of sadness from her expression. Why she managed to feel so much more when he was around, she had no idea, but right now, she didn't want to worry him.

They had this moment. It would have to be enough.

"Good morning," he said, his voice scratchy from sleep.

"Morning."

He brushed back a strand of her hair, a smile on his face. "Sleep okay?"

She nodded. "You?"

"Yeah." He smiled, something in the expression like maybe she'd had a lot to do with that, and it made her heart swell with an odd sense of joy.

She pushed away from the bed slightly, sliding up to reach his lips and kiss him. His arms wrapped around her, drawing her on top of him, and she could feel his cock against her, hard and ready for more.

Against his lips, she smiled, writhing her hips on him, and he made a hungry noise, his hands sliding down to grab her ass and hold her to him. "Tease," he murmured.

"Always."

He chuckled.

From deeper in the house, she heard the sounds of people moving around, and she glanced over her shoulder.

She felt Wes tense below her, and she looked back. "What?"

He hesitated. "Your hearing. It's really..."

She realized where he was going with that, and she turned away.

"It's all right." He kissed her cheek gently. "We're going to figure this out, yeah?"

She looked down at him, struck breathless by support and resolve in his eyes. "Yeah."

Kissing him once more, she climbed off him. Searching

around, she gathered her pajamas, only to pause when she realized what her family would see when she left the room.

Shit. As if things weren't uncomfortable enough.

Taking a steadying breath, she pulled her pajamas back on and gave Wes a smile before she headed out of the room. Henry was in the kitchen, cooking a pan of eggs over a camp stove.

"Morning," he said politely as she made her way from the hall.

Lindy murmured a greeting, her cheeks burning. Walking fast, she hurried toward the other guest room down the opposite corridor to gather her clothes. A short visit to the bathroom saw her cleaned up and dressed, and she came out to find Wes sitting on a bar stool near the kitchen, sipping coffee while Henry continued making food.

Her brow rose at the sheer normalcy of the scene.

"Ah, Lindy?" Henry stepped out from behind the breakfast bar. "Moment of your time?"

Trepidation prickled through her, but she walked closer.

"I went hunting this morning." He nodded toward the patio door on the opposite side of the kitchen. "It's hanging out back."

She stared at him and then turned to Wes, who shook his head at her unspoken question of whether he told the man exactly what she'd been eating.

"Hurry now." Henry smiled. "Before your little brother gets up, eh?"

The urge to deny knowing what he was talking about pressed at her, but hunger got there first, gnawing at her insides without giving a damn for how uncomfortable it all was.

God, she hated this.

But explaining to Frankie would be so much worse.

Ducking her face away, she hurried for the back door. The cold air bit at her as she stepped outside, but her eyes immediately went to the rabbit carcass hanging from what looked like a planter hook at the end of the wood patio.

Shudders coursed through her. *Hate* wasn't a strong enough word.

A few minutes later, she returned to the door only to find Henry already there, offering her a small towel. Eyeing him suspiciously, she took the cloth, wiping her face and hands. "Who the hell are you?"

"A friend."

It wasn't remotely a sufficient answer, but something about his smile left her feeling like it was the only one she'd get.

She stepped past him and headed for a bar stool beside Wes. He reached over when she sat down, putting a hand to her leg, and she gripped his fingers, trembling.

Her father came down the hall. "Good morning! You all about ready?"

Henry nodded, surreptitiously stuffing the bloodied towel into a drawer without even a hint of what he was doing in his expression. "Soon as you folks are ready, we can head out."

"Where is this place we're going?" Lindy asked.

"Not far." Henry gave her another one of his enigmatic smiles before returning to wash a few dishes in the sink.

Andrew headed for the coffee maker. "You sleep okay, honey?"

She glanced at him, but he didn't seem to be implying

anything. "Um, yeah," she managed, feeling like a teenager caught out too late.

Dishes clinking in the sink became the only sound.

"I-I'm just going to go get my bag," she stammered.

Hanging on to the friendly expression, she fled the room.

AFTER SO MANY DAYS OF TRAVELING ONLY WITH WES, trooping through the woods with the others felt terrifyingly loud. Never mind that she could probably pick up on any Allegiants or draugar that were nearby. Every crack of a branch made her tense. Every slough of snow from a tree left her jumpy. When it had just been the two of them, she knew they could take care of themselves.

But now Frankie was with them. Her dad too. Both traveling through the woods to meet potentially dangerous strangers, accompanied by a guy who clearly knew far more about this than he was letting on.

How could she be sure it wasn't a trap?

She stayed behind Henry, eyeing him warily as he led the way, ready in case he made a threatening move. The forest was eerily quiet around them, without even a bird or small animal in the underbrush. Overhead, the sky was a sickly shade of gray, and between all the trees, no breeze stirred the air. The strangest feeling they were being watched nagged at her senses, though she couldn't detect any trace of the Order or draugar.

A small motion caught the corner of her eye, and her focus snapped over to it.

In a clearing to her right, a large brown bear stood,

staring at them. A thick scar marred its face and more crisscrossed its sides like a mad roadmap of old injuries. Lindy froze, alarmed, but Henry just kept walking, nodding briefly to the creature like he was saying hello before continuing through the forest.

The bear eyed them, and chills crept over her skin at the sudden impression of fury in its gaze, but after another moment, the creature simply huffed and turned away, disappearing into the woods more silently than anything that size should have been able to move.

Lindy stared after it. That impression had to be her imagination. But regardless, even if she didn't know jack about bears, she was still pretty sure they didn't wander off at someone's nod. Unless Henry trained them. But then, who the hell trained bears in the forest? And trained them just to wander on after watching the group pass them by, as if the bear was...

Standing guard.

No.

Incredulity stole her breath as an impossible thought rose. The berserkers. Bear shifters. But they'd been wiped out by the Order, hunted down to the last cub and sow in the forests outside Coeur d'Alene, Idaho, nearly twenty years ago.

Her eyes turned to Henry, the pictures in his den sending shivers through her for a whole new reason. And maybe she was wrong. Maybe he was just good with nature, and all the animals around here knew him, and his wife divorced him years ago but he'd never gotten over her.

But it would explain a *lot*.

Except why he'd offered to help her or her dad.

Biting her lip, she eyed the forest and Henry alike.

What if this was a trap? Some way the last of the bear shifters wanted to get revenge on the Order? She and her family could be walking into a hostage situation for all she knew, where they'd threaten her dad and brother if she didn't somehow become the berserkers' weapon instead.

Her heart raced, the darkness inside her churning and whispering with bloodlust and hunger. Like a live wire, her skin tingled with energy just waiting to lash out, scorching anything that came near. She needed to tell her family to turn back. That this was a bad plan. Of course Henry baited them with the offer to help her, but that didn't mean he really—

The man glanced back over his shoulder. "It's okay," he told her calmly.

From the corner of her eye, she could see her father and brother glance at her, alarmed.

"You all are safe. My friends and I won't hurt any of you." The edge of his lips rose in a sad smile. "I swear to you on the graves of my cubs."

Wes's footsteps hesitated even as Lindy blinked and turned to her dad. Neither Andrew nor Frankie reacted at all to the choice of word.

They knew?

Nodding as if to himself, Henry turned and kept going, and her family followed immediately. Glancing at Wes uncomfortably, Lindy trailed after them.

Another hour passed before the thick forest finally came to an end. The tree cover fell back to reveal a spacious clearing filled with beautiful log cabins. Smoke drifted up from chimneys above peaked green rooftops. Window boxes, empty now due to the cold, sat beneath brightly colored shutters. Stone-lined paths led from one house to the next, and more surrounded spaces that would probably be gardens if the sun ever returned to the world.

After so much destruction in the rest of the country, the entire place felt surreal, like an idyllic painting come to life.

At the far-right end of the clearing, the front door of a large cabin opened and a woman stepped out onto the porch. Like Henry, she was tall and broad, giving the impression of a sturdy tree that would damn the wind that tried to knock her over. Dressed in a sweater and a skirt with what appeared to be pants underneath, she strode to the top of the stairs leading down from the porch and regarded them all like they were disappointing school children late for their first day of class.

Chuckling to himself, Henry headed toward her, leaving the rest of them to follow.

"You made it," the woman called like she wouldn't have been surprised if they'd failed.

Lindy moved to put herself between Frankie and the woman, and from the hard glance she received, she was fairly sure her action hadn't gone unnoticed. Sharp eyes lingered on her a heartbeat longer than the rest, only to slide back to Henry when he stopped at the base of the steps.

"Maeve," Henry said. "Meet Lindy and her friend Wes."

The woman harrumphed. "Might've guessed that, Henry Blackburn. Half-starved thing that she is. You're fighting it, aren't you?" She fired the question at Lindy and didn't wait for a response. "Good for you."

Her voice was harsh, like the words might be a compliment, might be an insult, and the woman hadn't yet decided which.

Henry appeared amused as he turned back to Lindy. "This is Maeve Thorncastle and her son Otis."

Lindy blinked, and only then did she register the boy peering past the gap of the doorway, his body nearly the size of a teenager, but his face and eyes like those of a child. When she spotted him, he flinched and then retreated into the house like a turtle tucking back into its shell.

"Thank you for having us again, Maeve," Andrew said. "It's good to see you."

Maeve scoffed.

A scuffing sound behind them made Lindy look back sharply. A dark-haired man stood several yards off, a machete strapped to his waist and a rifle on his back. He was built like Henry—tall and broad, a wall in human form —but not as old. Maybe in his early thirties with a trimmed beard and dark eyes that seemed to catch everything. A jagged scar crossed his face, stretching from his hairline over to his opposite jaw and then down his throat, giving him a savage look. That he was most likely the bear from the forest seemed obvious. A quiet air of stilled motion hung around him, like a knife hovering just at the edge of breaking skin, and something in her wanted to snarl at the sight.

Anxiety prickled through her, and she fought the sensation down. It felt wild. Inhuman. Like a predator worried another predator was encroaching on its territory.

But how the hell had he come up behind them so quietly?

Henry simply nodded at the man. "Knox."

"Clear?" Maeve demanded.

The man nodded once. "Nobody followed." His voice was low and even like a still pond.

Maeve harrumphed as if the fact barely passed muster. "Well, best come in, then. No sense standing around in the cold."

Henry chuckled like the woman amused him. Without a word, he climbed the steps.

Knox watched them all a moment longer, and Lindy couldn't bring herself to move until he did, like the first one of them to flinch would be lunch meat. His gaze flicked past her to land on Wes only for a heartbeat.

Fury flashed through his eyes. Lindy suddenly wanted to growl.

But the man made no move toward them. Giving only a brief glance to her, Knox turned and walked away without a sound.

As her family trailed Henry toward the house, Wes came up to Lindy's side. "You okay?" he asked softly, watching Knox too.

Taking a steadying breath, she nodded. Keeping an eye over her shoulder to the man's retreating form, she followed her family.

Past the front door, an airy living space waited. A rust-colored tile floor ringed the edges of the room, while the entire center was sunken several steps down. In the middle, a carved wooden table stood covered in books and papers. Bookcases lined the room, and overhead, a cathedral ceiling rose to a point with a chandelier of antlers hanging down. Windows and a sliding glass door at the far end of the space revealed a wooden deck overlooking the backyard, while a fireplace burned merrily to the left and a cozy kitchen waited to the right, a pot smelling of spices and cider boiling on the stove.

The entire place radiated the comfort of the library in

the woods, somehow still standing even though the rest of the ordinary world was gone.

"Everett!" Maeve called. "They're here."

Footsteps came from a hall to the side of the door, and a man easily equal to Henry in size walked into the room. He wore denim jeans and a thick flannel shirt of dark-green plaid. A bushy beard covered the lower half of his face, the shade nearly matched by the copper curls atop his head. At the sight of them all, he nodded while he continued drying his hands on a towel that was dwarfed by his size. The boy, Otis, was nowhere to be seen.

Trepidation tightened Lindy's smile into a flinch of her lips. "Henry says you can help me?"

Everett made a neutral noise. "Maybe."

"Well, she's brought a wolf with her, of all things," Maeve commented, continuing past them toward the kitchen again. "So there's that."

Lindy looked between them. "What are you talking about?"

"You left this to us, didn't you?" Maeve frowned at Henry.

"Just wanted to make sure I got the details straight," the man replied neutrally.

Harrumphing, Maeve shook her head.

"Maybe you all would like to explain?" Henry continued.

"What I'd *like* is for you not to have brought—"

"Good enough," Everett interrupted.

Maeve gave him an irritated look and then glanced at Frankie. "I could use some help in the kitchen." The statement was flat and blatantly untrue.

Andrew nodded and motioned for Frankie to go on.

"I'd like you to take a look at this," Everett said to

Lindy, ignoring the others. He headed down to the sunken space at the center of the room.

Swallowing nervously, Lindy walked down the steps, and she could hear Wes follow her immediately.

It helped.

"Do you recognize any of these?" Everett said, pointing to the books laid out on the center table. The pages were filled with text in languages that were only vaguely familiar and others she'd never seen at all. But the pictures...

She trembled. In image after image, a figure stood at the heart of black smoke. In some, people fought around them. In others, there was nothing but death. An old tome with illuminated pages lay atop the rest of the books, and in the painting there, the shadowed figure crouched beside a throne like an animal, a leash of smoke running from a thick collar on its neck and held by a figure with its opposite hand raised in benediction.

Countless wolves and bears lay dead around them.

Her eyes lingered on the crouching figure. It had no face, no eyes, though sharpened teeth glinted in tiny notes of silver where its mouth would be. Blood glistened on the ground beneath it, and smoke rose in swirls of gray and black from its hunched shoulders.

Beneath it all, the words *Scythe of Niorun* glinted in flakes of gold.

She shifted her shoulders uncomfortably. "What's your point?"

"That you knew what was waiting for you. That you chose this anyway."

Anger flared in her chest. "Is that why you brought me here? To prove I deserve what's happening to—"

A hand caught her arm, and she realized she'd taken a

step toward the man. She looked back to see Wes holding her wrist, concern on his face.

Closing her eyes briefly, she took a rough breath.

"No," Everett said calmly. "To see what you're willing to do now to change that."

Lindy shuddered. "Anything."

"Are you sure?"

She stared at him, incredulous.

"Can you help her or not?" Wes interjected, his hand still gripping her wrist.

Everett eyed him for a heartbeat. "Yes." He tilted his head to the side. "Possibly."

"How?" Lindy demanded.

The man sighed. "With a theory. The only one we have." He sank down onto the cushion seating around the edge of sunken space. "As you both know, the Order has made it their mission to wipe out any shifters on this planet—and they've nearly succeeded. The ulfhednar were scattered even before Ragnarok began. And the berserkers…" He smiled, something cold in the expression. "Well, the world thinks we've been dead for decades."

Lindy trembled, her suspicions utterly confirmed.

"Our theory, however, is that there was a reason for that genocide, beyond the Order's hatred of anything 'impure.' As I'm sure you learned as a child, the Order wishes to take the world back to their vision of perfection. 'The good old days,' as it were. They want to do away with what they view as chaos and the rest of us simply call *life*, and instead create the epitome of 'order.'" He scoffed. "Nothingness. Oblivion. To destroy all of creation and return it to the abyss of Ginnungagap because what is a purer example of order than zero? A category comprised only of itself. No passion or color or variation or diversity.

248

Merely the darkness of the abyss and the opportunity to rebuild the world as they see fit."

Wes shook his head. "But that's backward. That's not how the myths go. The *abyss* was chaos. This—" He gestured to the house. "*Life* was order. That's what the ancients believed."

The other man chuckled. "No one ever said the Order of Nidhogg was sane."

Lindy shivered.

"But basing our actions off of what *we* believe of prophecy is foolish," the man continued. "Who's to say how events truly will unfold? Prophecy is a blind scribe, scribbling the edges of things and giving us precious little definition at the core. To hear the stories, we should all be dead now, the sun and moon consumed by Sköll and Hati, the land drowned and then poisoned by Jormungand's rise. And where are the gods? Has Odin marched his armies forth? Is Heimdall locked in battle with Loki? Seemingly no. To the gods, time is not the same, and this apocalypse could play out over centuries or end tomorrow for all we know."

"So what are you saying?" Lindy managed.

"That nothing is certain. That perhaps the Order *could* succeed in recasting reality. We cannot assume they'll fail —or, conversely, that we're all doomed. Even some prophecies speak of survivors after Ragnarok walking forth into a new world, though others speak of this being the end of all things. But if there are survivors, and if *we* mean to be them?" Everett shook his head. "We have to understand what the Order is after because they have many strings to pull, and we have precious few."

"I-I don't..." Lindy shook her head warily. "What's your point?"

Everett leaned forward in his seat. "We believe it's why they sought to kill the shifters. Why they feared us enough to seek our utter destruction long before Ragnarok came to pass. Because in the battle of order versus chaos, shifters..." He chuckled. "We're neither. And both."

Lindy's brow furrowed.

"At their core, shifters are both animal and human, and neither at the same time. Just as a bridge touches on both things it connects, and yet is simultaneously *not* those things, so too are shifters creatures of both the wild and the civil, order and chaos, neither and both all in one body. 'Corruption,' as the Order calls us. But a 'corruption' that has some members who are fully capable of using seidr, of wielding it and controlling it and using it to thwart the Order's plans. Thus, while the Order have made themselves into something new with the advent of Ragnarok, we have *always* been something outside the dynamic of order and chaos." Everett smiled. "And that means we can stop them."

"How?" Wes demanded.

Taking a breath, the man leaned back against the cushions again. "Tell me," he said to Lindy. "Had you still been on the Order's side and had your transformation to the Scythe proceeded according to their plans, how would it have gone?"

His tone sounded almost rhetorical, but he waited for her answer all the same.

She fought back the urge to fidget with discomfort. Where the hell was he going with this? "Like that." She pointed to the pictures without looking at them.

Everett nodded. "But it didn't. You're fighting what the Order wishes you to be, which means some of you is still, for lack of a better term, *human*. And therein lies your chance. What's been done to you, we suspect, is a process designed to destroy every last shred of your humanity, and yet maintain your human form as an anchor, turning you into a creature of pure—well, we would call it chaos. They would call it order. Through you, they wish to claim nightmares from Niorun's realm and put that power under their control. Ultimately, we believe they even intend to channel the power of the abyss Ginnungagap into this world, manipulating the destruction and molding it to their desires. The spells they wrought upon themselves are mere shadows of that effort, and the powers they control are as well. But then, they wish to retain their identities. Yours, I suspect, is meant to be consumed."

"So what do we do?" Wes asked.

Lindy couldn't even bring herself to look at him, and she could feel his grip on her wrist shaking.

"Your humanity is the key. With some part of it still intact, you might yet escape the trap the Order has created for you. But only if you are removed from the dichotomy of order versus chaos and made into something else entirely. If, for example, you were bitten."

Lindy blinked, her mind hiccuping in attempt to process his words. "Bit... bitten?"

"We suspect the effect of a shifter's bite upon whatever remains of your human side could thwart what the Order has attempted to do to you. A shifter and what you are becoming cannot, by their very natures, exist in the same body. And while what the Order has attempted is powerful, the forces that make a shifter are far older and have changed many, many people over the course of the millennia."

"But..." Her father's voice came from behind her,

sounding horrified. "That could *kill* her. Henry, dammit, you never said—"

"There is that chance, yes," Everett interrupted with a remorseful tone. "Bitten shifters have a hard enough time surviving the change in the best of circumstances, and these are far from that." He met Lindy's eyes solemnly. "Your odds of survival would be low, and what you would experience would be... extreme. But that is why it's best to act quickly. The more of your humanity that remains, the better chance you have." His head moved ambivalently. "Given that your alternative is to become what the Order wants... This is the best solution we could devise."

"But..." Her mouth moved. "What would I... I mean..."

"There is no way to know for certain what would happen. It is only our theory, but it is the best we found."

Lindy shook her head. "I could become a monster even worse than the Scythe."

"It's more likely you would simply die," Everett said, a note of apology in his voice.

Her mouth moved again, and she couldn't find words. This wasn't what she'd wanted. What she'd hoped when Henry and her father said they knew of a way to help her.

But then, in the face of certain death by becoming a monster, even a sliver of a chance to escape that fate was worth something... right?

"Now," Everett continued. "If you choose to go through this, the choice is yours. Maeve and I have already discussed it. Either one of us would be willing to"—he bobbed his head as if seeking a better word and then settled for the obvious—"bite you, if that's what you wanted. But seeing you now..." His eyes twitched to Wes behind her. "I'd say you may have another choice in mind."

Her breath went still, and then she turned, seeking Wes.

He was frozen, his eyes locked on the middle distance with an unreadable look on his face.

She couldn't find her voice, staring at him now with her father and total strangers all around. But something stirred in her belly as she floundered, warming with desire at the idea of truly being like him and of being with him in *that* way.

If she survived.

"Wes," she started.

He flinched hard like he'd been hit, and when he looked up at her, his eyes were like nothing she'd seen from him. Horrified. Lost. Staring as if all of hell was opening up in front of him and he was inches from falling in.

His head shook.

"Wes." She took a step toward him. "What—"

Before she could even finish the word, he turned, fleeing the house like all the Order was on his tail.

# 2 2

## WES

This was hell.

*His* hell.

Gods above, somebody wake him up.

He fled the house, barely seeing cabins around him as he strode for the forest, aimless, seeking nothing but an escape. The wolf inside him clamored in protest because of course that rabid bastard did. It wanted to bite her. It probably loved the idea of him finally, *finally* becoming the same as the monster who'd covered him in scars and brought the beast into his life.

And with *her.*

His fist slammed into a tree, pain rioting through his knuckles but doing nothing to fix what he felt inside. Days of protecting her, of fearing for her, of fighting the feelings rising up inside him because what sane person could ever be with a wolf like him, and now…

He'd be the one to kill her.

A scream tore from his throat, bursting through the forest around him and sending a pair of ravens cawing up into the sky. Why this? This, of all the ways to help her. Why *this*?

"Wes?" Lindy's voice came from a distance behind him, and of their own accord, his feet stopped, rooting him to the ground with his body as rigid as the trees around him, quivering with rage.

Her footsteps carried through the forest.

He closed his eyes. She couldn't ask this of him. *Him* of all the wolves in the world. Because if he bit her... if he took the rabid sickness that made his wolf what it was and spread that to her, and let that foul bastard who'd bitten him gain one more victim...

"Wes..." Lindy's voice was breathless behind him, as if she'd been running.

"You can't ask me to do this," he said without turning around.

"Please. If this is the only way—"

"No!" He whirled to face her.

She stared at him, pain and confusion in her eyes. "But—"

"Don't you get it? I can't. I *won't*. The monster that made me this..." His head shook. "I won't do it."

She gave him a helpless look. "But... what's the alternative?"

"I don't know!" His voice rang through the forest, and he scrubbed a hand over his face, trying to calm down. "One of the bears, maybe. They could—"

"You'd let them be the ones who bit me?" Hurt filled her eyes. "You'd let me become *that* instead of... And it wouldn't matter to you?"

"You have no *idea* how this matters to me."

"Then how could you let them—"

*"Because I can't kill you!"*

255

She looked at him like she couldn't understand him at all. "*This* is killing me, Wes."

Guilt wrapped a stranglehold on his throat, pressing all the air from his body. How did he solve this? How did he help her and yet make her see that he couldn't possibly do what she was asking? *Because* he cared. Because he...

He loved her. Loved her so much his bones ached, and his heart wanted to rip itself from his rib cage. His entire being screamed with the need to help her, but he couldn't. Not like this. Not when it would kill her or else destroy every good thing she'd trusted him to save.

And yet if he did nothing...

His wolf thrashed inside him, howling in misery, and he bashed it down so hard his chest hurt. "I can't, Lindy. I'm sorry."

Turning from the anguish on her face, he made himself walk away.

# 23

## LINDY

The ground rocked beneath her feet as she watched Wes walk away.

How could he? After everything they'd been through, all the ways he'd stuck by her side despite the Order and draugar and the rest... how could he abandon her now?

She turned away, pressing a hand to her face. That answered the question then. The one of whether there could ever be anything between them. When offered the chance to save her from certain death and be with her at the same time...

He said no.

He left.

He didn't care whether she became a bear or was taken by the curse or about anything at all. He just cared that he wouldn't be the one responsible for it.

Her brow crumpled with confusion, tears trying and failing to rise in her eyes while her chest ached like someone had replaced her lungs with red-hot metal. But maybe the lack of tears wasn't about the curse at all.

Maybe it was just pain.

Hugging her arms to her middle, she started back toward the house. This was it, then. No Wes. No chance at being ulfhednar, and who needed them anyway? Sure, she couldn't imagine life as a *bear* of all things, but if it was that or die...

Screw him.

Her feet picked up the pace, carrying her through the woods. Damn that wolf. Damn him to every kind of godforsaken hell. If that's how it really was, then so fucking be it. He may have showed her who he really was inside, but so what? She wasn't going to die. Not now that she finally had anything resembling a chance.

Maeve sure seemed like a bitch, but maybe she was just a... Lindy chuckled to herself, the sound raw and ragged to her ears. A Mama Bear. But regardless, the woman didn't seem like she'd have much of a problem biting the hell out of anything.

Lindy included.

She pushed a branch aside, her body feeling like somewhere between the cabin and here, everything inside her had turned to lead. But it didn't matter. She'd get over it, and by God, she'd be alive.

That was all that mattered.

And she'd never think about that damn wolf ever—

The blast wave hit her only a heartbeat after the roar of the explosion. Her feet left the ground and then the earth found her again, slamming into her back, knocking the wind from her chest. Heat blasted her face, and she cringed away for a moment before trying to scramble to her feet.

Smoke rose from the direction of the cabins.

Oh God.

She took off running, the snow slipping beneath her feet. Screams carried through the air, driving her heart into her throat.

In her mind, the shapes of draugar flared to life, impossibly close yet she hadn't picked up on them at all.

She faltered, looking around frantically. How—

Her mother walked from between the trees.

Horror rushed like ice through Lindy's veins. A black robe covered Carolyn, but the hood was thrown back, and waves of her honey-brown hair hung past her shoulders, longer than Lindy had ever seen it. Green auroras drifted over her skin, and dark shadows painted her cheekbones in sharp relief. Draugar stumbled and staggered through the woods behind her, flanking her on either side.

At the sight of Lindy, Carolyn's lips curved in a smile. "Hello, darling."

Lindy retreated a step. She couldn't feel the woman in her mind at all, but power seemed to be rolling back into Carolyn, pulling away like a veil to reveal the draugar on all sides. "Mom... how did you—"

"Oh, I've been tracking you for days, my girl." Carolyn's hand rose, shadows twisting around her palm, and Lindy's skin tingled in response. "I knew sooner or later you'd lead me to Andrew and my son."

Horrified, Lindy's mouth moved, no words coming out. Her mother had been... she'd...

Lindy had led her right to her family.

"Now..." Her mother's smile vanished, her fingers curling into a fist. "Kneel."

A choking sensation wrapped Lindy's neck like a vise and then yanked her forward. Her knees slammed onto the snowy ground, and her fingers clawed at her throat but there was nothing. Only her skin, burning like acid. Only the shadows in her mind surging higher and higher.

"Mom, please…" Her vision swam. "Don't—"

Carolyn walked closer, and her fingertips brushed Lindy's cheek, leaving trails of cold like the touch of ice. "Time to come home, Melinda."

Her mother turned away. "Take her."

The draugar charged as Lindy crashed to the ground, her world going dark.

# 24

## WES

The blast wave nearly took him from his feet, but it had no trouble with the snow.

Digging his way from beneath a cascade fallen from a nearby evergreen tree, Wes gasped, his eyes darting around frantically.

Smoke billowed into the air, black and thick from the direction of the cabins.

Oh, no.

He scrambled out of the last of the snowdrift and bolted toward the houses, trying to trace Lindy's scent. Where had she gone after he left? Back to the cabins? Deeper into the woods?

Oh, gods, he *left* her. Left all of them. What the fuck had he been thinking? Stupid, selfish bastard. It wasn't safe to—

Shrieks of draugar reached his ears a heartbeat before the creatures poured from the woods, their rotted mouths gaping wide and their arms outstretched for him. He skidded on the snow, his eyes flying around fast, but they were everywhere.

The shift ripped through him, burning away his clothes and coat as it surged through his body. Lunging forward, he tore off the arm of the nearest draug reaching for him, and the creature stumbled, knocked off balance. Another fell to his teeth at its rotting throat, the taste of decay barely registering on him as the draug turned to dust, while a third collapsed when he took its legs from beneath it. In a blur of putrescent flesh and grasping hands, he continued onward, the bastards turning to dust around him as he fought through the forest toward the cabin.

But there were so many of them. So many, and they were slowing him down, and their stench of decay covered everything, making it impossible to find—

Her scent.

He whirled, taking off through the trees. She'd gone this way, but he couldn't smell her tracks, only her scent on the air, and the snow was churned and stained by the passage of draugar.

They must have been chasing her. But there wasn't any blood, thank the gods. If they'd killed her, surely there would be—

He tore past the underbrush and onto a stretch of road. The footprints scattered, heading every direction and turning back in the direction of the cabin too, while tire tracks carved a path off through the snow to his right.

But her scent stopped.

Spinning a circle, he floundered. Where could she...

His eyes went back to the tire tracks.

Oh, gods, no.

Turning fast, he raced into the woods again, heading for the cabins beneath the billowing smoke. They'd gotten her. The Order. They'd grabbed her and taken her the gods knew where. But he couldn't help her as a wolf. He needed a fucking car.

The roar of a bear shook the woods around him, and shrieks came from the clearing ahead. He bolted from the trees to see draugar everywhere among the cabins, scrambling through windows and crashing past doors by sheer force of numbers. Screams and cries came from the houses as the draugar broke in, but the berserkers met them too. The enormous bears charged out into the horde, tearing down the draugar as they passed.

He took off across the clearing. Maeve's house was his best bet, if only because Andrew would be there. Hopefully, the man wouldn't mind driving a nearly rabid wolf on a mad chase after his daughter.

Maeve's front door stood open, and Wes's adrenaline surged higher. He leapt up the steps and raced through the opening, only to skid to a stop in horror.

The rear wall of the house was gone, timbers and debris scattered everywhere, and shattered glass glinted on the red tile. Bookcases had fallen from the walls, and in the kitchen, a massive bear lay crumpled in the corner. The air was a riot of scents, from draugar to bear to the few people he recognized.

And blood.

A groan came from beneath a bookcase half-buried beneath wall debris.

Oh, fuck...

Wes rushed over, and Andrew's scent grew stronger. The man was pinned and only the chance fall of a table beside him had kept the enormous oak bookcase and the destroyed wall from crushing him entirely.

Pacing anxiously, Wes debated for a moment and then

lunged into the gap beneath the bookcase. Wedging his feet beneath him, he snarled as he shoved upward, struggling to lever the heavy furniture and the wall debris higher. The scent of blood filled the space, and his wolf growled at smelling it.

Fucking beast. It wanted to bite something, and like hell that'd be Lindy's father.

Andrew stirred with a pained sound.

Wes barked at him, praying the man could move enough to get out of here. The broken table had shifted position when he moved the bookcase, and if the thing fell now, the weight of it and the wall might crush them both.

Groaning, Andrew moved to drag himself free. The shelves dug into Wes's spine, and he could feel the timbers of the wall moving above the bookcase, creating a shifting distribution of weight that he fought to keep balanced. He couldn't let the wall debris roll onward to hit Andrew, not when it might stop him from getting free.

Or staying alive.

A deep roar came from near the doorway of the house. Trapped beneath the bookcase, Wes cursed internally. He couldn't move to see the threat, and if that was an enraged bear ready to kill someone, there was no telling what might happen.

History didn't remember the berserkers as being crazy for nothing.

Andrew cleared the edge of the bookcase. Relief joined Wes's adrenaline, but now he had a new problem. How the hell was he going to get out from under here in wolf form?

Growling to himself, he worked his way backward, the edge of the shelving raking across his back. Gods, this was going to leave a mark. But he didn't give a shit, not when the sooner he got out, the sooner he could get a damn car and go—

The shelving lifted away from him. Quickly, he scrambled backward to find an enormous bear holding the bookshelf up. The creature growled, the sound like a command, and jerked its head to the side as if telling him to get out of the way.

He retreated fast. The bear let the bookcase drop.

Wes was already moving, hurrying around to Andrew. The man groaned and tried to rise, only for another growl to come from the far end of the room. In the kitchen, the bear that had been on the ground was stirring, glaring at them all with a furious look that he'd swear had to belong to Maeve. Clambering from beneath her, a bear cub who probably was her son Otis retreated into the corner, visibly terrified.

Another bear came from the hallway, towering upright with bundles of clothes in his front paws. With a gruff sound, he tossed the clothes down in front of both Wes and the bear who'd lifted the bookcase before continuing on around the debris to reach Maeve and Otis.

Everett, Wes would guess. And something about the bear in front of him seemed like Henry. He couldn't communicate with them the same as he did with his pack —with the wolves, communication was nearly effortless, a mixture of their body language and the pack bond that let him feel the others' location and more—but some part of his mind seemed to understand who he was seeing, even if the people around him were in bear form.

Henry crouched down beside Andrew, who was struggling to push to his feet. With a massive paw, the bear held him down gently, a huffing sound leaving him that seemed like an entreaty to stay still.

"My kids…" Andrew protested, shaking his head grog-gily. "They have Frankie. I've got to find Lindy."

Wes cursed internally. Taking up the bundle of clothes, he raced for the closest room, shifting fast once the door shut behind him. The clothes were several sizes too big, but the bear had thought to grab a belt, which helped—as did the fact Wes didn't give a shit. He'd wear a burlap sack if it got him after Lindy faster.

Yanking the door open again, he strode back into the living room. Maeve was gone, and Otis too, though he could hear voices down the hall behind him. Still in bear form, Henry paced by the hole blown in the wall, eyeing the forest like he was daring it to attack, and Everett was nowhere to be seen.

Wes paused beside Andrew, who was blinking blearily at the ceiling. "Can we move him?" he called to Henry.

"I wouldn't."

Wes glanced back as Everett came from the hall.

The big guy shook his head. "Not till Maeve gets—"

"Don't you *dare* move that man." Maeve pushed past Everett to crouch down beside Andrew. "You stay still, you hear me?" Not waiting for agreement, she set to checking the man over with ruthless efficiency, muttering deadly imprecations against the universe the whole time.

Wes retreated, giving her space. "I need to borrow one of your vehicles," he said to Everett. "Please. They took Lindy too."

The male looked toward Henry, his face solemn. The bear shook his head, turning away.

"What?" Wes demanded.

A rustling sound came from the doorway. He looked over to see a handful of people by the door, their builds large like bears and their ages ranging from young and old alike. Knox stood at the forefront of them, his face solemn.

"Last of them are gone." Knox's jaw clenched. "They got Annie and Tobias."

Everett muttered a curse, shaking his head.

"Please," Wes said, trying to keep his tone level. "I'm sorry for your losses, but I need to go save—"

"There isn't any saving," Everett said.

Wes whirled back to the male, a snarl on his lips.

"They're going to end her, son. They've got their hands on her now. Lindy won't survive it."

Wes made an incredulous sound. "She will if you give me a damn car to go help her! And what about Frankie? If they're going to do to Lindy what you say, then he's—"

"They've already done it," Everett interrupted. "*Years* ago, before you ever met the girl. If they've got her, they're taking her humanity as we speak, and there isn't a thing you can do to stop that. Not in time."

"Like hell!" Wes scanned the room quickly, seeking any basket or hook holding keys.

There was nothing. Debris everywhere and destruction and nothing.

His heart raced. "Please," he said to Everett. "Do you really want to stand here and tell Andrew that... what? You gave up on his kids? And what about you?" He turned to the bears by the door. "Do you want to risk your families if there is even a *chance* you could stop this?" He shook his head, his heart going a hundred miles a minute. "What they will do to her, *none* of you will survive. But if you help me, then maybe—"

"The wolf is right."

He turned sharply to see Maeve pushing to her feet.

The female regarded the bears around her with an iron expression. "Helping Andrew's children is the only shot we have at survival. With Lindy under their control, we lose everything."

Everett shook his head. "We've survived this long by staying hidden from the Order, not by rushing straight into the thick of them—especially when they just got done murdering more of us!"

"You hand them that girl, Everett Thorncastle," Maeve countered. "And it won't matter where we hide."

The large male turned away.

"I just need keys," Wes urged. "Please. I can—"

"You'll need a damn sight more than that," Maeve retorted. "Reckless wolves. You never think." She looked to the others by the doorway. "Knox?"

The dark-haired male nodded. "Sawyer, get the Humvee. Kaylee, make sure the tire chains are secure. Alex, Amelia, go tell the other Bloodclaws we're heading out. I want one team with me and the rest stay here to stand guard, understood?"

Four of the people in the crowd hurried away while the rest eyed Wes nervously.

Ignoring them all, Maeve looked at Everett, who sighed.

"Very well." The male glanced at Wes. "But I have to warn you, without any idea where they've taken her, this isn't going to be much of a rescue mission."

Wes's heart sank. He'd hoped the bears would know. And with the whole continent as an option and the Order getting farther away every moment, the odds of tracking her were—

Pain shot through his temple like the wolf was trying to

break out of his skull. Clamping a hand to his head, he winced, his vision swirling. Snarling and snapping like a wild thing, the beast thrashed beneath his skin.

"Son," Everett began warily. "Are you—"

Wes groaned aloud as the rabid bastard inside his head clamored, howling that they had to go southeast right the fuck now because she was there. Dozens of miles off. Maybe more, moving farther with every moment.

Toward Minneapolis.

With a snarl, Wes shoved the animal down, his heart pounding like a cannon in his chest. He blinked hard, trying to steady his vision, and when he looked up, he found the others staring at him.

"What just happened?" Everett asked.

Wes shook his head and then winced when his brain felt like it sloshed against his skull. But the residual need to go southeast remained, like an invisible river pulling him that direction.

And it was insane. Some holdover of that crazed fucking wolf with its ridiculous notions of tracking her, just like it had carried on days ago when she first left.

When it nearly drove him off the highway, straight toward her.

Chills crept through him. It wasn't possible.

But if there was even a *chance* this strange sensation led to her...

He had no other plan.

Breathing slowly, he concentrated hard on holding the beast back while still feeling for the strange pull toward the southeast. The wolf fought him, thrashing in his mind, but he had years of experience keeping the bastard under control.

He looked back up at Everett. "I can find her."

"How?" the male demanded.

"Doesn't matter," Wes said, not about to discuss the madness of the feral wolf inside his skull. "We need to go. Now."

25

# LINDY

The first thing Lindy felt was a hard surface beneath her.

The second was the dark.

It swirled through her mind now, a living thing weaving behind every thought, every residual trace of emotion. Her sense of self seemed thin, as if she were watercolor paint on glass. And beneath...

There was nothing.

Breathless, she opened her eyes. Wires hung from the bare framework of a drop ceiling above her, and pipes ran every which way behind it. Beneath her hands, the floor was rough like cement. She lifted her head and tried to rise, but her body felt strange, like her muscles and bones weren't quite in sync.

The room was enormous, a sprawling space with pillars inexplicably paneled by cracked mirrors and a floor of chipped tile with concrete beneath. Weak gray light filtered into the space from somewhere behind her, unable to penetrate the far reaches of the room, but above an archway to her left, brass letters glinted on a lopsided sign, marking the space beyond as Dressing Rooms.

A department store, then. Abandoned. But she'd just been in the forest…

Memories filtered back, and her thin remnants of self became terrified. Her mother. The draugar. Where had they—

"Hello, Melinda."

She scrambled all the way up, wobbling unsteadily on her feet. Behind her, Carolyn stood atop a raised section of the floor. Three steps led up to a platform that extended the width of the room, and dusty windows stretched from the ground to the distant ceiling behind her. Nothing lay beyond them but gray sky.

In her robes, Carolyn looked down, a hint of the cold and satisfied smile on her face that Lindy remembered so well. The sight had filled her with pride as a child—the rare expression of approval. The proof that Lindy was worthy.

Now, chills crept through her. When she'd imagined this moment as a child, she'd hoped that expression was what she would see, and now here it was.

And nothing Lindy had done to avoid this had mattered at all.

On either side of Carolyn, other members of the Order stood, their hoods shadowing their faces, their hands folded in front of them. But at the far end of the raised floor, two of them held Frankie, the boy gagged and bound.

His eyes were terrified.

"Let him go," Lindy demanded.

Her voice came out flat and dull, in spite of the rage and fear filtering through whatever was left of her.

Carolyn's smile broadened. "Oh, I think I did that for long enough. It's time for you both to come back where you belong."

Lindy shook her head. "We won't. We're never going back, and I won't become what you want."

Her mother made a rueful noise. "This obstinance is tiresome, Melinda. You accepted the mantle of the Scythe. That comes with obligations, ones you *cannot* deny no matter how you fight. Despite the foolishness your father filled your head with, the mark claims you all the same."

Carolyn nodded toward her.

Lindy risked a glance downward and froze.

Only her tank top and underwear remained on her, but somehow, she hadn't felt the cold or lack of her clothes. Her body was a numb, distant thing, not responding to her immediately when she wanted to move. But jagged black marks like vines twisted and tangled across it now, as if the tattoo had spread over her while she'd been unconscious. Her eyes snapped up to one of the cracked mirror panels on a pillar, finding shards of her broken reflection. Of her body, only her neck and face were still her own.

"Every second brings you closer to the moment when you will finally become the Scythe of Niorun. Yet still you fight, and we grow weary of it. The time of the Scythe is at hand. The berserkers and the ulfhednar and *all* who refuse to submit to order must be brought to heel. So let us make an end of this, shall we?"

Lindy's feet finally moved, backing her away from the platform as her head shook. "No. I won't do it. You force me, *Mother*, and I'll throw myself out of this damn building. Do you hear me? So just let us go and—"

"Silence."

Carolyn's hand snapped out, twitching sharply, and

Lindy choked, grabbing at her throat. She couldn't feel anything on her skin, and yet her body swore something was wrapping around her neck like a collar cutting off her air. Her skin ached and her muscles spasmed in tiny lurches like something else was moving through her body.

Her eyes snapped up to the mirrored panels, and horror suffused her. The black lines of the tattoo twisted on her skin like a thing alive, growing and climbing over her collarbone. From her body, smoke began to rise, tendrils twisting out from her like the wispy fingers feeling their way through the air.

"You will submit to this, Melinda."

The tightness around her neck increased, and Lindy crashed to her knees, one hand catching her to keep her from falling to the concrete entirely. The skin of her finger-tips turned pitch-black as if she was dipping them into ink, and her nails lengthened, sharpening into dark claws. Up her hands and forearms, the stain spread as the smoke around her grew thicker, wafting into the room like tentacles.

Her head shook, and when she spoke, her voice was a rasp. "Never. I'll never—"

"Franklin?" Carolyn called.

Panic tinged the ashes of Lindy's emotions. "No."

Carolyn regarded her with a smile before turning to Frankie with a solemn expression. "Franklin, your sister will cease to exist unless you help her, do you understand? Melinda is about to die, and you will never see her again. But you can save her if you take the mark. Become our Scythe. Save your sister, or else decide you don't love her enough to spare her life."

"No!" Lindy cried hoarsely. "No, Frankie, don't listen to her!"

Her mother turned back to her. "To become the Scythe of Niorun requires willingness, Melinda. Only to the willing will the mark be passed on. You already agreed years ago, but that doesn't mean another can't be chosen now."

Lindy's ink-black hands clawed at her neck as her lungs fought to breathe. Her skin burned, but with cold rather than heat, as if everything that made her alive was draining away, even as the smoke swirled around her. "No, Frankie," she begged, staring at her baby brother. Behind his gag, she could see Frankie sobbing, his teary eyes locked on her in terror.

Carolyn smiled. "Submit, Melinda. Or else Franklin will."

Frankie's mouth moved, shouting behind his gag, and Lindy knew what he was saying. She could read his face if not his lips, and the way he was screaming to take the mark in her place.

All that was left of her heart ached. There'd been hope, but now it was gone. Wes wasn't here. The wolves and the bears and the whole damn world hadn't been able to spare her from this moment.

The one that had always been coming.

She locked her eyes on her brother, praying he could see some trace of emotion past the ice that was spreading through her core. "I love you, Frankie. Always remember I love you."

Lindy closed her eyes as the darkness swelled around her for the last time.

# 26

# WES

At least the bears had been pretty damn prepared for the apocalypse.

Wes climbed from the Humvee, staring down the street at the tower of glass and steel right at the edge of the chasm torn through the heart of Minneapolis. Part of a sheltered walkway extended from its second floor, torn in half by the destruction in the city; whatever it connected to now lay somewhere deep in the chasm, gone forever. The snowy streets were still and quiet, not even a whisper of a draug's shriek on the breeze.

Behind him, the bears pulled weapons and supplies from the vehicle. The Humvee had been reinforced until it was basically a tank on snow tires and chains, with an arsenal of weapons and armor in the back—most of it sized entirely for shifted bears. The journey here had lasted an eternity, though with no need for speed limits or stoplights, it probably hadn't taken as long as it could have. But every second was a lifetime. Every minute, hell. Lindy was inside that building, somewhere high above them.

She had to be. The wolf was convinced of it, and the beast clawed at the sides of his skull as if trying to dig itself out.

If only to get to her faster.

"I take it she's up there?" Knox commented, walking up beside him. The male's voice was flat and cold.

Wes couldn't respond. He could tell the dark-haired male disliked him, though the gods knew why. He just didn't give a shit right now.

After a moment, the male sighed, and when he spoke again, an unexpected hint of sympathy softened his tone. "Hope you know what you're doing." Without another word, Knox headed for the rear of the Humvee.

Wes didn't take his eyes from the damaged building. It didn't matter, really, whether he knew or not. He was still going up there. The wolf scrambled through him, pressing on his skin, making his bones feel as if they were about to break. But shifting wasn't the plan, not for him.

If he needed to speak to Lindy, he had to be human.

Around him, seidr rushed through the air as several of the bears shifted. Everett's enormous form was even heftier than the rest, but they all were huge. Cinnamon fur covered a few, while dark-brown fur covered Knox, who was nearly equal in size to Everett. Scars covered the younger bear—an oddity considering most old wounds to one form didn't show up on the other—but Wes scarcely cared enough to wonder about it. Their job was to take the lead and the rear, eliminating any draugar on the way, all while hoping the building didn't fall into the chasm or that Lindy wasn't gone already.

Shivers ran through him. She wouldn't be. He'd find her first.

And then...

His wolf pressed against his skull, fit to give him a migraine. The rabid bastard wanted to bite her. Of course it did. Ever since he'd heard the theory that biting her could stop what the Order was doing, the wolf had practically been bashing itself into the walls, ready to sink its teeth into that beautiful woman.

Ready to take everything away from her, same as the Order, just in a different way.

"Good to go?" Henry came up beside him, offering him a machete. A backpack hung from the male's shoulders and a large knife in a leather sheath was strapped to his waist.

Wes nodded, taking the blade and trying not to think how it reminded him of Lindy.

But he'd figure out a way to save her. Even if he hadn't come up with a single damn solution all the way here, he still would.

And she'd still be *her* when he reached her.

With the bears pacing along beside him in human and shifted form, he started down the road. His fingers gripped and re-gripped the machete's hilt, his every sense attuned to the slightest sound or hint of movement. Ice and snow crunched under his boots, and the wind whistled past them as if to tug them forward over the edge of the chasm. Beyond the ravine, there was only gray sky and fog, with no sign of the other side.

Like the world ended where Lindy could be found.

Shivers crept over his skin. Where was the Order? Or the draugar, for that matter? The heart of Minneapolis was as abandoned as the snowy fields of Nebraska, and not even a symbol for those robed bastards was splashed across a window or doorway nearby.

For all their arrogance, surely they hadn't assumed *no one* would come after them?

He glanced at Henry. Tension lined the male's ordinarily jovial face, and his jaw muscles jumped like he was holding back a snarl. On either side, bears paced forward, their enormous paws leaving clawed marks in the snow and their muscles rolling beneath fur and body armor. But nothing on the street moved at all, and when they reached the glass door of the building, the foyer looked utterly empty.

"This is too easy," Henry murmured.

Wes nodded.

"Don't suppose you have the wrong building?" the male continued, eyeing Wes askance.

Studying the foyer beyond the glass, Wes didn't answer. He knew he was in the right place, though only the gods could tell how. But every fiber of his being said she was several floors above him, scared.

Hurting.

"She's here." He reached for the door, pausing before taking the handle. If there were traps here, he couldn't feel them, though that didn't mean much. Someone like Hayden may have picked up on something, but for him...

What other option was there?

Wes pulled the door wide.

Cold air reeking of death and decay rolled out at him. In bear form beside them, Everett rumbled a low growl.

"Draugar," Henry muttered.

With a noise of agreement, Wes walked inside while Henry motioned for a few of the bears to keep watch. Shadows hung thick in the foyer, clustering in corners, swallowing the hallway ahead. To his left, a collection of chairs and potted plants sat near the windows, while a U-shaped front desk waited across from them, a cup of pens scattered across its top and papers on the floor nearby. A cafe with round tables and stylized metal chairs occupied the right side of the space. Bags of coffee beans lay strewn across the floor where they'd fallen from the shelves, and a moldy croissant decayed next to a spilled coffee cup on one of the tabletops. No corpses were nearby that he could see, though there were too many places for a draug to hide.

His nose twitched. The strongest smells came from the hallway up ahead, where brass signs said the stairs and elevator could be found. Without electricity, the elevator wasn't an option, and that left the stairway.

The narrow, confined, level-after-endless-level of the stairway.

Perfect place for an ambush. Or a slaughter.

He glanced at Henry to find the male regarding the hall. "How good is your night vision?" he asked the male.

Henry swung the bag on his back around, not taking his eyes from the hallway. He drew a pair of clip lights from inside. "Better with this." He offered one to Wes and then clipped the device to his chest, clicking it on. Wes did the same.

They headed for the shadowed hall, the bears flanking them. The bright beams of their lights reflected like a small sun from the brass doors of the elevator and glinted from the silver handle of the stairway door. Odors of rot and decaying meat stung his nose and made his eyes water. Without a word, Henry walked to the door and paused shy of taking the handle. Glancing back, he held up a hand to Everett and Knox in bear form, ticking his fingers in a silent countdown.

And then he yanked open the door.

Draugar poured out like a flood, their rotting faces thrown into sharp relief by the lights Wes and Henry wore. Snarling and shrieking, the creatures scrambled over each other, clawing at the bears. Knox lunged forward into the dark stairwell, surging over the top of the rotted horde and slamming down on the creatures, his claws and teeth tearing through them and reducing them to dust. Everett came after him, catching any who managed to get past the younger bear and shredding them.

Gripping the machete, Wes followed as they forged ahead. Shrieks rang from the cement walls, and when the bears started upward, he couldn't even see the stairs for the horde climbing over each other to reach them. Dead bodies in business suits and maintenance worker uniforms flashed into the beams of light, their rotted mouths fighting to bite anything, while their hands scrabbled at the bears' body armor. The two berserkers acted like a snarling, fur-covered wall, catching draug after draug, but there were so many.

Even as he reached the first step, a draug flung itself from the banister above, clawing toward him as it fell. His machete tore through it, and one of the bears behind him made quick work of the creature as it tried to drag itself toward him anyway, but then more were coming, falling through the darkness from the floors overhead, ricocheting from the banisters on their way down, and grabbing for Wes and the others as they plummeted to the ground.

He swung until his arm grew sore, and his legs ached as they climbed level after level through the darkness. Blood and gore splattered him when rotted draugar tumbled past, falling to the machete or tumbling from the stairs. Dust covered his clothes, turning them gray, and exhaustion weighed on him. He hadn't caught sight of a number on the walls in a while, and all he knew was that Lindy was still above him, up there somewhere.

Gods, please let her hold on.

And then Everett slipped.

Wes's eyes went wide as draugar slammed into the stumbling bear, tearing him down. In a tumble of fur, the bear careened down the stairs, and there was no time. No space to avoid him.

Lunging to the side, Wes grabbed the banister and leapt out of the way, bracing himself by his feet and one hand on the opposite side of the railing, his other hand holding the machete and nothing but an endless drop of dark, empty space below him. Draugar plummeted from above, slamming into Wes's shoulders and scrabbling for purchase on him as they fell. Sodden with blood and grime, his grip on the railing began to slide, gravity pulling him toward the drop.

Henry grabbed his wrist. "Climb!"

Wes scrambled over the railing again. Slamming into the wall of the level below, Everett surged back to his feet, while up ahead, Knox roared and hurled a draug over the railing where it fell, shrieking and flailing to the distant ground.

"How much farther?" Henry called.

His heart pounding, Wes forced himself to refocus, trying to feel for Lindy.

Relief hit him. "One more level."

"Thank the *gods*." The exhaustion in Henry's voice was palpable. Clapping Wes on the shoulder, the male continued up the stairs, slashing at another draug when it got past Knox.

Adjusting his grip on the machete, Wes followed. Two more turns around the stairs led him to the fire exit. On the surface, the door looked no different than the countless others they'd passed, a slab of steel painted gray and bearing scuffs from years of wear and tear.

But the hairs on his arms rose all the same. Something was wrong beyond that door, and his wolf stretched and scraped claws across his insides at the feel of it.

Henry grasped the handle. "Ready?" he called to Knox and the rest. "Three, two—"

"Wait!" Wes shouted.

He was too late. Henry yanked the door open.

The feeling grew worse by a hundredfold. Seeming oblivious, Knox snarled and jerked his head as if motioning the others through. Henry charged in, and behind Wes, the other bears growled as if urging him to go on.

Apprehension flooded him, and his wolf pressed at his skin, torn between the instinct to flee and the fact Lindy was there.

Lindy won.

He ran up the steps and followed Henry through the opening. An abandoned storage area waited on the other side, a black abyss of space in which the beam of his light picked out empty metal shelves against the walls and a few empty cardboard boxes and broken plastic hangers on the floor. Behind him, the bears slammed the door, sealing out the draugar.

His light landed on a door on the opposite end of the room. Lindy was there. Everything in him screamed she was there.

So was whatever the hell he was feeling.

Henry hurried toward the door, and the other bears bumped past Wes as they followed.

Wes's head shook. "Something's wrong."

Henry didn't glance back.

"Dammit, I said—"

"First one who sees her," Henry ordered the bears, ignoring him. "You go for the girl. Bite her if you can, take her out if you have to. Got it?"

Cold shot through Wes. "*What?* That isn't—"

"I'm sorry, Wes." Henry looked regretful. "We can't risk them controlling her." The male pulled open the door and charged through, the bears on his heels.

Wes raced after them. A concrete space waited on the other side, and a thick pillar with cracked mirror paneling stood only a few yards ahead, blocking his view. The bears fanned out, rushing to other pillars on his right and left, moving more silently than anything their size should have been able to move. The shadows were thick, but weak light came from up ahead, diffuse and gray.

He hit the shelter of the pillar and threw a look past it immediately, scanning the enormous room, praying he hadn't been wrong and that he got to her first.

A nightmare met his eyes.

On her knees before a platform where half a dozen Order members stood silhouetted against the daylight, Lindy was surrounded by smoke that moved like a thing alive. Shadows poured from her bare skin like water, hitting the ground and twisting out like tentacles through the room. At the far end of the platform, her brother stood, bound and gagged in the grip of two Allegiants, while at the center, a woman stood, the hood of her robe thrown back and her brown hair backlit by the weak light.

"Submit, Melinda." Cruel satisfaction filled the woman's voice. "Or else Franklin will."

Oh, gods.

Wes shoved away from the pillar, tearing across the

cavernous room toward Lindy. Ahead, he could see the bears charging through the shadows, aiming for her. Adrenaline poured into his muscles, fueling his ulfhednar speed.

"I love you, Frankie," Lindy called, her voice weak. "Always remember I love you."

Horror flooded Wes.

A bear lunged for her.

The shadows around Lindy surged like they had been supercharged by a lightning bolt. Darkness rushed out from her like a wall, slamming into Wes and all the bears alike.

His feet went out from under him as the wave of smoke ripped past him. Pain shot through his body as his shoulder crashed into the ground, the padding of his coat seeming to do nothing.

Because it wasn't there.

His head spinning, he fumbled at his chest, finding only wet, bare skin that hurt like hell when he touched it. Confused, he flinched back and stared in horror at the blood coating his palms.

Deep gouges were torn in his flesh, tracing the paths that used to be scars. Blood poured from them, swallowing the tattoos he'd used in a vain attempt to cover the wounds.

But they'd never really be gone.

Trembling, he tried to brace himself on the ground, but the concrete seemed to give like dough, wobbling and warping beneath his feet. Cold fear sank icy claws into his chest. He couldn't even see the room, not really. Everything was fog and smoke, and past the ringing of his ears, he could barely make out the sound of fighting beyond the mist.

And the rumble of a deep growl.

Terror turned his feet to lead weights. He knew that sound. Heard it in every nightmare, despised it each time its echo came from his mouth.

The wolf paced from the fog.

His muscles turned to water. He was eleven years old again, the scrawny boy who'd hurried home through the woods when his father couldn't pick him up from school. He was the kid who'd run and fought and screamed, and it hadn't mattered in the end. Yellow eyes the color of pus pinned him as firmly as skewers through a bug, so much intelligence in their gleam that even then, long before he'd known of the ulfhednar, he would have sworn they were almost human.

But nothing in them was sane.

A low growl rumbled from the wolf, drowning out the noise of fighting, becoming the only sound in the world.

Wes's feet stumbled backward but the floor didn't cooperate, and he fell, the gelatinous concrete snaring his hands, his wrists.

The wolf's lips pulled back in a snarl he would swear was a grin.

In an instant, the beast was on him.

Claws tore his chest, driving him into the ground, and he screamed as teeth sank into his shoulder, ripping through muscle all the way to bone. The bite burned like acid was flooding his veins, scouring away his life and anything he might have been. Lifting its head again, the wolf stared down at him with blatant satisfaction, Wes's blood dripping from its jaws.

And it lunged for his throat.

Tearing his hands from the concrete, Wes caught the creature before it could kill him once and for all. Shoving it back with all his might, he scrambled upright as the wolf rolled and came up ready to lunge at him again.

Gray eyes met his own, the color of the fog at the end of the world, and he knew them.

He saw them reflected back in every lake and pond when he paused after a long run.

A snarl pulled at the beast's lips, its hackles raised.

Wes leapt at the wolf.

The creature met him halfway, slamming into him in a tangle of fur and claws, hands and teeth. Tumbling to the ground, he punched at the wolf while the beast thrashed and snapped, gnashing into his flesh and ripping at his grasp.

But he'd be damned if he lost to it this time.

Tearing at the beast with his bare hands, screams of rage and obscenities poured from his lips. This was the bastard that had taken everything. The reason he'd lost his home, fucked up though it was. The reason his parents stopped loving him, and the reason he'd had to start life over at eleven years old—except the entire concept was a joke. Because love was impossible. Because he'd met Lindy and couldn't ever be with her for fear of destroying her too.

Now he could finally end it once and for all.

Blood soaked his hands and slicked the wolf's fur as he and the creature rolled, biting and tearing into one another. He could feel the creature weakening, feel the way its attacks slowed with every passing heartbeat. This was it. This was where, at long last, he'd shred the beast alive.

But the man was hurting his mate, and he couldn't lose to him now.

Confusion fractured Wes's rage, but the wolf was still

coming for him. Lindy was in danger. It had to protect her, no matter the cost.

With a shout, he thrust the wolf away. The creature tumbled across the concrete and scrambled to its feet, facing him again, teeth bared.

Wes stared. In the misty expanse, the wolf stood, its bloodied sides heaving as it watched him.

"I-I'm not—" His head shook. "I wouldn't hurt—"

But he had.

Pain filtered through to him, coming from the wolf. A thousand moments of pushing it aside. A thousand more of shutting it away. And the creature didn't care, not really. It was used to the pain.

But now he was hurting her. Because she needed him to do the one thing he wouldn't. Because he could save her, and instead, he'd sided with the old monsters who'd failed to kill him, and this time he'd let them win.

Shock took Wes's feet from beneath him, and dumb-struck, he sank to the ground. "I... I didn't..."

The wolf's eyes never left him.

A shuddering breath escaped his chest. That was the truth, wasn't it? All these years of tearing himself apart to prove he wasn't everything his parents said when they beat him in penance to their god... and it hadn't mattered. Deep down, he'd believed them the entire time. Sure, he'd trusted his pack, loved his friends, and shifted when necessary.

But he'd still bought the lie. Still thought the wolf—*his* wolf—was an abomination. Because it came into his life through violence. Because the bastard who bit him was a monster, and the wolf was something he'd never risked trying to understand.

Because he'd been a scared little kid, and somewhere inside, he'd believed them.

Every day, he'd set the wolf apart from himself. Every day, he'd fought it, beating it down and denying it was ever truly *him*. Because he thought it was ugly. Untrustworthy.

And all the while, he'd been hurting himself too.

Through the gray mist, the creature walked closer, wary distrust in its eyes, and it hurt to see. Who was more the monster? A wolf or someone who hurt those they claimed to love?

Wes reached out a hand, and carefully, the wolf's snout brushed his palm. He couldn't say if this was delusion or reality, and somewhere beyond the gray, he knew the bears were fighting to survive.

But something in his chest loosened all the same.

The wolf's eyes met his, and for the first time in his life, Wes opened himself fully to the creature who was his own heart, and who'd never wanted anything but to be loved.

His vision cleared as the wolf merged into him like a fading dream. Shadows still roiled through the room. In a tangle of claws and fur, the bears fought one another, and blood splattered the floor around them.

And at the center, Lindy crouched, watching the destruction. One stained hand braced her on the floor while smoke poured from her skin, surging in waves of madness throughout the room. Dark tattoos like talons framed her face now, as if a monster had her in its grip. A thick band of ink wrapped her neck like a collar, and a black leash of smoke extended from it up to the hand of a woman on the stage, as if Lindy were nothing more than a dog.

His eyes never leaving her, Wes rose to his feet and let

the shift roll through him, burning away his clothes and coat and every damn illusion he'd ever held. He'd been a fool, and maybe it'd cost Lindy everything. He could only pray he wasn't too late.

Teeth bared, the monster turned, wearing the face of the woman he loved.

Wes leapt for her.

# LINDY

I n the darkness, Lindy died.

Memory slipped away. Hope and pain too. There'd never been anything beyond this moment. Only the darkness was left.

Coursing with power and the need to use it, only the darkness was still alive.

A leash ran from the neck of the darkness, first as a shimmer of air and then solidifying into a sinuous line of black smoke. The rope extended to the hand of the One, its master and source of meaning. Impulses poured down through the leash, forming the darkness's will, its thoughts. The darkness was called the Scythe. Its purpose was to cut and rend apart all whom the One sought destroyed.

And so it did.

Beautiful madness rolled and surged through the room, twisting the minds of those who opposed the One, turning them against their corrupted allies, making them see their worst nightmares instead. Blood splattered the ground as they fought, causing saliva to well in the Scythe's hungry mouth, and whispers came from the One, promising a feast later.

But now something was wrong.

Anger from the One made the Scythe turn.

A wolf stood behind it, and the One's wrath curled the Scythe's lips back in a snarl. The wolf needed to die, now, quickly. With blood and madness, rent limb from limb. Waves of shadow poured from the Scythe in immediate response, but still the wolf was coming, charging forward with teeth bared, a corrupted creature whose blood would taste like sweet wine when the Scythe devoured it whole.

*Wes.*

Fury poured from the One, and the Scythe faltered, confused at anger that suddenly seemed equally directed at it as much as the wolf. The One's commands raged through the leash, and more shadows raced from the Scythe in response, waves of darkness slamming into the wolf over and over as it lunged.

*To save her.*

The corrupted beast slammed into the Scythe. With clawed fingers, the Scythe tore at it, ripping gashes from the wolf's fur while all around the bears shredded each other and painted the floor red.

But the wolf didn't fall. Didn't stop. No matter the wounds and the blood, the creature snapped and snarled and lunged—

Until its fangs sank deep into the Scythe's shoulder, down into muscle, down into bone, and pain erupted through the world like flames.

## 28

# WES

Lindy's blood filled his mouth, and inside his mind, man and beast howled. She thrashed in his grip, clawing at him and screaming. Surges of black shadow flooded from her, buffeting him like raging waves, warping reality around the edges and filling it with cries from all he feared. His pack dying. His parents beating him. The world on fire and Lindy dead and everything that mattered to him burned to ash.

But man and wolf were united in this purpose, and they'd never lose their focus again.

Digging his teeth into her and begging her to forgive him for the pain, Wes tried to drag her backward. Smoke lashed at him, striking like scorpion stings, and a rope of black mist ran from a thick band of ink around her neck, tethering her to the woman on the platform ahead.

"Stop him!" the woman shouted, grasping the leash and hauling on it to keep him from taking Lindy. "Kill the wolf!"

The Allegiants started down from the stage, but the

fighting bears tumbled past them, cutting them off. Wild and erratic, the berserkers were everywhere, some seeming to be battling only air, slashing at nothing, while others tore into their friends, rolling and biting across the floor in a rage. In a corner, Henry cowered against the wall, screaming in terror.

His heart racing, Wes's eyes darted around. How the hell was he going to get her out of here? Draugar almost certainly remained on the stairs, and if he let her go, the woman would haul her away from him. And that didn't even bring into it the way Lindy was thrashing around. She'd stopped hitting him now, her body flailing instead, as if she was trapped in the throes of a nightmare. But still, he couldn't—

In his grip, Lindy suddenly convulsed as if struck by an electric shock.

A wave of shadow erupted from her, surging across the room, and all the other shadows were driven ahead of it. Like the wave of an explosion, the power slammed into the walls and windows, shattering the glass and spreading fractures through the concrete like it'd been punched by a giant. The ceiling groaned for only a heartbeat, and then the space above the platform came crashing down.

The Allegiants scrambled as an avalanche of concrete and pipes poured down, and Wes stared in horror as Frankie was lost behind the cascade.

Lindy went limp in his grasp.

Wes looked from her to the platform and back. The tether was gone, though the dark collar and tattoos remained. Cautiously, he released his bite on her shoulder.

She sagged to the ground, her white tank top stained red with blood. The wound on her shoulder was so deep, but if the change took, she'd heal and regain full use of her arm.

If she didn't die.

He looked up, frantic. The platform was a mountain of rubble, and of the Allegiants, he could see no sign. The bears no longer fought, though they were badly hurt. Some stumbled, clearly dazed, while Henry braced himself on the wall and staggered to his feet.

Wes barked at him, cursing the fact he couldn't communicate clearly. But the male turned toward him and then followed the jerk of Wes's jaw.

Horror spread through Henry's body language. "Frankie!" The male staggered toward the destruction on the platform. "Where are you, boy?"

No response. Wes's heart sank, dread settling over him.

"Here!" came a muffled cry from behind the debris.

Henry scrambled over a pile of concrete. A moment later, the rubble shifted.

The big male hefted Frankie over the destruction and then climbed after him. Blood stained Frankie's ankle, and he tried to stand only to fall back with a cry of pain.

Henry put a hand to the boy's shoulder as if to keep him from trying to move again. "Everett, you think you can carry the kid?" Henry threw a look at the bear. The berserker was seated on the ground, wavering as if he was only a heartbeat from collapse. "Oh, hell. Knox?"

The scarred bear grunted, appearing exhausted, but he walked closer, limping as he moved. Hobbling on one foot, Frankie clambered onto the bear's back.

Wes looked down again. Lindy's closed eyelids twitched and her body spasmed like she was having a seizure. The smoke was gone, but the jagged tattoos remained, twisting across her bare flesh and up like claws on the sides of her face.

He nudged her, but she didn't wake, and his heart sank. Gods, how was he going to get her out of here? If Frankie was okay, the Allegiants and that bitch with the leash might still be alive too. But Wes couldn't drag Lindy all the way down the stairs and back to the Humvee.

Footsteps crunched on the debris, and Wes's head snapped up to find the berserkers pacing toward him.

He growled a warning, stepping past Lindy to put himself between her and the bears.

They stopped.

"Easy there," Henry called.

Wes's lip curled back.

Holding his hands up peaceably, the big guy walked toward him. "We need to go."

No shit.

"I'll carry her. She's safe with me, I swear."

Said the male who wanted to kill her only a few minutes ago.

"Come on, son. What choice do you have?"

A low growl left Wes, but Henry was still right. Short of shifting and carrying her down the stairs while he was bare-ass naked, there weren't a lot of options.

Henry stepped forward carefully as Wes inched back. Scooping her up in his arms, the male nodded toward the door. "Let's get the hell out of here."

On that, at least, Wes couldn't agree more.

Barreling downward through the remaining draugar proved less difficult than forging upstairs through the horde, though Wes suspected the bears' desire to be out of this place helped. With Lindy in his arms, Henry charged after them, and Wes never let the male out of his sight, terrified the bear would drop her over the banister or leave her for the draugar to destroy.

And Lindy never woke. Not when they reached the Humvee, nor all the way back to the bears' cabins. Her eyelids twitched and her muscles spasmed while her skin began burning with a fever that only grew worse. They lay her in a bed at Maeve and Everett's house, and the female swung into action like a force of nature, muscling nearly everyone out of the room.

Wes didn't budge.

But no matter what Maeve tried, Lindy wouldn't respond and her fever didn't either. Delirious murmurs and whimpers left her from time to time, and beneath a sheen of sweat, her skin was ashen. Every so often, she would thrash, but the movements were weakening, as if she simply couldn't keep fighting as hard. And even though the female never said it, he could read the look on Maeve's face. Lindy was dying.

His heart was dying with her.

A rustling made him look up from where he clutched her hand. Andrew sat by the bed, and when Wes moved, the man's eyes flicked up to him.

"It's not your fault," Andrew said quietly. "You tried."

Cold shame sank over Wes, and inside him, the wolf howled in pain. The words weren't true. If he'd been faster, if he'd bitten her when she asked instead of running like a coward...

Lindy might have survived.

He turned back to her. Beneath his grip, he could still feel her pulse beating like a trapped bird, faint as a whisper.

And his head shook. "I killed her."

At Andrew's silence, his shame deepened, crushing the air from his lungs. He couldn't do this. Couldn't sit here, watching her die. There had to be something else. Something he missed. In leaving the building in Minneapolis, they hadn't stopped to see if any of those Order bastards were still alive. But if he found one, if he forced them to tell him how to reverse this damn curse, then maybe... maybe...

A weak spasm shook through her, air rattling in her chest.

He thrust to his feet and fled for the hall.

In the living room, Everett and the others looked up in alarm as he rushed by, heading for the door.

"Wes!" Henry called.

He didn't stop, shoving past the door and striding out onto the porch. The Humvee was parked just outside, and if the bears were anything like the wolves, then the keys would still be in the—

"She's your mate, isn't she?"

Henry's voice stopped him. A shudder coursed through Wes, his body aching as if every molecule of his being was in pain.

Boots reverberated on the porch as Henry came up behind him.

"I have to save her," Wes managed, unable to make himself turn around. He started down the stairs again.

"Does she know? What she is to you, did you tell her?"

Wes's chest quivered, his face tightening against the agony that made him want to howl.

WES

A breath left Henry. "Tell her, son. Now. Be there with her. You—" The male paused, and when he spoke again, his voice was thick with old pain. "You'll never forgive yourself, if you're not."

Henry's boots scratched on the porch as he turned and went back inside.

Shudders rolled through Wes, and he strode toward the Humvee. He wouldn't accept this. He wouldn't just give up, not when she was slipping away with every passing moment.

His hand froze on the door handle.

Hours of driving. More to find an Allegiant. And what if they didn't have an answer?

What if she woke up and he wasn't there?

He looked back at the cabin. If he stayed, she wouldn't make it. But if he left and he was too slow again, she could—

The sudden sound of wings made him tense. Fluttering down from overhead, two ravens landed on the snow in front of him.

Instantly, they shifted into human form.

Wes froze. Tall and thin with black cloaks of feathers covering them, the two regarded him with imperious expressions. He couldn't tell if they were male or female, and when they spoke, their voices seemed to reverberate in his ears.

"We want—"

"—to see the girl."

One spoke and then the other finished, seamless, as if they were simply one mind with two mouths.

Without another word, they turned, walking toward the cabin door.

"What?" Wes took off after them. "Who the hell are you?"

They didn't respond, striding up the steps in perfect sync.

"Hey!" Wes sped up, but somehow they stayed ahead of him even as he chased them past the door.

The bears shoved to their feet, alarm clear on their faces. Ignoring them entirely, the two raven people veered left, heading down the hall.

"Wes," Henry said. "Who the hell—"

"No clue." He raced after them. "Get back here, damn you."

The two people pushed past the door. Andrew made a sound of alarm, and Wes's heart hit his throat. He charged through the opening to find the raven people standing at the foot of the bed.

Lindy moaned, thrashing harder than he'd seen her fight in hours. Sweat still coated her bloodless skin, and her eyes rolled behind her closed lids.

Wes rushed over to her, keeping one eye to the ravens as he grabbed her hand. "Lindy? Lindy, please, can you hear me?"

Her breath spasmed in her chest, ragged gasps that set her lurching on the bed.

"What are you doing to her?" Andrew demanded.

The ravens cocked their heads to the side, the gesture entirely birdlike.

"This one—"

"—is something new."

In the blink of an eye, they moved, suddenly standing by the headboard on either side of the bed. In perfect sync, they reached out, each putting a hand to her.

Lindy gasped, her body spasming so hard that her back

arched up from the mattress. Her eyes flew open, staring unseeing at the ceiling while her mouth opened in a silent scream.

And then she sagged back to the bed, her eyes falling closed again.

Alarm rolled through Wes in a cold wave. She wasn't breathing. Oh gods, she wasn't breathing.

"Lindy?" He patted her face and then looked up at the two people standing like silent sentinels on either side of the bed, cold expressions of satisfaction on their faces. "What did you do? What the hell did you—"

The ravens disappeared.

# 29

## LINDY

Whispers carried through the dark, twisting around her like someone moving past only to come around again. The sound was ethereal, like a lullaby carried on the wind. Familiar too, like a mother soothing her child after a nightmare, even if her own mother had never done any such thing.

But Lindy couldn't make out the words.

Mist swirled through the darkness before her eyes, gray over black, but refracting light around the edges like a rainbow. She couldn't focus; the world was a blur swimming in and out of view with only whatever was right in front of her seeming to have any definition at all.

But what was in front of her made no sense.

Firelight played through the shadows and danced on a dark wall. Something moved past her, but she couldn't make out the shape of it.

"Hello?" Her voice slipped away as if drawn down a long tunnel.

A young woman's chuckle drifted around her, pleasant, friendly.

Lindy tried to look around, the world blurring as she turned. "Where am I?"

*Not there yet.*

The young woman's words came as if in a dream, passing into her mind even though she couldn't say who had spoken.

"What does that mean?"

Again, a chuckle passed around her as if on a breeze. *You did well.*

Lindy floundered, confused. "I don't understand."

*The poison was not poison. The poison was the idea.*

"What?"

*Come.*

She felt a hand take hers, drawing her forward through fog and firelight. Ahead, a figure in robes like ashes and embers moved in and out of view, leading her onward. Rainbow light danced around the edges of the form, as if the shape didn't quite share Lindy's same reality.

Memories rose of old stories, and her confusion deepened to wary alarm. The goddess. The one for whom the Scythe was named. Lindy's voice trembled as she spoke. "Niorun?"

The figure turned, the deep hood of her robe hiding her face entirely, and yet somehow, Lindy would swear she smiled.

Pressure on her hand returned, drawing her forward, and the shadows grew thicker. She couldn't see the figure anymore, only feel a grip on her hand, but from the darkness the sounds of growls and shrieks arose, along with a flapping of wings like birds flew somewhere nearby.

Fear closed her throat. What was this? Where was

Niorun taking her? Lindy was back to herself after nearly dying, and...

Maybe that was just it, though. Maybe she wasn't back.

What if she was dead?

The realization pressed on her chest like a fist. All this time thinking her life was over, and now it was. She thought she'd be ready for it, but now she knew there was no such thing. Life was possibility. This was nothing. No hope, no future. Utter finality. And to it, she'd lost Wes, lost her family and friends. Lost everyone to spend eternity here, in the darkness, just another one of the monsters, and for what? She hadn't even saved anyone.

She'd failed.

And she'd give anything to go back and live again.

Niorun paused, and then a hand cupped Lindy's cheek, cool and soft, and a feeling of gentle comfort stole over her like a warm blanket on a winter's night. *Child...*

Again, she felt as if Niorun smiled, though in the swirls of deep shadow and darkness, she couldn't see the goddess's face at all.

*The poison was not poison, but something new.*

White light shone in her eyes, and she gasped. A high ceiling rose above her, distant and cloaked in shadows like an enormous cathedral. She lay on the floor, the surface cold and slick like marble beneath her back.

She sat up. The cavernous hall stretched away on all sides around her, and pillars like white trees rose from the ground to support the distant ceiling. Daylight burned beyond the towering archway to her left, while far to her right, the space emptied into a long, dark corridor where the walls danced with firelight. In all the great space, she was utterly alone, except for one old man dozens of yards away, pushing a broom slowly across the floor.

"Where am I?" she called. "Where's Niorun?"

The old man kept sweeping.

Shivers rolled through her, and she started to chafe her arms against the chill, only to pause. Dark tattoos still covered her body, and her fingertips were black as if dipped in ink. She trembled, looking up at the old man again. "Am... am I dead?"

He glanced over at her, his head bobbing slightly as if to allow for the possibility. "Perhaps."

Without another word, he returned to sweeping.

Wetting her lips nervously, she pushed to her feet. The dark corridor stretched beyond the old man, curving so she couldn't see the other end even though the walls were cast with a patina of firelight. In the distance, there was the sound of laughter and joyous song. But her chest tightened at the idea of heading toward it.

Somehow, she wasn't sure she could ever come back.

"The battle is coming." The old man's tone was conversational, as if he'd merely commented on the weather, and he never stopped sweeping.

Lindy's attention snapped back to him. "What?"

"The pieces are moving into place. I would have the strong at my side, even if there is little chance we will prevail." He turned toward her, half his face in shadow while a smile pulled at his lips, and when he spoke again, zeal filled his voice. "But the battle will be *glorious*."

Two ravens suddenly flew down from the shadows overhead to land on his shoulders, and in front of her eyes, his body seemed to change, as if two images were suddenly laid overtop one another. A battle-scarred warrior stood before her, a patch over his eye and a spear in his hand, his body towering with strength. And a wise old man with a staff regarded her, a knowing look in his one eye while the rest of his face was lost in shadow beneath his broad hat.

The man smiled, merely a caretaker once again. Carrying the ravens on his shoulders and the broom in his hand, he turned and walked away down the dark hall.

"What do you mean?" she called after him. "What is this place?"

A breeze stirred behind her. She turned.

In the archway, a beautiful woman stood with her body surrounded by sunlight. Wide open fields stretched away behind her, on which the distant forms of people moved as if they were sparring in preparation for battle. On the horizon, towering mountains stood capped in crisp white snow beneath an endless sky.

"You did well," the woman said.

Lindy trembled, not sure how anyone could say that after everything that'd happened. "Who are you?"

The woman laughed, the sound like distant chimes carried on the wind. "I taught seidr to the gods in the days before man."

An uneven breath left Lindy. "Freya?"

With graceful steps, the woman walked closer, light dancing around her like gold. "They never were opposites, you know. Chaos. Order. They need each other." She smiled and gently placed a fingertip to the center of Lindy's throat. Something felt like it snapped, only for her skin to burn where the woman's finger touched.

Freya lowered her hand. "For what is to come."

Lindy reached for her throat. Something tingled under her skin.

The woman looked into her eyes, her voice echoing as she spoke. "Time to wake, child. They need you."

Lindy opened her eyes to gray light and the feeling of something soft beneath her. A warm hand clasped her own. The logs of the cabin ceiling stretched overhead, and cool sheets covered her body.

Which hurt.

She groaned and immediately heard a gasp somewhere to her right as someone tightened their grip on her hand. She looked over to see Wes crouched at the bedside, and wet lines traced where tears had fallen down his cheeks. Her father stood behind him, staring at her with shock.

A smile pulled at her lips to see them both alive, though worry threaded through her for why Wes had been crying. "Hey," she managed, her voice weak. She tried to rise and go to him, but everything hurt.

Immediately, he moved to help her. His hands slipped around her shoulders, taking her weight and lifting her.

Something stirred beneath her skin. Dark, but not like the voracious power that craved to devour and kill. Strange and wild, it rippled through her in an instant, only to brush against something that felt like it was inside him, whispering across it like smoke over fur.

Wes froze.

Eyes locked on him, she couldn't breathe, but he didn't die. Didn't scream in madness or terror. Instead, he blinked at her, something almost holy moving through his gaze, as if she'd taken his breath away.

Tenderly, he lifted her until her back was against the pillows.

"What..." She cleared her throat. "What happened?"

The two men looked to each other, and Wes's mouth moved like he was struggling to find the words.

"We thought you were dead." Her father's voice was tight.

She stared at them both as foggy memories played back. A hooded figure in shadow and rainbow. A grand hall of marble and distant firelight. An old man with ravens, and a woman who—

Her fingertips brushed her throat. The skin tingled inside.

*For what is to come.*

A shuddering breath entered her lungs. "Is Frankie okay?"

Her dad nodded.

Lindy hesitated, feeling her way toward the words gingerly. "And Mom? The woman with the… the leash. Did she…?"

Andrew looked away. "They tell me Carolyn, um…"

"The ceiling collapsed," Wes said quietly when her father couldn't finish. "It fell right where she…" He grimaced. "I'm sorry."

Something in her chest ached in spite of everything, and it didn't feel like the grip of her mother's power.

It felt like a child wanting her mother to have been different than she was, and for that person to still be alive.

Lindy closed her eyes.

Her father made a soft noise. "I'm going to go let Frankie and the others know you're okay."

Nodding, she tried for a smile.

The door shut behind him. Her eyes slid to Wes to find him watching her.

"Are you okay?" she asked quietly.

The corner of his lip rose. "I should be asking you that."

Her gaze dropped away.

"I am now," he amended gently. A heartbeat passed, and when he spoke, his voice was tight. "I thought I'd lost you."

"I thought you had too."

He took her hand, and she squeezed his fingers hard.

"I'm sorry, Lindy," he said, pain thick in his voice. "I should've... I *shouldn't* have walked away from you. Or left you. Or not done what you asked. I... I just spent so much of my life scared I might hurt someone with what I am that I..." He shook his head, a futile expression on his face. "I'm so sorry. Can you ever forgive me?"

Her heart ached. "You came for me. Against the Order and my mother and the whole damn apocalypse, you came. Yeah, I forgive you."

He looked up, relief in his eyes, and she reached over, putting a hand to his cheek.

"Thank you," he said softly.

She smiled.

Gently, he helped her to her feet, and her legs wobbled beneath her before steadying with Wes's strong arm holding her close. Carefully, she made her way toward the clothes folded on a nearby dresser, only to pause when she caught sight of herself in the mirror.

A quivering breath entered her. The marks were still there. Dark and jagged lines like tattooed vines tangled across every inch of her body. Black shapes like claws extended from the back of her neck and past her temples to frame her face, and around her neck, the thick ring of a collar showed on her throat.

But it was broken in the center, right at her voice box.

She walked closer, her eyes roving over the marks, and as she passed through the light from the small window to her left, something flashed at the center of the break in the tattooed collar on her throat.

Her brow drew down, and carefully, she twisted her head left and right, peering at it more closely. A hint of gold shimmered in the center of the gap, but she could only see it at certain angles, like it was embedded in her skin, a filament of gold barely visible unless someone knew what to look for. The shimmer formed a trail of runes she didn't recognize, each one small and placed in a vertical line.

She looked back up at herself in the mirror. Black clouds stained the whites of her eyes, and inside her mind, she could feel strange shadows. The curse the Order gave her, but it was different somehow. Even though it permeated her, it wasn't numbing or dead. Wasn't even frightening anymore. The shadows were hers, and even as she thought of them, they twisted away from her skin like delicate wisps of smoke.

"What am I?" she whispered.

"Something new."

She whirled, her breath catching. "What did you say?"

Wes hesitated. "There were some people here. Earlier. Before you..." He cleared his throat. "They were ravens, and then they weren't, and when they came in here, they said you were something new right before they disappeared."

Lindy turned back to the mirror, her eyes tracing the marks. "Do the bears have any idea what that—"

Shapes of the draugar surfaced at the edge of her mind.

She gasped and turned to shove the window curtain aside, scanning the forest. The trees were still, and nothing moved beyond them, but in her mind she could feel the Order and the draugar encircling the cabin like a snake.

Right before they vanished entirely.

"What is it?" Wes asked.

Chills moved through her. She knew that feeling, like something being erased from view. She'd felt it only a short time ago when Carolyn captured her in the woods.

"Lindy?" Wes prompted.

She headed for the door. "They're coming."

# 30

# WES

Wes raced after Lindy from the room, his mind bouncing between alarm for whatever she was sensing and alarm at what had just happened. What the hell was she? And what had he felt when she first woke up and he touched her? If he had to describe the sensation, it would have been wolf-but-not-wolf, ephemeral as smoke and yet nuzzling up against him.

And gods, it felt good...

He shoved the thoughts aside, not wanting to get his hopes up. Besides, he needed to focus. They weren't out of this yet.

From their seats around the sunken living room, the bears looked up in alarm as the two of them rushed into the room. Everett sat with an arm around Otis, the large child clearly nervous based on the way he seemed to be fighting the urge to suck his thumb. Across the space, Henry was sagged into a seat, his wounds bandaged and his face haggard. Maeve was in the kitchen, while Knox stood by the door as if still keeping watch, just in case. The dark-haired male's neck and shoulders were wrapped, and hints of bloodstains marred the white fabric. Near the hallway, Andrew was crouched by Frankie's seat. The man gripped his son's hands as if in encouragement, and tears glistened on the kid's face.

"Lindy!" Frankie cried. The boy shoved out of his chair, sending the thing rocking as he rushed over and threw his arms around his sister.

While Lindy hugged him, she gave a quick look to the others. "They're coming. The Order. The draugar. Do you have any weapons?"

The bears were frozen for less than a heartbeat.

Knox shoved away from the wall and headed for the door. "Stay in the house." He tossed the order over his shoulder like he didn't have a doubt about being obeyed.

Everett headed for the hallway, muttering something about weapons, while Maeve drew Otis to her, the kid giving up the fight not to suck his thumb. With a grunt, Henry maneuvered to his feet and hobbled toward the tarps covering the broken windows at the back of the house, looking past them as if checking in case anyone was sneaking up where the bears couldn't see.

Wes eyed the broken windows and then the door. His wolf rolled beneath his skin, ready to shift and attack.

"Dad," Lindy said. "Can you get Frankie somewhere safe in here?"

Andrew glanced at Maeve, giving her a questioning look.

"This way," the female said, bringing Otis with her.

Lindy's family hurried down the hall with Maeve urging them on like an irritated school matron.

"Y'all ought to head back with them," Henry said to Wes and Lindy from his post by the tarps.

Ignoring him, Lindy headed for the windows beside the front door.

"Dammit, girl. The last thing we need is those folks getting their hands on—"

"They're here," Lindy interrupted, stopping cold a yard shy of the door.

Wes came up beside her. "Go protect your family. We've got this."

Her face tightened, her expression torn.

He clasped a hand to her arm and then continued past her, yanking open the door and stepping outside, letting the shift rush through him as he moved. It'd be a pain to find more clothes, but the bears seemed to have a stockpile. And there wasn't time to strip down all nice and neat, anyway.

Shrieks from the draugar carried from the woods, closing in fast.

A huffing sound came from behind him, and a bear walked onto the porch. Everett, he thought. A glance through the open doorway confirmed it, as he saw Henry shift quickly by the back window.

Lindy stood, one hand on the doorframe and her eyes on the forest, unmoving.

Wes made a gruff sound, urging her back inside. She glanced at him, and he couldn't read the look in her eyes.

The shrieks grew louder. He barked at Lindy and then whirled back toward the woods. Branches snapped and cracked. In the distance, the trees rustled, like a wave was rushing through the forest on all sides.

And then it died.

Heart pounding, Wes glanced around warily. On the

snowy ground, shifted bears stood in front of their homes, watching the trees, while at his side, Everett growled, the low sound filtering out almost as if by instinct.

But the rushing sound was gone. The rustling too. Shrieks and howls rose from all sides, as if the forest itself had become a monster, while the choking scent of decay spread past the trees.

Where the fuck were the draugar?

Green smoke rolled out between a row of evergreen trees like a noxious fog.

Allegiants walked into the clearing, more than he'd seen even at the building where they had Lindy. Behind them, the draugar shuffled from between the trees, not moving past them but instead waiting like a silent, decaying host at the backs of the robed figures. The virulent clouds of smoke drifted around them, as if the snow itself were vaporizing into toxic mist.

And at the center of it all stood Carolyn.

A growl left Wes. Her hood thrown back, the woman eyed them with disgust. Her bearing was ramrod straight despite how she was limping, and the shadows on her face gathered dark and severe in the hollows of her cheeks, giving her the look of a skull. Like the other Allegiants, her robes were torn, and from them all, he could smell blood, the scent sour like curdled milk.

Carolyn took another step forward, her face twitching with rage. "Where... is my... *daughter*?"

Wes bared his teeth and snarled. Nearby, a large brown bear growled and all around him, the other bears stepped forward, pacing toward the Allegiants.

Carolyn made a contemptuous sound. "Then I'll find her over your corpses."

Her hands moved, stirring the air, and the green smoke rose around her.

Cold resolution settled over Wes. The magic was deadly, he knew. He'd seen its effects in Mariposa, days before, when it'd nearly killed them all.

But it had to touch them first.

He started down the stairs, still growling. All around him, the bears moved forward as well, and on either side of Carolyn, the other Allegiants shifted their weight, as if bracing for the attack.

A door shut behind him. Swiftly, Wes risked a glance over his shoulder.

Lindy stood on the porch.

Ice shot through him. What the hell was she doing?

But at the sight, Carolyn chuckled. "Well, hello, Melinda."

The woman hurled a hand forward, and smoke rushed from her palm, surging past him. The black line hit Lindy's neck, and twisting her wrist sharply, Carolyn snagged the tentacle of smoke as if gripping a rope.

Wes's heart hit his throat. Not again. That leash thing—

"No." Lindy jerked her head to the side. The black line flew apart like shattered glass.

Rage flooded Carolyn's face. "You are the Scythe of Niorun! You are the weapon of the Order, and you *will* obey!"

"Never again."

Iron filled Lindy's voice, and Wes turned back to Carolyn, growling with pride. That was his mate. He could practically feel the strength rolling off her as if it were electricity charging the air.

And it grew.

A pulse thudded out across the clearing. It burned the

air when it passed him, racing for the draugar and the Allegiants, and he recognized the feeling. The same blast had ripped by him in Nebraska when she first destroyed the draugar, only now it felt infinitely stronger. In a moment, it slammed into the noxious clouds as if to shred them like a hurricane.

Sparks erupted, and the green fog blazed so bright, he flinched away, spots in his eyes.

The draugar still stood when the light faded.

Carolyn smiled. "You think we weren't prepared for you, Melinda?"

Cold stole over Wes. What the hell kind of power was in that fog, if whatever Lindy had done couldn't stop it?

At his back, he heard Lindy take two steps forward on the porch, and then a new wave of seidr rushed out, tingling over his fur. In a single bound, she leapt past him, her body changing as she moved. The confines of her clothes burned away with the power of the shift, and when she hit the ground, she wasn't human.

But he'd never seen anything like her wolf.

Her fur was black like the tears through the sky, dark as the depths of space, but it drifted up like she was made entirely of smoke. When she threw a look to him, her eyes glowed green and light twisted up from them like auroras. It wasn't the sickly color of the Order, but instead, a vibrant shade like fresh life in springtime, shining out in the gathering twilight.

And he could feel her. Like one of his pack, he could, and joy bubbled up inside him despite everything.

Satisfaction blossomed in her eyes as she regarded him, becoming iron resolution as she looked back at her mother.

A low growl left Lindy.

The contempt on Carolyn's face vanished into rage.

With an imperious gesture, she threw out her arms and the power around her thudded through the air like an explosion. Shrieks rose from the forest again, turning to a flood as more draugar poured from the woods into the clearing.

Carolyn smiled, utter cruelty in her eyes. "Get them."

The draugar charged.

# 31

# LINDY

The draugar raced right at her, green smoke rising from the forest behind them, and yet everything felt right.

Seidr coursed through Lindy's new form and joy flooded her body, as if something inside her had been waiting all her life for this, and now, at long last, it was here.

The Scythe of Niorun, never to be chained again.

Shrieking and howling, the draugar charged from the smoke, clawing madly to reach her, but instantly, pure instinct took over, telling her what to do before she even had the conscious thought. Lunging forward, she tore into the draugar, shredding them to ash. To move on four legs was awkward for a moment, like crawling at high speed, but she could feel herself adjusting. Some part of her mind seemed to understand this, to *know* this, and effortlessly instructed the rest of her on what to do even as she sped through the horde. To her left, she somehow could feel

Wes's presence, and she knew he was unharmed for the moment, destroying the monsters same as her.

It was exhilarating.

Her eyes scanned the flood of draugar around her, their bodies strange in her new vision. The green smoke rose behind them like a backdrop, not moving forward though she couldn't understand why. Meanwhile, lines tangled around the draugar like ropes, not black or green but somehow an absence of both, as if reality was inverted where the vines were. Anti-space. Negative color. The sight was disconcerting, and confusing too, and then she spotted one of the Allegiants.

Understanding hit her. Some of the lines led back to the man, gripped in his fists like leashes. This was what the Order had done, different than what they'd tried with her but powerful all the same. This was their twisted, corrupted seidr controlling the monsters, marshaling them to the Order's task.

But why wasn't the green smoke coming with them?

Lunging forward, she snapped her jaws through the lines, and the invisible ropes broke, floundering around like cut tentacles for a moment before vanishing entirely. The draugar to which they'd been connected suddenly staggered, all of them stumbling around like autonomous puppets suddenly free of their strings.

Satisfaction filtered through Lindy, and she charged forward, biting through more of the leashes and leaving confused draugar staggering into each other in her wake. The Allegiants shouted, whipping seidr through the air in an effort to ensnare the monsters again, catching some, missing others, while all around, chaos ensued.

But something was wrong. There'd been more Allegiants here only minutes ago, yet now at least half were gone.

Including her mother.

Alarm spread through her, and Lindy inhaled sharply, testing her new sense of smell. Her head snapped to the right. There, a trace of her mother, threading a path through the draugar and toward the side of Maeve and Everett's house.

Her mother was going after Frankie and Andrew again.

Digging her paws into the cold snow, Lindy took off, tearing past the draugar as she raced after her mother's scent. Like hell, Carolyn would hurt them. *Touch* them. Like hell they'd ever live in fear of that woman again.

Lindy rounded the side of the house, and there she was in a space between the wreckage of the porch and the edge of the forest, with green smoke hanging in the woods beside her as if the noxious cloud extended all the way around the clearing.

And Carolyn wasn't alone.

Lindy skidded to a stop, her eyes darting over the Allegiants with her mother. The robed figures stood in a half circle, their arms outstretched. Behind her, Lindy could feel more of them closing in too, their shapes in her mind almost obscured by the draugar rampaging through the clearing to fight the bears and Wes.

Her mother grinned. "Look who's come back anyway. You're ours, Melinda. You'll always return to us." Carolyn glanced past her to the Allegiants closing in. "No matter what you've done to yourself."

Lindy growled.

Carolyn scoffed, clearly disgusted. "Now!"

As one, the Allegiants shouted. Chains of glowing green

smoke surged up from the ground all around her, lashing across Lindy before driving back into the earth as if to anchor her there. She staggered, fighting and failing to keep her feet as they tightened and dragged her down to the snow.

Thrashing beneath the magical restraints, panic pounded through her. She was trapped. Pinned to the snow and frozen grass like...

Like an animal.

Carolyn walked closer, ignoring the others as they continued to chant strange words Lindy only vaguely remembered from her childhood. "You are such a disappointment." Her mother's lips curled up, cold and cruel. "But you'll still obey."

The woman bent closer, contempt in her voice. "You let that wolf bastard corrupt you, *daughter*. You should have died rather than let that filth touch you. But no matter. We'll still do what you couldn't. Every other disgusting animal is going to die in these woods, drained of life and screaming their last. And him?" She chuckled. "You swore yourself to us, Melinda. You will be our tool. So I'm going to skin that cur alive, and hand you the knife right before the end, and you *will* obey when I tell you to cut that animal's throat."

Stepping back, Carolyn raised her hands and the green smoke rose too, churning high above the trees like a wave ready to crash down and snuff all life from the clearing. Around her, the Allegiants chanted louder.

The chains over Lindy's body began to tighten, making her yelp in pain. Panic drummed through her, for herself, for Wes, for all the bears who were going to die if those green clouds came slamming down. But no matter how she thrashed beneath the chains, she couldn't break free. With every passing heartbeat, the restraints sank deeper into her, their touch like death that bit like needles. Her strength drained even as something else seemed to seep into its place, as if the chains of smoke planned to drink down all the power inside her and fill her with their poison instead.

Her thoughts slowed. *The poison was not poison. The poison was the idea.*

Why try to take her strength? Why try to drain what they'd helped create?

*Child...*

Lindy looked up, her eyes finding Carolyn and all the Allegiants, their faces so sure, so confident.

For no reason at all.

They didn't make this power inside her. Not really. Sure, they'd twisted it just like they twisted everything, corrupting Niorun's gifts and seeking to turn them into something else. Something they thought belonged to them, just like they thought about the ulfhednar runes and seidr and the whole damn world.

*The poison was not poison.*

It was their ideas.

Lindy had never been theirs. These powers weren't either.

They'd come from Niorun.

A snarl left her. One at a time, she drove her paws into the snow, bracing herself as she reached deep into the shadows inside her, welcoming every last one. Every nightmare. Every old fear. Because they weren't terrifying.

They were her.

In a roaring, tumbling wave, the shadows flooded her veins, building higher and higher like an electrical storm. Snapping and snarling, they coursed through everything she was, teeming with nightmares and dreams and hopes and fears.

All of life and everything beyond.

The chains shattered. Rising to her feet, she swept her eyes over the Allegiants as smoke and shadows rolled out around her, billowing and churning, filled with the echoes of terrified cries. The Allegiants stumbled back as the wave of darkness hit, horror suffusing their skull-like faces. Inside the dark pits of their sockets, their eyes darted around like they were suddenly seeing their darkest dreams come to life.

And Lindy growled.

Their screams tore through the air. Scrambling backward, they raced into the forest as if fleeing for their lives.

Lindy turned to find her mother standing stock-still before her. Instinct whispered what to do, same as it had on the porch when the draugar arrived, and with only a moment's concentration, Lindy felt the shift rush through her.

The shadows stayed as she straightened in human form, the black mist draping around her like a dark robe and drifting away like smoke at the edges. Beneath her bare feet, the snow felt as cool as spring water, and overhead, the green smoke hung like frozen clouds motionless in the sky.

Carolyn drew herself up with an imperiousness that would have been frightening, if not for the fear Lindy could see making her mother tremble. "You can't do this," the woman insisted. "You're a tool of the Order."

Pacing forward, Lindy lifted her hand. Tongues of shadow like candle flames twisted out from her ink-black fingers. "I'm nothing you own."

Carolyn's eyes darted from Lindy to the dark fire.

Lindy twisted her wrist, letting the black flames dance higher. "You will never hurt me or anyone I love ever again, do you understand?"

A whimper slipped from Carolyn before she clamped her lips shut tighter.

"Do you *understand*?"

Her mother's feet slipped backward as she flinched away.

For a long moment, Lindy regarded her, torn on what to do. She couldn't kill her mother. No matter what the woman had done, no matter what Carolyn *was*, Lindy couldn't bring herself to do it.

But she could make sure her mother never came near them again.

Tendrils of shadow twisted out from Lindy. Wrapping around the woman, the darkness sank deep into her, finding Carolyn's fears, drawing them out like pulling threads from a cloth. Overhead and throughout the forest, the green clouds dissipated into nothingness while her mother staggered back, batting at the shadows tangling around her, unable to escape.

Lindy stepped closer, her voice becoming a growl. "This family is *mine*."

Carolyn shrieked, cringing away.

A hint of a predatory smile crossed Lindy's face. "Run."

The shadows parted around Carolyn, releasing their grip. Instantly, the woman stumbled backward and bolted for the woods like the hounds of hell were on her tail.

A slow breath escaping her, Lindy watched her go, her hand lifting to the break in the tattooed collar and the tingling gold runes on her throat. Even if she wasn't sure what she'd done, something inside told her the woman wouldn't escape it.

Possibly ever.

And that was the point. Protection for her family, for the shifters, and a message too, one sent to the Order and Dal Hegnar himself. The Scythe of Niorun wasn't their property.

Never again.

Shrieks of the draugar came from beyond the edge of the cabin, and she could still pick out their shapes amid the shadows in her mind. Striding back the way she'd come, she rounded the corner to see the bears coated in ash, still fighting the horde. But there were dozens of the monsters still standing. Maybe hundreds scattered throughout the berserkers' compound. Even now, some of the draugar turned, spotting her, racing toward her with their mouths open wide and their rotted teeth bared.

A strange feeling stirred in her, a sense of a brighter shape in the shadows, but not threatening. Familiar.

Wes, she realized, held back by the never-ending horde racing her way.

Something inside her howled.

Instantly, shadows surged away from her, roaring out across the compound in a black and tumbling wave. It swept past the bears and Wes, leaving them untouched like islands in a dark sea, and struck the draugar.

The monsters shattered into dust.

Mid-strike, the bears paused, looking around in shock. One by one, they spotted her, several of them growling while others took a step back in alarm.

Her eyes were only on Wes.

Renewed trepidation stirred in her as she saw him staring at her too. What would he think of this? Of her?

And the strangest feeling suddenly filtered into her

mind, like a warm breeze on a summer's day. Comfort, but somehow from outside of her.

Her brow furrowed in alarm. It was him.

She walked across the clearing, her bare feet scarcely chilled by the snow, and the bears retreated from her path. When she reached him, she crouched down, meeting his gray eyes.

The warm feeling strengthened. On instinct, she reached out, putting her arms around him, and he nuzzled his head against her, a low rumble in his chest like a contented growl. Because he was with her, and she was with him.

*Her mate.*

She paused. The thought was... right. Peaceful and soothing, it spoke in a voice that was at once both new and yet her own.

A wolf.

One who, more than anything, was finally free.

AMONG ALL THE FOOD AND WEAPONS AND SUPPLIES THAT Maeve and Everett apparently had stockpiled, they'd thankfully included plenty of clothes.

Unfortunately, none of them really fit.

Lindy cinched a belt tighter, scrunching the jeans around her waist, and regarded herself in the bedroom mirror. The knit sweater hung like a multicolored carnival tent on her with the sleeves rolled up to keep them from dangling past her hands. Above the wide collar, dark tattoos like claws still framed her face, and the golden runes glistened on her throat.

A wry chuckle escaped her. As looks went, she supposed there was worse than "goth met garage sale."

Though, now that she thought of it...

She glanced at the mirror. Earlier on, she'd been able to draw shadows covering her back inside with only a thought. But that dark smoke wasn't the only part of this power.

Her eyes narrowed at herself in the mirror.

The tattoos vanished like ink drawing back into her flesh, leaving no trace they'd ever marked her skin. Only the shimmer of gold at her neck remained, a thin line of runes that shone only in the right angle of light.

A breath left her, and her trembling hand lifted to her cheek. No black stain marred her fingers any longer. No tangle of jet-black lines wrapped her palms. Shoving the sleeve of the sweater aside, she gasped.

The Allegiant tattoo was gone.

Her lips moved, but she couldn't make a sound, happiness choking her with an elated sob. Somewhere inside, the darkness still twisted, but it was hers now. Not a death sentence, but a gift. Power from a goddess who'd never cursed her at all. And if she needed them, somehow she knew the shadows would be there and the marks would return. But until that time, they slumbered peacefully inside.

Knocking came on the door, and then the handle twisted. "Lindy?" Wes stuck his head in.

She turned, and his mouth fell open.

"Oh, merciful gods..." He stepped inside, shutting the door behind him and never taking his eyes from her. "How...?"

Shaking her head, she shrugged, grinning. "Like shifting into a wolf. I get to choose."

His brow twitched down as he absorbed the words, and then he was rushing across the room to her, lifting her in his arms. Tears spilled down her cheeks as she hugged him, laughing while he spun her around. Setting her back down, he looked down at her, such joy in his eyes, and then his lips found her own.

She melted into the kiss, her hands tightening on him to keep him close, and she never wanted to let go. His fist clenched on the back of her baggy sweater, holding her to him as his tongue plundered her, every inch of her body pressed to his, and when he broke from her, she could barely breathe from the way her heart was racing.

Her hand reached up, cupping his cheek as she looked deep into his eyes. She never would have imagined she could find a happiness like this, and yet here it was.

With him.

*Her mate.*

The words pressed at the edge of her lips, but she didn't know how to say them. How did wolves handle that? She was so new to all this, and yet... even with how wonderful things were between them, what if, when it came to *that*, he didn't feel the same?

A concerned look crossed his face. "Are you okay?"

She started to nod, only to hesitate. "Yeah, I just—"

"Lindy?" Henry's voice came down the hall. "Wes? You decent?"

Wes glanced at the door briefly before looking back to her. "What is it?" he asked quietly.

She hesitated, apprehension tangling up so badly it choked her. "Nothing."

His brow furrowed, but he nodded, and when he took her hand, she gripped it tightly as they walked to the door.

At the end of the hall, the bears were waiting in the living room with her father and brother nearby.

"We've come to a decision," Henry said when they walked in. "This place isn't safe. The Order knows we're alive, and they know we're here. Now, we could ask you to stay put and help defend this place, but"—he glanced at Knox, who looked away, scowling—"strategically there are too many potential liabilities. But you told your father you had somewhere safe."

"We want to know where it is," Maeve said.

Lindy drew a breath, glancing at Wes. He gave her a small nod.

"His pack has a place outside Mariposa, Colorado," she said. "A fortified manor and a *very* secure bunker too. And my best friend, Hayden, she's, uh… pretty amazing with seidr. She and the pack defend that place, and the draugar and the Order can't reach anyone there."

"Would there be space for us?" Everett asked.

"We'll find it," Wes assured him.

"Thank you," Henry said, nodding.

Wes echoed the motion.

"Tell the others," Everett said to Knox. "Pack everything. We'll take the Humvees and leave within the hour."

The bear looked like he was grinding his teeth, but he gave a quick jerk of his head all the same.

As the others hurried away, Lindy sighed. With a setup like the bears possessed, driving back wouldn't be as hard as it'd been coming here. Moreover, her powers were under her own control now, and with Wes and the berserkers around them, her family would be safe.

They'd all make it. And when they got back…

Anxiety knotted her stomach. What would her best friend think to see her now?

Wes tightened his grip on her hand, and she glanced at him.

"You sure you're all right?" he asked.

"Yeah."

He nodded at the response, still watching her.

Lindy shrugged awkwardly. "What... what's it like, being..." She floundered. "I mean... being bitten and then meeting the wolves and..."

"They'll accept you."

She looked back up at him.

"They're my family. And Hayden... she's your friend, right?" He drew her closer. "We'll explain what happened —as much as you're comfortable with—and go from there. But..." He grinned. "I think you're going to like being part of the pack."

Warmth and hope bloomed in her chest, all tangled up in one. Being part of a pack had never been anything she'd imagined for herself and yet, it felt right too.

But that left one thing...

Lindy drew a deep breath. "Wes... Outside, when I saw you after the draugar—" She bit her lip, avoiding his eyes. "A word came to me."

He was silent for a second. "Oh?"

"Yeah." She looked up at him. "My, uh... mate."

Air left him.

She ducked her face away again. "I... I love you, Wes. And I'm not saying you have to feel the same way, I just—"

He drew her to him, his lips claiming hers. The strangest feeling spread through her, as if a dark and powerful wolf was wrapping around her, protective and loving and so gentle despite all its strength. And inside herself, the shadows and darkness rose to meet it, not dangerous, but filled with so much love, it took her breath away.

Wes pulled back to stare into her eyes. "I do."

Her mouth moved, all her words escaping her.

He smiled. "You're my mate, Lindy. From the moment I saw you, no matter how I tried to deny it, my heart was always yours." He kissed her again. "I love you with everything I am. Forever."

She looked up at him, tears in her eyes that were only joy. "Forever."

# 3 2

# KNOX

This was a mistake.

Climbing from the Humvee, Knox eyed the enormous ulfhednar manor. Three stories of stone and plaster towered over the courtyard and the burnt trees around it. To hear Wes and Lindy tell it, a bunker of even larger size sprawled underground beneath it, though all on its own, the building could probably house an army.

Noises of relief came from the civilian bears still sitting in the Humvee behind him. After days of driving across country—not to mention years of hiding in fear of the Order—someplace this secure had to look like they'd arrived in nirvana.

They didn't know the wolves like he did. What the ulfhednar were capable of.

What they'd done.

"Stay in the vehicles," he ordered the civilians and his Bloodclaws alike. "Keep the engine running."

Fear scents from the civilians prickled his nose, but they all obeyed.

"Alex," he continued. "Amelia."

Without a word, the twins left the Humvee and came up to his side. From the other vehicles, Everett and Henry climbed down, along with Wes, Lindy, and her family.

Knox's teeth ground as he and the twins walked toward them. He didn't care what the wolves or those humans did, but the berserkers were his responsibility and they shouldn't be moving without guards.

"We need to secure a safe location for the civilians," he growled to Everett, eyeing their surroundings. "We shouldn't just—"

The manor door opened and the bear inside him snarled. Wolves in their human forms rushed out, along with so many actual humans that it made his body shudder with the urge to shift. Lindy and Wes said the town residents were staying with them, but he'd thought perhaps they were exaggerating the numbers.

There were dozens. Likely more below, and his skin crawled at the realization.

"Lindy!" A dark-haired wolf female raced across the courtyard, engulfing the new shifter in a hug. "Oh my God, I was so worried."

"I'm sorry." Lindy squeezed the female right back, her voice choked with tears. "I didn't want to scare you; I just didn't know…"

Knox turned his attention to their surroundings. He hadn't cared to learn the identities of the wolves they'd be meeting—names were irrelevant; their intentions were what mattered—but he'd heard enough to know that must be the friend. Hayden. The one holding the defense around this place.

Surely a bubble of seidr wouldn't be enough.

More voices rose around him: humans and ulfhednar

introducing themselves to Everett and Henry, and then Lindy introducing her family to the wolves. In only moments, Everett was motioning for the berserkers to leave the vehicles and join them, and Knox bit back a growl.

"Bloodclaws throughout the courtyard," he snapped to Amelia. "Stay on guard and keep the civilians in sight. No one goes off on their own, got it?"

The female nodded and strode away quickly to tell the others.

"You made it!" cried a human young woman, relief radiating from her as she raced up to Lindy and Wes. A large man with a red-splotched face followed, a teenage girl and an elderly woman behind him.

"Thank you so much for telling us about this place," the older woman said.

"Yeah, it's, uh—" The big man glanced around. "It's not bad."

The young woman scoffed, but there wasn't any anger in the sound. "Don't listen to Anthony. He loves it."

"I didn't say it wasn't good, Yasmeen," the man protested.

Knox dismissed the argument. This was pure madness. The berserkers should have met the wolves away from their stronghold and determined how to proceed from—

"Wounded this way. We have medics ready to help you."

His blood turned to ice, the voice snapping his attention toward it as if on a tether. By the door to the manor, a wolf female stood, her white-blond hair slicked back in a ponytail. Her pale eyes skimmed from newcomer to newcomer around her, and she smiled as one of the young bears asked her a question.

He could barely breathe, old memories rising around him, so visceral. Her tear-streaked face in the rearview window. His throat raw from his own cries, and his knees skinned by the gravel where he'd fallen as he ran, chasing her and the vehicle with no hope of catching either.

But maybe he was wrong. This wasn't her. It'd been years, after all. A lifetime and more.

"Who is that?" he asked Alex, keeping his voice flat and uninterested in total defiance of the way his heart was pounding.

"Hmm?" The bear followed his gaze. "Oh. Um..." He thought for a second. "Looks like that might be Luna. One of Wes's pack. Real close-knit group, from the sound of it."

Luna. Gods above, it *was* her.

His eyes darted around. Were the others here? The bastards who couldn't hurt him now, but by the gods would still pay?

Alex glanced over his shoulder as his sister Amelia called to him. "You need anyth—"

"Go on."

The Bloodclaw hesitated at the tight tone Knox couldn't hide. But after a moment, he nodded. "Okay..." Still eyeing him, Alex hurried away.

Knox looked back at the blond wolf. She hadn't glanced in his direction. Probably had no idea he was here. Shepherding the newcomers was taking all of her attention, her voice so kind and her smile so gentle.

Trembling rippled through him. She'd always been gentle.

Nothing like him, especially anymore.

Her eyes moved toward him and Knox turned away sharply, still shaking. She wouldn't recognize him. Not after all these years. Not with so much life and damage between them. Things she didn't know about.

Things she never would.

He drew a steadying breath, shoving down the memories and the pain and everything that had come after, just as he always did. The berserkers never should have come here. *He* never should have, not for a thousand reasons, and definitely not for this one.

His heart ached. This had all been a mistake.

And reuniting with Luna would be the biggest of them all.

Thank you so much for reading Fated Curse. Be sure to continue the series! Grab **Fated Hearts: Book Three of the Shifters of Ragnarok** today!

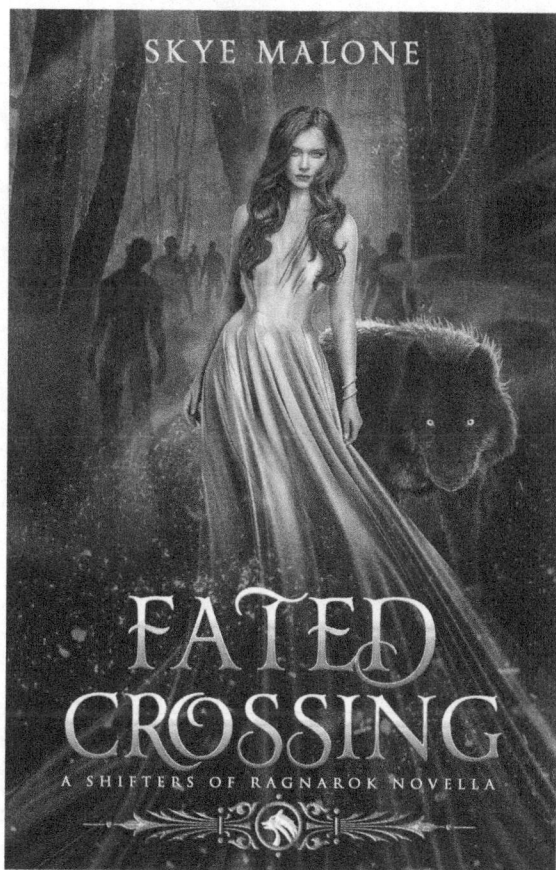

# TITLES BY SKYE MALONE

ADULT PARANORMAL ROMANCE
The Shifters of Ragnarok Series
The Demon Guardians Series

YOUNG ADULT PARANORMAL ROMANCE
The Awakened Fate Series

YOUNG ADULT URBAN FANTASY
The Kindling Trilogy

# ABOUT THE AUTHOR

Skye Malone writes action-packed fantasy and paranormal romance. A fan of magical books since childhood, they adore stories that pit ordinary characters against extraordinary odds and reveal the strength within. Abandoned buildings are their passion, along with old castles and deep dark parts of the forest where anything is possible. A graduate of the University of Illinois with a degree in English literature, Skye lives in the USA Midwest with a retired racing greyhound and a three-legged mutt.

🅐 amazon.com/author/skyemalone

BB bookbub.com/authors/skye-malone

f facebook.com/authorskyemalone

g goodreads.com/skyemalone

📷 instagram.com/authorskyemalone

♪ tiktok.com/@authorskyemalone

Made in the USA
Monee, IL
30 January 2025